Three Tales of Passionate Japan

LAURA ANTONIOU
MIDORI
CECILIA TAN

For more information contact:
Riverdale Avenue Books/Circlet Press
5676 Riverdale Avenue
Riverdale, NY 10471

www.riverdaleavebooks.com

Design by www.formatting4U.com
Interior art for The Way of Heaven by Autumn Sacura (Alexandra Gladysh)
Interior art for The Secret of Silk by Michael Manning
Interior art for The Bonds of Love by Trevor Sutherland

Digital ISBN: 9781626015296
Trade ISBN: 781626015302
Hardcover ISBN: 9781626015340

First Edition December 2019

TABLE OF CONTENTS

PAST   1
    The Way of Heaven
    by Laura Antoniou

PRESENT   91
    The Secret of Silk
    by Midori

FUTURE   201
    The Bonds of Love
    by Cecilia Tan

The Way of Heaven

Laura Antoniou

The Lady General, Hagane Masako, Mistress of the Five Provinces, Conqueror of the Battle of Kiyoshi and Special Retainer to the Imperial Prince Yoshinake bowed her head down to the woven mat and held her position until the barely perceptible movement of her lord's little finger. Although no one else in the room was permitted to keep their arms, her blades glittered from their polished scabbards, one before her, one still thrust through her sash.

"I like this little," Lord Okubo sniffed, leaning delicately toward his companion Lord Hattori. "This upstart peasant female owns the puissance of a lord twice her age and four times her breeding! The prince is too much swayed by her."

"Oh, yes, that is surely so," Lord Hattori flirted back, lowering his eyes demurely.

"And yet, she had served us well upon the fields of battle," interjected young Lady Miyamoto Asa, who was the prince's cousin. The three of them watched as the general's back straightened, and her prince acknowledged her. Her armor moved underneath layers of brightly colored woven and knotted silk, bands of crimson and gold overlaid with the modified chrysanthemum symbol of the royal house. Her long black hair was bound behind her and a wide band was wrapped around her forehead, battle style. No other fighter ever dared to enter the court dressed in such an outlandish way. Even the lowest ranking soldier knew to change into formal kimono and sandals. But not the Lady General.

"Her victories only serve to make her more dangerous," Okubo snarled. "One day, she will rise up and betray the prince, mark my words."

"You are a fool," whispered the elderly Lord Senji. His bones creaked like armor when he shifted his posture so the younger retainers could hear his carefully modulated words. "You must observe everything, else know nothing. Observe; does she not show him great deference in her every move, in her very choice of inflection? Do her eyes never leave his person, ever following the plumes of his breath, her body taut with eagerness to obey? Does not the great prince always take his Lady General into private session after her report, in order to hear what is meant only for his ears? And does he not always return from such meetings refreshed and full of vigor?"

"This is so, Old Lord," Lady Asa murmured, "but what is it you are suggesting?"

"That the Imperial Prince is pillowing with his general?" Hattori muffled a snicker. "Oh, surely not! With a commoner?"

"A further outrage!" Okubo hissed. "She will perhaps try to entice him into an alliance... or to make her a concubine... or even... even!" He stopped, his face coloring to near mulberry, grinding his teeth.

"To be his wife? You know that is impossible," Lord Senji chided. "Our lord has always been a man of great personal discipline in all things. Has he not already accepted the Lady Umiko to be presented for a potential betrothal? He knows he must have a lady of the proper age and blood and rank. He is no fool for women; he has not kept a concubine, only hires the very finest of diverting ladies to beguile him, and then only rarely. No, nothing can come of this, save the continued loyalty and love of his general." He glanced at the two of them conferring at the front of the room, oblivious to the surrounding audience of retainers, guards and petitioners. "No, children," the old man sighed, "there is no danger from the Lady General. He has tamed her with his controlled passion, bound her to him through his power. She loves our master and will serve him loyally until death."

Lady Asa nodded and turned her nose away from the gossiping lords, ignoring the slight curl of contempt in Hattori's lips.

Lord Okubo straightened his own back and composed his handsome face. "She is a viper," he assured Hattori.

"Oh, she surely is," Hattori agreed.

* * *

"And finally, my lord, here are the agreements of the provincial governing lords, and their written oaths to you. They will arrive in the capital before the first harvest to offer their obeisance in person and beg leave to present you with such gifts and tributes as you desire."

Masako's voice was low and gravely, the voice of a woman long used to raising commands above the din of a battlefield. Her weathered face framed dark eyes, gray as storm clouds. Under the exaggerated mantle of her formal battle dress, her shoulders looked broad and strong. Her hand, extending the rolled sheaf of papers to her lord, was brown and marked with winds, reins, and hilts, crisscrossed with old scars.

Prince Yoshinake took the scrolls with one clean, smooth, and manicured hand. Although his palms and fingers were also marked by the sword, he had not seen battle from any position closer than strategic overlooks. Imperial princes were not supposed to take to the field personally; their lives were far too precious to expose to the dangers of open combat. And why should he? He had been fortunate in finding and obtaining the service of the greatest general in the land. With her strength and his wisdom, he had nearly succeeded in uniting all of the provinces in his suzerain, as they were when the land was new.

"We are pleased with our general," he intoned, nodding gravely. He was a young man still, barely into his third decade, a child when his father died and left him the swords and fan of his branch of the imperial clan. His hair was black as a crow's wing and swept up onto his head in the style favored by royalty, his cheeks clean and his skin ruddy as the purest wheat, smooth as finest silk. But he was a serious and calculating lord, full of plans and insights, and he had earned the respect of his retainers.

"We shall now retire into privacy to hear that which is for our ears only," he said, nodding to the room. As one, his court bowed, and his bodyguards sprang up to make way for their lord. He rose while his court was still bowed into rows of colorful backs and nodded briefly at the sight of their heads all bobbing slightly above the floor. His general waited until her lord was walking to raise herself and followed him at the correct distance.

"A viper!" Okubo whispered.

"As you say," murmured Hattori, fanning himself.

* * *

Takeuchi no Yoshinake Shinno, Lord of the Five Provinces, Protector of the Shrines, Bearer of the Sacred Kinumora Fan and Prince of the Blood, immediately threw himself down onto his belly when the doors behind him slid shut. He lay there, trembling and quivering like a minnow trapped in a receding tidal pool as the sounds of his personal guard echoed away into the distance.

"You are so like a worm," Masako commented, stepping over him.

"Oh, yes, my lady," he eagerly offered back, not daring to raise his head.

Masako kicked him once, hard, catching him in the side, near his ribs. "You're forgetful, oh prince."

"My general! My glorious general!"

"Do you know why you are like a worm, my prince?"

He stiffened and his fists tightened in the effort required to answer her. "I squirm upon the very earth before you, my general?"

Masako kicked him again, this time catching him in the thigh. "No, you cretin. It is because you are blind, yet useful in catching great prey. As to that matter, have you formally accepted Umiko?"

"Yes, my general!" Eager to be recognized for doing something right, the prince raised his head, just a little bit. "As you instructed me, my general! She arrives in 16 days!"

"Good," Masako murmured. She walked the length of the room, and shrugged her shoulders under the armor. "You may approach me, my royal manling."

Yoshinake leaped to his feet and tried to contain himself as he crossed the mats to where she stood, rigid and waiting for his ministrations. Carefully, he untied the silk ribbons of her over mantle, and then the straps and ties of her body armor. With the ease of a man who had seen it done thousands of times and learned from the royal valets themselves, he acted the perfect personal servant. Without betraying his nervousness, he used his own stand to lay her armor aside. He handled each piece with care and delicacy.

"I remember when you lacked these skills," Masako chuckled. "I suppose that you do have some more use after all."

She turned toward him. The next layer between them was the leather under padding, soft with use where it was not stiff with repeated washings in sweat and blood. He blushed sweetly, like a maiden. She flicked one finger in his direction. With trembling fingers, Yoshinake carefully untied the knots that held the padding together, and without brushing her skin with his bare hands, drew it off.

Her hard body, brown where the layers of silk and armor failed to cover her, and harder and pale where it did, made him moan, a tight sound barely held in check as he scurried to lay the padding down and return with a light cotton robe. He noted with familiar pangs of sympathetic pain her calluses and her scars, the bruises from her latest engagement and the white lines and ridged stars that mapped out past ones. Her body was a constellation of wounds, most taken in his service.

"You are a goddess," he murmured, slipping the cool cotton over her shoulders.

"Flatterer," she snorted. "When you meet a goddess, then may you compare. But I do permit your worship. Show me your devotion, my prince." She seated herself on his mats, pulling one leg up in a vulgar fashion never displayed before such an august presence and poured herself some of his sake.

Yoshinake knelt before her and parted his own robes. His scarlet sash was heavy brocade, wound through with precious threads of gold, but he cast it aside without a thought and eagerly parted layers of silk to reveal his artfully folded loincloth. When he unwound it, his tumescent manhood, awakened since the first appearance of his goddess, stirred over the clean, round spheres housing his future generations. But cast through the head of his royal cock was a device no household servant had ever seen.

It was a large ring, carved of ivory. It was not a complete circle, but gapped, leaving two points separated by a finger's width. The entire ring could be contained in the circle he made with his thumb and forefinger. On one end of the ring was a knob carved from the original tusk and depicting a chrysanthemum bud. The other end of the ring came to a sharp and narrow point. Covering the point now was a golden ball with a pin through it.

The ring went into his organ through the little slit at the end. He remembered how he had strained against the elegant silk ropes, his mind flooded with entreaties to his ancestors and all the gods that the pain would be endurable and he would show no cowardice. He did his ancestors proud in that respect, although he privately doubted many of them approved of the nature of the pain he endured so well. But that was not his fault; these were different times. It was no longer the custom of a prince to actually do battle in the field, even when his talents led that way. He must therefore have his mettle tested in more esoteric endeavors.

Masako had affixed this ornament herself, hammering the gold around the point with the edge of her chop. Yoshinake could have easily removed the appliance had he wished, but he could have never duplicated her own design in the soft gold if he marred it in any way.

The Lady General gazed at the displayed royal genitalia and nodded. "You have been good, my prince," she said generously. "And you are still pretty as a girl."

He beamed with pleasure, another thing his court never saw. "Thank you, my general!"

"Come closer," she commanded.

Eagerly, he shuffled forward, and displayed his handsome body for her pleasure. His bare chest shone with scented oils. He was strong and healthy and in his prime. The sedentary life at court did not prevent him from engaging in regular exercise with swords and bows or long rides through the countryside, hunting and taking the air. His nipples seemed somewhat larger than those of other men, but that was also because of his goddess.

Even now, she reached for them first, testing them with tight pinching and a light slap of her rough fingertips. Yoshinake sighed with pleasure.

"These shall have to be schooled again," she said softly. "They are unused to attention. I have brought with me wooden pegs that we shall employ later. Eventually, I shall have made matching rings, so that you may be decorated here as well."

He opened his eyes and bit the inside of his lip. "My general... nothing would please me more... yet... my general surely knows... it will be very difficult for me to hide such rings! I will have to dismiss my dressers entirely and forbid all from my bath... and never strip to the waist during competition!"

Masako nodded, a slight smile on her lips. "Yes, that is true," she acknowledged, flashing him an appreciative glance. "But by that time, you will have already firmly established your... eccentricities. Your court will believe this to be some new fad of yours, and you will create fashion. It is already said in the capital that the most civilized of men will never bare their generative organs to less-than-equals. Perhaps, should you choose to reveal them, other men will seek similar decorations, and bear them with pride." She smiled again and moved her fingers down to stroke the length of his shaft. It swelled pleasingly at her touch. It was also clean and sweet smelling, smooth as heavy silk. She stroked it absently, like a pet, until it rose and jutted into the elegant curve that was his alone, and Yoshinake sucked in a quick breath to prepare for the usual response to such behavior.

Her hand swept away from the royal cock and then back, slapping it sharply. Yoshinake ground his teeth but stayed still, his muscles tense. She slapped him again for good measure, and he arched his back slightly, appeasing her by offering yet more.

"My brave, strong prince," she chuckled. Her voice was warm with approval. She returned to sipping at the wine, watching him recover, his flesh pulsating with discipline and desire, his body betraying nothing of the minor pain she had caused him.

Together, they breathed in the rich scent of power. When it began to dissipate, Masako sighed and shook her head. "Unbraid my hair," she said, pouring more of the wine. Yoshinake crawled behind her and began to undo the practical windings of her hair with gentle and skilled fingers.

"My general," he ventured, as he reached for the second braid, "your miserable servant has... a concern."

"Yes?" There was just an edge of impatience in her voice.

"The Lady Umiko..." He faltered, despite having practiced a myriad of methods for approaching this delicate subject. "She is to be my wife..."

Masako chuckled again. "Yes, my prince. And therefore, we shall have to remove this special ring so that you may present her with your royal spawn. But it will return as soon as your princely duties are done."

He sighed and brightened immediately. "Then... you shall meet me before and after every visit to the lady?"

"At first. Until Umiko learns herself how to remove and apply it. Or I may have one crafted for you to wear even during her use of your handsome shaft. A smaller one, perhaps with a raised design, to increase her pleasure."

His fingers fumbled and he drew them out of her hair in panic. "My general?"

"Finish what you are doing, fool. That will cost you many stripes later." As his fingers returned to working out the weaving of her tresses, she smiled, knowing that he couldn't see her face. How delightful it was to surprise him! Even the wise prince could not possibly guess all of the twists and mysteries of her imagination. She hardened her voice, for her pleasure and his. "Were you so foolish to think that after capturing your manhood myself I would not care how you used it elsewhere? No, my prince. You have been mine from the moment I first held you down and opened you. You shall remain so to the day I leave this world and go to meet my ancestors."

"B-but... Umiko!"

"She will learn to see to your needs and hungers," Masako stated. "I will teach her myself. Umiko and I have... discussed these matters." She coughed out a laugh, a low sound like the growling of a hunting cat, and she could actually feel the stillness of Yoshinake's fingers as he realized the whole of this new chapter in his tale.

"She is amenable to your situation," Masako continued. "Indeed, eager. In 16 days, when she arrives, you will pretend to introduce her to me, and I will continue to instruct her personally on how to properly train you, use you, keep you both challenged and pleasing. In time, you will be hers just as you are mine. I will teach her all she needs to know."

"But what shall I tell my court? That is most irregular!" His panic had grown considerably.

"Bear yourself like a man! Are you a prince or some turtle shit slave afraid of what you cannot see?"

11

Masako snapped. "You will tell your royal bottom kissers that the lady requires training in arms, as any good prince's wife should have, and since you have the greatest female fighter in the world at your service, you are using her to instruct your bride. This first meeting shall formalize the betrothal; I have decided the fifth day of the Month of Affection will be auspicious for the wedding. In the time between, I shall visit her if my duties allow. Should your foes be so discourteous as to require my attention, I will merely be forced to wait until she becomes your wife for more esoteric instructions."

His mouth fell open in amazement and he buried his attention to his task, running his shaking fingers through her hair until it shone in waves of shimmering ink. Oddly, his mind fastened upon the word auspicious, and he wondered if his general had actually consulted the appropriate astrologers. Then, he remembered the astonishing revelation about his future bride and scampered on his knees back in front of her, where he bowed deeply.

"Most honored general," he whispered, his forehead touching the surface of the mat. He held the position, his back muscles tense with the strain of the formal posture. "Your worthless slave begs for your attention!"

The Lady General gazed down on the bow that his back made. It was strong, bent like a cedar limb under great weight, an expanse of wheat blown over by a southern wind. She could see the faint lines she had once drawn with bamboo rods, broken across that expanse, tearing flesh and marking him the way everything she did marked him forever.

Ah, but that had been magnificent! To indulge their drives so strongly that blood flew between them and the very earth rumbled with pleasure in their frenzy. But it had been some time since they had such freedom. Marking him was a dangerous, and therefore rare pleasure. There was only so much that could be explained away by sparring and accidents.

Especially when her lord was so lithe and graceful. Few managed to strike him in combat; he moved like a golden carp in a clear pond, flashing and drawing the eye, then darting away with a sinuous ease.

He was everything a prince should be. The gods were generous in giving her the strength of arms and will and cunning to earn a place as his retainer; more so to grant her the ability to satisfy his powerful lusts and desires.

"You need to be taken," she said finally, her voice soft. "You need to be held, like a girl child before pillowing, an elder in the coldest night. And you need to be tested as a man, driven to near-madness in your agony and strength, conquered again and again to force you to rise, triumphant and resilient and fierce as a god. It is not fitting that I, a descendant of questionable heritage, be your lady, so there must be another. And Umiko is perfectly suitable, a Fujikama lady of great beauty and grace. She is agreeable. Young, strong, and eager to serve you in the ways you desire. And you will show her all the honor the wife of a great lord deserves, and she will be your taker, your lover, and your keeper."

The imperial prince shook as he raised his head to gaze at his beloved general. His questioning eyes were bright with devotion, his lips parted only slightly. "This crawling one is overwhelmed by his general's forethought and generosity," he whispered. "But he fears for the loss of his one true master. He begs the general reconsider. Please do not leave this one to the hands and whims of a child!"

"You know the tones so very well, my princeling," Masako admitted, leaning forward. "And you flatter me with them. But do not fear; Umiko may be a child, but she will be no true novice to the use of a man such as you. Did you believe that I would cast you into the care of an incompetent? That I would abandon my glorious ruler to the fancies of an empty-headed girl? Oh no, my prince. I have planned what shall become of you, and chosen a lady who is eager to meet your insatiable desires with desires of her own. And there are many more years in these scarred limbs of mine, many more battles to your eternal honor and power and glory. Should you—or your honorable lady-wife—require my services, oh, how eagerly I shall obey." Her voice had turned slightly teasing, with what passed for humor in her usual stoic demeanor.

He met her eyes, measured what he saw there. Did he have the faith? The sublime trust so necessary to their sport?

He bowed his head again in mute acceptance and shivered as she drew her fingers along his jaw.

"Before I go to face my ancestors, I will know you are master of many domains and thousands of swords, surrounded by little brats of royal birth to carry your sacred blade and fan when you have returned to me in the Other Kingdoms. And should the gods will it, and you ascend to the throne of your ancestors and become a god yourself... ah, Yoshi-chan, then still shall I be your general and guide your legions in the very heavens to your even greater glory."

"As you say, my general," he sighed. He pressed his cheek into her hand, breathing out against the skin.

"My most honored and treasured prince," she murmured, patting his cheek and smoothing her hand over his head, stroking his perfect warrior's knot. "I will serve you unto death and beyond. Come to me, my worm, my dog, my boy whore, and my exalted master. Come and please me. Perhaps if you do, I shall permit you to achieve clouds and rain tomorrow, or the day after. And perhaps I will not." She sighed, leaned back, and parted the light robe she wore. "Come to me, beautiful man. Show me your gratitude and how you shall please your wife, when she permits."

Princely worm that he was, Takeuchi no Yoshinake Shinno crawled forward to the divided thighs of the Lady General, Masako, Mistress of the Four Provinces, Conqueror of the Battle of Kiyoshi and Special Retainer to him.

*　*　*

Fujikama Umiko slid open the window of the palanquin despite the chill in the crisp spring air. Wind swirled off the road, drawing up eddies of fallen petals. Already, she missed the sharp scent of the tall, dark pines surrounding her family estates. The Black Mountain was more than her home; it was the ancient heart of her family's claim to divinity. The mountain and the familiar coasts and the land between, dotted with the treasured silk farms, were part of her family's

15

great resources. To be apart from that land, even over one boundary stone into the neighboring districts, was strange and a little frightening. She sighed and breathed deeply, trying to catch a breeze. Her lady attendant, confidant, and best friend Chiyo sighed and pushed the window closed again.

"Your hair will be a bird's nest when we arrive!" she chided, tucking one loosened lock back into the heavy coil she had so patiently helped arrange that morning.

"What does that matter? He will take me in full regalia or in rags," Umiko muttered, slumping a little. She stroked the chest next to her, running her fingers over the elaborate bronze fittings.

"Or you will take him," Chiyo said, her tone wickedly bawdy.

Umiko wondered if it had been wise to share everything she knew about her soon-to-be husband and lord. But Chiyo knew so much else; wasn't she the first to teach her how to achieve clouds and rain by herself? Didn't she bring her erotic pillow books and pretty youths to divert her melancholy thoughts on many a chill and lonely night? And wasn't she the one who had brought the note from the Lady General during that incredible visit to the seaside shrines?

It was during the annual pilgrimage to honor Ohonamochi, guardian of silk worms and the making of silk. Banners of colored silk and tassels of knotted silk ropes were strewn and draped and tied everywhere; even the meanest peasants in the district were allowed to decorate their hovels and bodies with scraps and threads. There would be special cakes made, offered, and devoured. Children would play spinning and weaving games, while their parents drank a special mulberry wine. And the maidens of the village had their own gay custom—they would tie ribbons of silk to their hair, wrists, ankles, or, most daringly, to the obi cinched at their waists. At nightfall, they would run through the village and fields, daring the men who had no woman yet to catch a ribbon. It was always amusing to watch as ribbons magically appeared when certain handsome youths were about, revealed by the hitching of a kimono or a flick of one wrist.

The Kinumora village lord was a vassal who had given his house over to her and her party with elaborate apologies for such a wretched dwelling, completely unworthy of anyone of quality. Of course, the house was a beautiful and elegant cliffside retreat, rustic and charming with gleaming, polished cedar framing the doors and first-quality tatami mats on the floors. The sounds of the crashing waves below them made a stirring music to sleep by, the salt in the air a spice to match the sharp scents of her father's mountain fortress. The night before the ceremony to honor the god, Chiyo came with a carefully written and folded note requesting a meeting with the famous Lady General, Masako.

Opinions were divided on the outlandish yet undoubtedly successful general. Samurai women were not often tutored in swordplay and battle strategies, although there were historical and mythic examples of great female warriors. There were a few in the current living generations, including within the Fujikama family.

Umiko's second cousin, Shiori, was quite skilled with the naginata, a traditional women's weapon, and had vowed not to marry any man who could not defeat her in battle. It was quite a scandal until Lord Kagehiko came to woo her with his own blade. Oh, how they clashed on a summer evening, sparks showering the air like fallen stars as they danced and wove their streams of silver. The shafts whirled and crashed, the blades sang, and finally Shiori's treasured heirloom was struck from her arms and she stood at the point of Kagehiko's halberd, chin out, hair wild, furiously beautiful. He did not laugh. He did not threaten or scold. Instead, he turned his own weapon in his hands and offered it to her.

"Defend our land," he said, his voice hoarse. "Defend our home. Defend our sons and daughters. And I swear I shall honor you all my days, and forever defend you and all that is yours."

Cousin Shiori was now contentedly awaiting the arrival of their second child. Songs were sung of their unorthodox courtship.

But a woman was not supposed to devote her life to the arts of war. And she was not even a proper noble! Her family had been samurai, but a long-overshadowed, vaguely disreputable, yet admittedly ancient branch in vassalage to one of the minor lords who had been quick to throw their banners behind Prince Yoshinake when he made his claims over the province. It was said their poverty had occasioned instances of inferior marriages to non-samurai, but no one cared enough to investigate. In her generation, there were no sons to take up her father's swords. Yet one day, she appeared, fully armored upon a well-caparisoned battle steed, incapable of defeat. Swearing herself to Prince Yoshinake and no other.

Or perhaps that was what made it possible; with no family of note to force her to marry and breed young and the good fortune to have found a patron who did not mind the service of an armed woman, Masako was uniquely situated to assume her position.

Umiko's mother disapproved; her father was much in favor. "A general who wins is a general who wins," he declared firmly. "A woman or a monkey or a eunuch, what does it matter if our prince is well-served?"

And it was thoughts of the prince that made Umiko say yes to the meeting.

From the first time she'd seen Prince Takeuchi no Yoshinake, she had desired him, which was astonishing since she'd only seen six summers. It was her first appearance at court, and she'd seen the young prince kneeling on the dais with his family, accepting the tributes and bows of the visiting lords and ladies. His glossy black hair and sharp, wise eyes startled her; his beautiful, arched cheekbones and slightly narrow brows captivated her. Despite her strict schooling in bows and greetings, she almost gaped at him like some oaf of a peasant; luckily, her mother gave her a firm push into a proper obeisance, and she closed her mouth so hard she bit her lip.

As a Fujikama, she knew she was meant to be the bride of a man who could possibly be emperor one day. That day, when she was but a child, she knew which one she wanted.

So, she had received the infamous Lady General with great courtesy and curiosity. No marriage offers had come from the prince as yet, although she was finally of the correct age. Her mother and aunts had conferred and agreed to wait for up to one year to

19

judge offers as they came, and it was only three months into that year.

Masako arrived by foot, dressed in her military style kimono, the imperial crest of the Prince prominent on her mantle. Her four young guards bore banners and haughty demeanors, obviously proud to accompany her; they waited by the gatehouse, served sake by one of the prettier housemaids. Umiko saw the Lady General attended only by Chiyo and her personal maid.

General Masako Hagane was everything Umiko had imagined; tall and strong, with a straight back and alarming dark grey eyes, like storm clouds over the sea below them. The only difference between the living woman and Umiko's imagination was her age. The Lady General was much younger than Umiko had supposed, still in the bloom of her years rather than the descent. After she bowed and offered formal greetings, Masako eyed Umiko with a measured gaze that was more exciting than insulting.

"Please honor this house by taking tea," Umiko offered. "It is very poor, I am afraid, quite unlike the fine tea you must have in the service of our esteemed Lord."

"You have gone to too much trouble for an old soldier like me," Masako demurred politely, much to Umiko's surprise. "I beg forgiveness for rudely disturbing the peace of your pilgrimage. You honor me well beyond my worth."

Why did I not expect her to be polite? Umiko wondered, as the maid poured tea for them. They continued the dance over little teacakes; Umiko offering them and apologizing for their poor quality while Masako praised them extravagantly. Umiko relaxed into the familiar rhythm and waited patiently until Masako reached into her mantle and withdrew a beautiful folded package, sealed with silk ribbons and wax.

"I apologize for rushing to the matter at hand," the general said, laying the folded paper down onto the mats between them. "I am a miserable messenger and beg you to forgive my directness. But it has been whispered that you would not be adverse to a marriage to my Lord."

Umiko could barely breathe with excitement. "Should your great Lord deign to be interested in my poor house, I am sure his suit would be welcomed," she said carefully.

"He is honored by the mere possibility," Masako said. "But it pains me to ask this most inappropriate question, my lady—do you, yourself, have any interest in my Lord?"

Umiko fell silent for a moment and then glanced at Chiyo, who waved the maid away and fell back to kneel some distance from them. Outside, the distant sound of waves and a closer cackling cry of crows seemed like drums of portent. So much could turn upon the wrong answer to such a bold and unusual question.

"That... is an odd question," Umiko said haltingly. "I will obey my family and I am deeply, deeply honored to be considered by such an august prince. But... do I... is it proper..." She faltered, looked back into those storm-grey eyes, and then gathered her strength. "Yes, General Masako. I have long desired Prince Yoshinake and beg you to hear this without thinking ill of my presumption and selfishness."

Masako knelt back comfortably and nodded, seemingly pleased. "It is your selfishness the Prince

21

would desire most of all," she said, with the raising of one scarred eyebrow.

Umiko stared at her for a moment, ran those words through her mind two times and turned them around to examine their meaning. Finally, she leaned forward and poured tea for the general. "Please tell me more," she said.

* * *

They spoke long into that night, and again the following day. No pillow book had ever described some of the more extreme practices her future lord and husband craved. But while shocked at first, Umiko rapidly warmed to the idea of holding him so enthralled. She imagined placing herself astride him in the classic position of Mounting the Stallion, with his glorious body bound in silk, his dark soulful eyes affixed upon her. She could ride him thus, perhaps in the slow, old-fashioned three-shallow, five-deep rhythm, which Chiyo swore was best when the lady was above.

She could score his chest with her fingernails, order him to tell her she was beautiful, take him the way she was taught she might one day be taken... and instead of being rebuked, she would be honored, praised, perhaps even... loved.

"I am not a depraved woman!" she had whispered to Chiyo when they were preparing to embark on their journey. "I must have been mad to say yes! How can I do all these things to my beautiful lord and believe he will think of me as a great courtesan or a more worthy lady? Won't he see me as wanton? What if I am not sufficient for him?"

"From what the Lady General told you, better you might worry that your harigata is sufficient for him," Chiyo giggled.

"Oh! Is nothing serious to you?" Even as she rebuked her friend and confidant, she felt the crimson heat of a blush climb her throat at the thought of even admitting she owned a harigata to a man. A man! Her prince! Her lord and possibly husband! How could she even handle it in his presence? True, it was a handsome piece, chosen after much study and consideration. Beautifully carved to the semblance of a man's noble organ, the shaft was cunningly decorated with delicate crossed ridges, reminiscent of strands upon a loom. At the base coiled wisteria blooms, artfully hand tinted, swelling out so silk cords might be fastened there.

Over several nights, Chiyo had two maids demonstrate the many ways one might be pleasured using a harigata. Of course, many of them mimicked the way of a lord with his lady, but several were intended only for a lady alone, or with other ladies. It had been a most thorough education! But somehow, in all the discussions and demonstrations of where and how a shaft may be employed for pleasure, introducing one into her husband's body was never even suggested.

Although Chiyo did show her a painting of a courtesan introducing a finger between a man's buttocks while embracing his root with her mouth. At the time, Umiko couldn't decide whether such an act seemed strange or simply ill-advised. But on that journey home, her imagination turned to how she might be called upon to please the great prince by doing things few would consider pleasurable.

23

* * *

And now it was time. In the center of a lengthy retinue of her father's retainers and her mother's attendants, family members and guests from her province, she was at last approaching the day of her wedding. She had not seen her husband-to-be since their betrothal, when they were presented to each other publicly with an array of traditional offerings from both families. He was even more beautiful than she could have imagined; truly a god in mortal form, sweetly favored, strong and graceful. His voice swept her heart and trailed along her sides, sending tendrils of pleasure up through her ribs and then down her spine. She was an instrument for him to play; how could she ever hope to be even the least of his retainers?

Yet, when their eyes met, she was surprised to find his widening with pleasure. The slight dip of his head as he ran his gaze over her showed a new shadow on his cheek, the faintest of smiles. When he met her eyes again, she could see a change had come over him. He was no longer as distant. Instead, he was curious. Perhaps even covetous.

Oh, if only she could be a singer or a dancer and could giggle, flirting with him like any lusty village girl! But instead, she said, oh-so-gently, "My Prince..." allowing the title to trail into a gentle question.

"My Lady," he responded.

With a wild rush of perversity, she felt her body change. All the ritual formality could not stem the sudden eruption of heat and moisture between her legs and the pounding of her heart. This was what the pillow books described, what the paintings of reddened women showed! It made her weak and bold all at once, and she dared to smile back.

Their families pronounced the meeting a grand success.

That night, in her chamber, a slender, folded sheaf of papers was delivered, sealed with the Lady General's insignia. It was the first of several cunningly written romances, much in the style of the great court Lady Takako. The chief difference became clear after a page or two of typical character introductions and descriptions of court life. When the naughty and bold Lady of the Misty Valley pressed the shy, poetic Lord of the Pine Forest down upon the floor and wrapped his own silk sash about his strong wrists...

Study had never been so fascinating.

* * *

It took nearly the rest of the season to negotiate the arrangements and her dowry, to spread the word by messengers to all reaches of the land, and to obtain the formal permission and blessing of the Divine Emperor. And for the ladies of her family to complete all but the final stitches of the unique wedding gift only her mother's line was able to craft and bestow.

Her dowry included gold, ingots of fine steel, bolts of raw silk and rare, precious gems. Also, there was an exquisite screen, so old and delicate it was transported in a palanquin of its own, several chests of first quality kimonos, a dozen books of fine poetry and two of history, hand mirrors and ivory combs, calligraphy sets with the finest of brushes and inks, incense imbued with the rich scents of the mountains and the sea. Among the unique offerings was a bronze bell said to be from the time of Queen Himiko, said to be enchanted, although for what purpose no one could say. Naturally, the Prince had the best swords and armor made for him, and there was no attempt to send such items for his direct use. But there was a handsome matched set of newly made bows, both the daikyo, for use standing, and a shorter hankyo, for use from a saddle. The prince's skill in archery was well-known, and no one made more beautiful bows than the clans of craftsmen in the mountains. With them came almost a thousand arrows of various sorts, from stout war bolts and slender hunting shafts to cunningly crafted singing shafts to strike fear into the hearts of massed warriors.

But beyond all of those priceless offerings was the single garment in the chest beside her. The chest was a treasure itself, carved with mulberry leaves and berries and perhaps as old as the enchanted bell. Inside was what appeared to be a lovely under-kimono, in the style of a shitagi: short, masculine, designed for wearing under armor or formal court garb. It was deliciously soft, brushed with the gloved fingers of every lady of the Fujikama family as they chanted blessings into it, knotted every seam with prayers for honor, protection, strength, vitality and wisdom. One line of stitches had been left unfinished until the marriage formalities were concluded. Then and only then was Umiko permitted to see it, touch it, and perform her duty.

But even as she was bathed, anointed and garbed for this task, she knew the labor of her mother and aunts and married cousins had been only the third stage of preparation for this garment. The silk itself was woven in secret, taken from a sacred grove where only certain mulberry plants were grown, and only a single sort of caterpillar was introduced to them. Only one family held the mysteries in this function, vassals to the Black Mountain Fujikama clan. They produced the silk made this way only once a generation, at best, and never more than this deceptively simple kimono. It was dyed the most opalescent pale peach, elegant, understated, and magical. It fell to her, the promised bride, to take up the precious, ancient bone needle and lay the final stitches. Completing the weave of spells infusing the garment was the last thing she did in the home where she was born, before starting this journey to be wed.

Crafted thus, blessed thus, prayed and meditated over, dedicated and passed between women only, it was designed to shield the wearer from shame and betrayal. This silk was a far more subtle armor than the most stunningly wrought, gorgeously lacquered battle panoply could be.

And it was Umiko's most precious offering other than her body, her womb, her bloodline. For she was her mother's only daughter, and the last lady in her generation who was unwed, delivered to her lord husband in a state of ritual purity.

He would take her in rags; he would take her even if she had not agreed to learn and even embrace his intimate desires. With the simple robe in this chest, placed upon him by the hands of his sworn lady, he would be protected by kami so ancient their names were lost in the mists of time. He would become invincible.

This is what I was born to be, Umiko reminded herself. And he is the lord I have wished for since I was a child. I should rejoice that my giri and ninjo align so perfectly! I am ungrateful.

And afraid. Afraid I may not be the lady he truly wants, afraid he is taking me as a weak, pale placeholder for his true desires, eager for the magic and status I bring. The four "romances" the Lady General sent her stirred her blood and desires; not as much for the actual activities described—did she truly want to beat her lord and husband with whips of knotted rope?—but for the promise of his pleasure when she performed them well. If his pleasure were great, then he would surely learn to appreciate her, respect her, honor her... or would he? Could she be a tormentor and a lady worthy to guide his household, counsel and console him, bear his heirs?

"You will be a good wife," Chiyo said with a sudden drop into quiet courtesy.

Umiko stared at her for a moment and then dipped her head. "I shall be the very best wife I can," she said. And that was truly all she could do now. She prayed it would be sufficient.

* * *

The ensemble for the wedding feast was a full 12 layers. The sleeves on three of them were so long they would trail the ground if she lowered her arms as she walked; it would be the last time she wore the maiden's kimono. Some of the garments were so gossamer-thin they seemed woven by the great silver spiders said to live in the western provinces. Her hair was also a triumph of the weaver's art, brought up in complex twists and loops in the latest imperial fashion. To her natural, nearly waist-length was added a fantastical wig, fastened with combs of hammered silver and strands of delicate pearls. The pearls were all perfect, white as the powder on her face. She was grateful for every layer between her and the world, for the training in keeping still, gliding her way elegantly through the crowds of guests and witnesses. It was like some grand drama she'd seen every season of rains, fantastic yet so familiar she could speak each line along with the performers.

She had felt the same earlier in the day, for the Shinto rituals binding them as husband and wife. Then, her clothing was limited to merely five layers, covered with a pristine bridal coat, so blinding white it hurt her eyes to gaze upon it. With her head bracketed by a large white hood, she did not see her prince until they turned to face each other.

Oh, how resplendent he was! His aristocratic bearing was well-suited to the elaborate formal mantle over his grand coat, the arching wings on his shoulders evocative as the steepled edges of the sacred temple in which they stood. The gold and crimson of his sigil were all set against a dark layer of the rare, deep purple mulberry only used by his father's line. His swords seemed to gleam with a light of their own, jutting oh so jauntily through the heirloom sash about his narrow waist.

And when he caught her eyes with his, lifting a sake cup for her, placing it into her hands, whispering, "Please, my lady," all sense of duty fled her once more, leaving only the most raw desire in its wake.

She could feel it like a heated wave, starting in her stomach and then washing through her loins, right to the center of her hooded pearl. The feeling again left her weakened in body.

But strengthened in resolve.

"Please, my lord," she whispered, lifting his cup to him.

Their eyes met and she let him see her desire. Praying it could be discerned through all the layers of protocol and custom.

Did his eyes just… darken?

Did his lips part… just so?

Did his tongue touch the edge of his perfect lip before he raised the cup and took his first sip?

No god had ever had so sublime a wine as what she tasted in her second ritual sip. She could die now, swept away by the streams of heat flooding her limbs. It was unbearable to stay still, to concentrate, to wait for the chance to meet his eyes again, to commune with his powerful, masculine essence. Costly incense of the rarest resins filled the air, spring blossoms and petals had been scattered along their paths, her own delicate maiden's scent of jasmine and lilies were nothing compared to the slight hint of steel and the tang of musk and salt that came from the man opposite her. She desired him more than life. More than honor.

At the third sip, her eyes misted, and she thought she was going to fall forward. Because his fingers trailed hers against the delicate porcelain of the cup, and it seemed a spark flew between them. His touch ignited the stream of heat through her body and she didn't know if she could stand another single moment without touching him.

Perhaps she was depraved. She could only hope it suited him. Because now, she wanted to find out what pleasures she could coax from his body, what he could awaken in hers.

But after they were wed in the eyes of the gods, she had to change into the festive 12-layers and rejoin him to accept the tributes of his vassals and enjoy the entertainment gathered from all five provinces to honor this auspicious day. It was all a web of contrast and confusion for her; bright colors and rich scents swirling around her like spirits. She managed to part her lips for the taste of a sublime ritual dish: the male essence from sea bream topped with a crisp horsetail shoot. As she bit through the delicate head of the root, she remembered the advice in one of her pillow books, to gently employ one's teeth along a rigid shaft. When she raised her eyes to her husband, she found him looking back at her in the same instant.

He is thinking the same thing! she realized.

The evening seemed intolerably long.

When it was at last time to retire, Prince Yoshinake offered his arm to her. The hunger for him had grown to a monstrous weight, more than every layer she wore, pressing against her chest. For a moment, her doubts returned, until she noticed in the honor guard accompanying them, the storm-grey eyes of the Lady General. Umiko paused, briefly, and nodded to her. The General bowed deeply, hiding from the court the fleeting smile she only allowed her new princess to observe. At the sight of that smile, Umiko straightened. She would prove worthy.

* * *

31

The steady thrum of erotic tension played through her body all the way to the private wing of the palace that had been set aside for them. Through the slow and careful attendance of her maids as they removed one layer at a time and took the priceless garments away, then led her to the second bath of the day, where she could at last shed the court-style cosmetics and the heavy wig threaded through her own hair. Then, Chiyo anointed her with a green tea-colored oil taken from a precious box made of a hollowed crystal. One touch on each foot, on the inside of each thigh, over her belly and between her breasts, at her throat and on her forehead. One maid lifted her hair while another passed a smoldering pan of incense below the tresses. These were new scents for her, set aside for her entry into the honorable state of wife. Her mother had used them: the rich, salty-sea aroma and the alluring, deep sweetness of the smoke in her hair were supposed to be reminders of a woman's fertility and ability to create a home.

They drew the whisper-soft sleeves of her sleeping robe over her arms and Chiyo wrapped the sash around her waist. Now, there were no complex knots anywhere upon her body or in her hair. She knelt before the ornate chest with the bronze fittings and drew out the sacred garment for her prince. She took one final moment to breathe in deeply.

There was a sharp sound like a pebble falling into a cup and she turned her head swiftly to see, but there were only the two maids and Chiyo, looking back at her with expressions of hope and joy. But behind them, along the wall where their shadows flickered between the lanterns and their bodies... what was that?

"Is there something wrong, mistress?" Chiyo asked.

"No... no. Nothing." Umiko blinked and looked again. Three shadows, nothing more. She took another breath, stillness broken and then gathered herself. "I will go to my lord husband now."

Chiyo opened the doors for her. Umiko smiled at her and gave her silent thanks and tried not to think of what she'd seen for one brief moment. Surely the sake, or the heat of the day under all those layers, or the excitement of the marriage bed awaiting her, had caused her eyes to play some mischievous game on this most sacred night.

Yet, for that single breath of time, she had seen but two shadows of women. And one sleek, long shadow, sinuous and vulpine, with a long and fuzzy tail.

* * *

"You are beautiful, my lady. And I am yours."

It was only proper he speak first, but Umiko was unprepared for such a bold and unconventional statement. One of her cousins reported her husband's first words were, "At last! Shall we play Hide the Eel now?" Her mother told her that Father said, "I hope I shall be worthy of you." But no one reported compliments. Or declarations of possession.

"Remember, his male spirit seeks a feminine one of power and confidence," the Lady General had advised her. "As a sword seeks a sheath, as the books say, neh? He will seat himself inside of you, yes, but you shall take him and shield his vitality, preserving it. You shall envelop him, receive his body in worship, his seed in fealty. Allow your desire for him, the part you called selfish, to guide you. If you do so with sincerity, this match will be blessed."

So, while every fiber in her being struggled against it, instead of saying something like I beg my honorable lord to accept me, though I am not worthy, she nodded, just slightly.

"I would have you pleasure me," she whispered, the shame of it filling her with an indescribable glee. "Before we proceed to our duty."

His eyes lit with joy! When he smiled, the most beautiful hollow appeared in the smooth flesh of one cheek. His shoulders had been slightly forward, his body stiff; now, he straightened and then bowed to her, an elegant dip of his body. It entranced her, the smooth power in the way he bent.

She'd never had a man of her class bow so low to her.

"Would my lady have me thus, or shall I be bared to her?" he asked.

Oh! The robe!

"Please accept this—" She had to stop herself from saying "poor offering." She paused and breathed in. "Please accept this sacred garment from your wife. It is the Guardian of Princes, the Shield of Silk. I offer it... I present it to my husband, that he may never suffer the pains of betrayal and shame. I would have my lord husband wear it for this night, that it may bind to him... and to our children... for generations to come."

He eyed the pale silk in her hand and sucked in an appreciative breath. It had been many years since a like garment had been made, and he knew its import.

"This undeserving man begs to make himself

worthy of his wife's immeasurable generosity and kindness." With one sweep of his arm, he undid the simple knot holding his sleeping robe closed and shrugged his shoulders. The thin, dark cotton fell away from him, leaving him entirely bared to her for the first time.

It was her turn to suck in her breath. What a magnificent body he had! Worthy of a hero, a godling. He had still the slender waist of a youth, but his chest was firm and she could see every breath he took in the ripples that ran down the ridges of his hard stomach. There was a scar along his ribcage, long healed, but curved like a cresting wave, the end of it pointing right down to his manhood...

Which was also curved, like the horn of a kirin out of the old books of legendary tales. And hard, his foreskin a thin ridge along the base of the head. He was entirely free of even the slight thatch of fine hair depicted in her pillow books, and that was perhaps why he seemed somewhat... larger than she'd imagined.

"It's bad luck if one's lord has a small member," Chiyo told her. "Men who are small and angry because of it are like fugu... puffed up and dangerous, although they look foolish."

No. Her husband did not look foolish. She let the sacred robe fall open in her hands and held it for him, and therefore got to see his elegant body twist as he turned for her. The sweep of his shoulders and the sensuous curve of his back were delightful, but oh... his taut, dimpled buttocks! They were not the curve of her own, which Chiyo assured her were perfectly peach-like, the type men hungered for. But just a little long, his hip motions sending the two sides rocking like pleasure spheres in her hands... his bottom was an invitation. It took her a few moments to remember to slide the silk up his arms.

Their first intimate touch was her fingers trailing the bare skin of his shoulders before she dropped the feather-light robe onto them. He shuddered, a delicious, body-length ripple in the flickering lamplight.

The pale peach color made his body appear as some kami of golden cedar, warm and glossed with life.

"You are so beautiful," she said.

He turned to her, his face bright with pleasure. He had left the robe open, and the frame it made for his body was delightful. "I am glad you find me so, my lady. You are glorious as a goddess; it is fitting I have been made to please your eyes. How may I give you pleasure of the body and the senses?"

Umiko didn't know how to answer. All the positions and all the intricate variations depicted in her pillow books and lively paintings, all the techniques described by the Lady General simply fled from her mind. There was only one thought remaining. Placing all her trust in her selfishness, she said, "I want to touch you."

He spread his arms wide, welcoming her.

His skin was brushed silk wrapped around heat. Her searching fingers started up on his collarbone, trailing it, pressing in until she reached the hollow under his throat and could feel the steady thudding of his heartbeat. It sped up as she ran her fingers down his chest. His nipples seemed... swollen almost. More prominent than those in paintings of men, certainly. When she brushed one, he gave a short gasp. She jerked her hand away, but he caught it neatly in his.

"Oh, my lady. Please. If my sounds offend you, I shall remain silent. But you may touch me where and how you wish. I am yours. Please."

She returned her hand to his nipple and brushed it again, and this time, he was silent. But his chest rose as though offering her more, and she gave an experimental pinch.

He smiled down at her. Playful! Daring her, perhaps?

She pinched again, adding a twist. Still he remained completely silent. His body, though... his hips swayed forward, making his manhood spring slightly, a bobbing invitation to grasp.

"So sorry..." The phrase came out without volition, so ingrained were the standard rules of etiquette! Umiko pressed her lips together and took a deeper breath. "It pleases me more to... hear my husband."

So she got to hear his long sigh as she ran her hands across the bands of muscle on his stomach, the languorous growl of pleasure as she finally ran her hand up and down his shaft. Oh, how nice it was to touch! She had never touched the enticing boys Chiyo had brought for her entertainment, merely watched as they danced and cavorted with each other and the maids. This tool was delightful! It was so much more giving than any harigata. And the sacred sack beneath it was heavy in her palm... until she looked up into Yoshinake's face and saw his lips part in a moan of pleasure.

Then, they were light as a warm breeze in autumn. She rolled them gently, and was rewarded with both a shudder and another moan.

He was pleased! No, more. He was excited. And

all from gentle touches? But he doesn't want them forever, she reminded herself. Carefully, she closed her hand, increasing the pressure. She almost looked away a dozen times, but she forced herself to keep watching his face. His throat tightened; he drew in a sharper breath. His dark eyes widened and he nodded. "Yes," he whispered. "Yours now, my lady."

Hers. Her prince, her lord, her husband… hers to use and enjoy. Umiko let his balls hang freely again and continued her exploration of his body. He had another scar on one hip. Finally, his lovely bottom was glorious in her two hands as she patted and squeezed it through the robe and then under it.

Her own body seemed radiant, as though she might burn her sleeping robe off with a twitch and a thought. There was a deep, seeping hunger between her legs now.

"Caress me," she said. "Touch me… and… and please me."

"Please forgive my ineptness," he said. And then, he dropped to his knees before her, which shocked her into stillness.

But he wasn't bowing… at least not in any proper social form. He folded down in a fluttering of silk from the robe, and before the edges touched the floor, his lips were pressed to the top of her right foot.

It felt like he had drawn a spark from flint and steel. She was ignited, instantly, from that touch of his mouth… his noble, sweet mouth!… upon her skin. He ran his lips from her toes all the way to her ankle and her flesh pebbled with the power of that simple caress. When she curled her toes, he dipped down to press gentle kisses upon them and then he swept to her left foot to repeat the worship. Then, without using his hands to part her robe, he nuzzled and ran his lips and his smooth cheek against her calves and slowly up her legs.

She wanted to tear her robe off and be bare for him, but the perverse pleasure of the light fabric being parted and falling, brushing against his own robe, the heat of his lips and the chill in his wake were all like threads on a loom, all suddenly necessary, rendering her incapable of making one sensation paramount.

He did not aim directly for her jade gate, or the pleasure pearl, as she thought he had planned. Instead, as he neared, he cupped one hand over her mound, as though shielding it. For a moment, she was puzzled, but focused on lifting the sides of her robe to better feel his body up against hers. He pressed his lips to her hip and then tongued the flesh slowly, a trail of heat that caught silk as it dropped against it… his silk or hers, she couldn't tell.

Then, she rocked her hips slightly forward and knew why his palm was there, between her legs. He captured her heat and made a cunning shell to reflect it back against her, and when she writhed even a little, she was held by that firm, strong, yet perfectly comfortable place to rest. Like rocking on a bolster in her bedchamber!

But so much better. She gasped out loud, as what was once a flutter of pleasure and desire became an insistent need.

"I want… I must… please, my lord…"

He stopped running his tongue across the curve along the top of her hip and pulled himself back. Before he could ask her anything, she folded neatly to her knees

39

before him, running her hands across the sides of his head, down his shoulders. "You... your..." She felt the searing heat, the fire within her demanding to be fed. There were no words for this. The romances failed her, so she pulled at him, drawing him against her. "Please," she murmured against his ear. "Please, now."

"As my lady wishes."

He surprised her by pressing her back. Not a playful tumble upon the luxurious futon and quilts laid out for them, but a slow, boneless glide of their bodies, like jellyfish undulating in the moonlight. His lips continued to caress her, but now from the top of her body and then down, nuzzling through her scented hair, across her ears, down her throat. Enraptured by his lips, the heat of his breath, Umiko cried out when he finally parted her robe entirely and their skin met. And when his hand returned to the well between her legs, this time she felt the stroke of his fingers opening and parting her.

Her earliest teaching in this art suggested she turn her head and avert her eyes to show her new husband how completely his she had become. But the Lady General had suggested otherwise. "The spirits of lust enter through the eyes for acts of this nature," she had written. "Capture his passion with yours. Most men are weak before the desire of most women; let him see yours."

So she kept her eyes upon his face and saw a moment of shock. But it flickered as quickly as a lamp in the wind and his beautiful eyes sharpened. And with a determined force she thrilled to see, he dipped his head and writhed against her, lithe as any pleasure youth, his disciplined body suddenly as sinuous as a snake. His lips fastened upon her breasts, sucking each nipple up briefly before resting against her heartbeat. Then, down, further down, across her belly, and she opened for his worship at her hidden pearl, now aching.

All at once, the storm of passion rushed through her, a bolt of lightning inside, and she burst like a ripe persimmon against his mouth, so quickly, completely without warning! He gripped her hips in his hands as she shamelessly arched up against him, and the sheer relief gave her license to cry out again, gathering fists of silk in her hands.

Still, he did not relent; he did not pause to allow her respite. Instead, he licked and sucked at her to bring forth another such wave, this time slower, longer.

"Please," she whimpered. "Now, husband, now, my lord, now, please…"

He crouched up and for a moment, she felt a thrill of fear. The threatened pain seemed almost a blessing; it would strengthen her, give her focus. When he fitted the turtle-shell head against her, she gasped. Oh! Oh, this was too much! Just the thought seemed likely to carry her away again! And he was slow, so slow, slipping and sliding along her, nudging at the pearl one moment and then gliding down her folds to the opening below. It was like the caress of the harigata, except he was warm, oh so warm, and the velvet softness of his skin was so pleasant…

But when she closed her eyes in a sweep of passion, thinking, now we shall do our duty it took barely a breath to snap them back open. Her duty!

He stopped his motions as her body stiffened.

"Have I hurt—?" He started to ask, but Umiko reached for him and touched his lips with her fingers.

41

"So sorry… I… my husband." She gathered every scrap of strength she had left. "Please. On your back, please."

With that tiny smile she'd come to realize was for her alone, he easily rolled and brought her along, his arms strong as steel bands as he lifted her up over him. Yes, the sacred robe fluttered around his body and under it where they were about to be joined.

Perfect.

Carefully, she guided his manhood back against her folds, and started rocking gently, as Chiyo had advised. "In this way, you shall grow accustomed to him and you will open like a flower," she'd said. "Rub your pearl, it may help. Or, let him, if he is deft in that art. I suspect he will be!"

He was. And he didn't need her to tell him. Instead, he immediately pressed into her, his fingers circling and then stroking, holding her in the way called the Ox Horns.

Slowly, she began to take him into her. All the ladies she knew disagreed about the discomfort of the first time. Chiyo had brushed it off as meaningless. One of the maids confessed it was terribly painful the first two times, and then never so again. One of her cousins sighed and admitted she'd barely noticed. Her mother merely told her what all mothers tell their children. "There is no greater pleasure in the world than doing one's duty correctly."

And so she was surprised at the moment of searing heat—had she done something wrong?—and then it was gone! They met, husband and wife, lord and lady, joined together, his erection enveloped completely by her body. She gasped, her hands braced against his chest.

"Ah!" he cried with her, arching his back. "My... my lady!" His face was naked to her, frightening in the intimacy she'd been granted. Wasn't it said that the men of his line had three faces and six hearts, each one buried deeper and deeper, until only the gods themselves could know the truth within them? Yet there he was, stretched under her, his chest a golden, flickering expanse of muscle and sinew, his throat pulsing, his face flushed and radiant.

Mine, she thought. Delirious, yes, she was mad, a crazed, depraved woman, writhing like an animal with her lord and surely she could never face him again...

But their eyes met and all she could think was mine, mine, he is truly mine.

* * *

She lay next to him; his strong body sprawled as loosely as a child in his repose. They both glistened with the exertion of their marital debut. The taste of him on her lips was sweet and briny all at once, like the finest urchin roe.

"It is good luck for a maiden to achieve clouds and rain at least once the first time with her lord," Chiyo had assured her.

We shall be blessed with luck, Umiko thought, smoothing her hands down her husband's body. Soft, soft, so soft, like a petal falling in a summer wind, like a wave of new silk thread before it had been captured on the loom. And when he slept, she raised herself to look at the robe cast aside in their ever more inventive coupling. Less than one segment from the coil of incense had burned away since she allowed herself a

43

glance at the sacred garment. Its pristine, pale peach had been crumpled, soaked, wrenched about and stained. The greatest stain was from where they had joined, a spot of darker pink mingled with glistening remains of his pleasure and hers.

Now, in the slightest glow of the lowered, flickering lamp, she could see quite clearly the area where the mark had been.

It was as unblemished as the day the silk had been brought to her mother. Their offering had been accepted. The Shield of Princes was now his, as she was. And he was hers. She could hear, in the distance, a rising wind, but her husband was a steady heat beside her.

* * *

Many remarked on the marriage of the young prince and how perfectly he had been matched with such an attentive, polite, and charming girl. His retainers smiled behind their fans when they saw how their lord brightened to see her and laughed in the boisterous way of men when he left them earlier than was his habit to go to her side and bed.

Old Lord Senji gave the younger courtiers of the household his knowing gaze as they were forced to admit their prince was a devoted husband to an entirely acceptable lady. Wagers were made concerning when they would receive the news she was bearing her first child.

And for the Lady General? Here even the strident Lord Okubo could not find even a hint of scandal to fret over. Indeed, the frightening woman seemed more pleased than anyone at the success of this union! She was punctiliously polite to the princess and was even instructing her in the arts of the naginata (the traditional halberd women used) and tessen, the war fan. When word had gone out of these lessons, many samurai women suddenly demanded fans of their own, and dozens were sent to the new princess as gifts and offerings. Naturally, she returned similar gifts, occasionally a fan painted with her family's wisteria blossoms mingled with the imperial chrysanthemum. To own such a fan became a mark of distinction as Princess Umiko began to establish her own court of ladies.

As the summer ended, several obstreperous lords to the south began to experience "bandit raids" which required the massing of armed retainers to "defend their lands." Prince Yoshinake was not foolish enough to believe the stories and dispatched his Lady General at once to deal with it. After sending spies, she gathered her own troops and marched forth.

The court settled in as the peasants harvested and the cycle of the year turned. They waited for their next prince to be announced, assuring the line of succession for this house.

By mid-winter, when the Lady General returned with the heads of two rebel lords and the stoic hostages taken from among their heirs, the court was still waiting.

* * *

"I have been examined by the finest onnano-miko, and so too, my lord husband has seen a healer from the Celestial Kingdom, well-known for his magic potions," Umiko said to the Lady General as they walked in the crisp, cold air. The gardens in winter sparkled with frost in the morning, giving way to reflecting droplets by mid-day. The General had given her report and formally introduced the hostages to the prince, but her usual post-report meeting had been brief.

"Please speak to my lady wife," Yoshinake had said, his eyes cast down. "My glorious General; I fear I have offended the gods in some way. Surely, this must be my fault, for the Lady Umiko is sublime and I have come to adore her. I strive to please her and do my duty as a husband... but..." He shook his head sadly. "I have failed her, and you, and my family... perhaps even the gods! Please. Go to her."

She went at once.

"I beg you to forgive my bluntness, highness, but is the prince all a man should be with you in the night? Does he rise and stay within you? Does he issue forth his essence?"

Umiko lowered her eyes for a moment, hiding a sad smile. "Oh, General... indeed he does. Even so, he has taken the potions, eaten of the finest in male-strengthening foods. And we have used..." She paused, glanced around. But her guards were far away, standing by the gates and up on the broad walls. "We used the higo zuiki!" Even whispered in private, it was almost too embarrassing to mention. The strands of carefully cut and measured fibers from a certain plant, soaked and then wrapped in layers around a man's member made it stand erect and engorged and slippery, all at once. It also made him... thicker. Once she figured out the proper weave to work around him, their gasps and sighs and hunger had been so great, she had been amazed at his vigor and endurance! Oh, that night she had called him her stallion.

But still no child had taken seed within her.

"We summoned the old monk of the valley, the one they called the Demon Scourge. He cast spells and burned sacred incense for us, and suggested the lord my husband cause a dosojin to be carved. That very night, he ordered one hundred made and dedicated!" The General nodded; the sacred stone kami were known to encourage fertility. One hundred might be excessive, but at the very least, they might encourage a healthy crop of peasants next year.

"Was there any change at all after the monk had cast his spells?"

Umiko gave a sad laugh. "Ah, for three nights, my lord was inflamed with lust, indeed. He was mighty as a bull, and begged me to bind him and then broke the fine ribbons I used! We were both sore the next day, yet eager again by night. We did all as the monk directed, but nothing happened save pleasure. In fact, my maid Chiyo became exhausted—she said we kept her awake and she needed to move to another house to sleep. The poor thing was taken by a fever kami and is still a little weak."

They walked on, past bare limbs and the bones of old leaves.

After a time in thought, the older woman asked, "And what of your pleasure, highness? Do you achieve satisfaction always?"

Umiko gave the slightest bow of assent. "He pleases me greatly, seeking my release before his own. I have learned many of the practices he hungers for,

47

and my lord honors me in saying I have become somewhat skilled. I know my meager efforts are not nearly what his loyal General offers, but I have prayed for more artistry. I... truly, I do not deserve his esteem, or his affection, as it seems I may be barren. Perhaps I am not the correct wife to serve such a perfect lord! He is so perfect, General, so beautiful and fine! I am blessed by his gaze, unworthy of his notice, let alone the kindness and generosity he shows me. It is as though I go to a god in the night..."

At this, the General paused in her steps. "Ah," she said. "I must consider this. Please excuse me, highness." With a deep bow, the General swept off, her own guards almost making a clattering sound as they hurriedly left their post by the exterior gates to catch up with her.

Umiko stood in silence for a few moments after that abrupt exit. Then, with a shiver and a frown of confusion, she slipped her hands into the warm sleeves of her coat and walked slowly back to her ladies.

* * *

"A pilgrimage? In winter? Folly! Or worse! It might some vile plot!" Lord Okubo charged, shaking one fist.

"It does seem strange," Old Lord Senji was forced to admit.

"A plot, it surely must be," Lord Hattori whispered, after casting his eyes about to ensure no one was listening in. "But my lords... have you noticed the strangest thing?"

"The strangest thing is our great prince having his

wife and the future mother of his sons go away to who-knows-where with that... that unnatural female and no proper retinue of guards! There should be one hundred swords accompanying her, and priests and monks to free her from the evil kami blocking her womb!"

"Ah, you go too far!" the Old Lord admonished.

Lord Okubo gnashed his teeth. "There is nothing too far in defense of our lord."

Lord Hattori glanced around again and then stepped in close. "Of course, you must be right," he said with a soothing purr. "But... has anyone else noticed the strange behavior of the court ladies in regard to this pilgrimage?"

Old Lord Senji frowned. "I have not. My wife has barely spoken of the affair."

"Bah! The ladies are useless! They should be talking sense into the princess, defending her with their lives! Instead, they have ceased their endless chatter, gossip, and meddling and behave like a flock of starlings when a cat's been loosed!"

Hattori nodded slowly. "Indeed it is so. That is the oddity."

They stood in the light of the winter morning and considered. And parted from each other, each determined to discover the source of this odd behavior.

The court ladies remained infuriatingly reticent.

"Of course the princess must do what she feels is right," they would say, their eyes modestly lowered, fans fluttering, voices serene. "Surely, we must trust our wise lord."

No amount of shouted demands or wheedled teasing would move them a single thread from those phrases. Lord Hattori was correct—this was a most mysterious development. The unity of those most baffling creatures, from high to low, mothers to chamber maids, was so unsettling, there was nothing to do but let the Princess Umiko and her tiny escort leave. She had two maids, a cook, two male servants, six bearers, and Chiyo to accompany her. And instead of an escort of 50 stalwart warriors, there were only a dozen, all from the Lady General's personal guard. They were fierce, arrogant, and young and handsome, none married and all deadly. Leading them was the General herself, outfitted for battle, banner raised.

No one from the court could suggest any force great enough to threaten such an escort, especially when the Prince himself blessed their journey. To where, no one knew. And to do what exactly, no one could say.

* * *

"I don't even understand this," Princess Umiko confided to Chiyo when the retinue had traveled three days. They were traveling along the mountain ridges marking the borders between Prince Yoshinake's capital lands and her family's territory. The familiar air was welcome, swirling around them with the scents of winter rain and the hint of frost. "I feel like such a fool, for the General has patiently explained it to me twice, and I fear asking again. But how can a forgotten god or kami help me?"

"Goddess," Chiyo corrected, pouring tea for her.

"God or goddess, what is the difference?"

"Ay! Do not ask this of her when she comes to speak to you!" Her eyes were teasing, but she lowered

50

her voice. "If she comes." Her previous illness, after the monk's visitation, had been finally overcome. Chiyo was back to her usual teasing nature. In fact, she was almost as effervescent as the spring they were heading too.

In the ages long ago, when the emperors were only a few generations from divinity, god and spirits roamed the land in numbers to rival the mere humans planting their rice and radishes and mating in the fields for amusement and fertility. Why, a wandering god might piss out a well of sake for a clever maiden, or grant a golden lance to the samurai who could slay a mighty demon-beast. Mischievous spirits lived in sake bottles and brooms, dire ones infested swamps and mountaintops. It was a less refined time, less bounded by ritual and propriety.

Remnants of that past remained everywhere. In stone lanterns worn down by the ages and set over mounds of bones to honor forgotten warlords; rustic gods and their shrines scattered alongside crossroads grown over with wildflowers and brambles. Ritual dances of entreaty and petitionary fervor amid harvest festivals seemed to stop just short of outright public orgies and bloody sacrifices. The seaside village where the sacred silk came from had posts carved with enigmatic art showing silkworm cocoons and moths alongside human figures of the same size. Were the people tiny kami? Did those primitive folk think they lived inside the cocoons, or perhaps helped form the precious silk so unique to the land? Who knew?

Men's magic still showed itself in the carvings and stone statues resembling the mighty male member, erected to entreat the spirits and gods for strength, virility, and fertility. In the fire dances where men

51

wore masks and became, for a night, petty gods, thundering and stamping their dramas and frightening demons from homes and villages. In the secrets of the forge, where they made the sacred arms of the samurai caste, blooded them and named them, hoping a powerful and bloodthirsty spirit would find them an attractive place to dwell.

And the women's magic—ah. That was a great mystery. Like the making of the silk and the robe, the women of the past ages gave great gifts to their daughters and granddaughters. But each secret, each ritual, each note in the song of life was held like a miser's treasure. A small token here, a whispered word there. Every generation lost a little more and prized what they held.

Thus, Umiko had heard of this mountain, and this stream and this spring… in a way.

There was a custom, when a child was born, to build a shrine and dedicate it in their honor. But when a daughter was born, the shrine was given a special incense made from the resin of pines found on this mountain.

There was a song, chanted as rice was pounded into cakes, that spoke of giving the cakes to a maiden who has passed her first moon blood and was sent to the stream to offer it to the kami in return for fertility.

There was a vine that grew along the stream, entwined with wild cucumber plants, that made a stout cord that was traditionally dyed red and used to tie off the umbilical cord of a first daughter. Umiko's mother had given her one in an undecorated pine box; all she said when giving it was, "I shall come to you at the hundred days and show you what to do with the cord."

And there was this pool, a pool that bubbled up

from the earth, steaming even through winter. It smelled foul sometimes. Some said it was because demons were captured beneath it, and therefore the waters would make you strong if you immersed. But others said it was a bath for mountain-dwelling creatures like oni, a kind of terrible ogre, and only smelled thus after they had bathed. But all agreed, stench or no, it had been at one time a sacred place for women.

But very few actually went there. From time to time, families would hire a wandering nun to ascend the mountain and fetch back a bottle of the water, which would be poured out over a new field or offered on a funeral pyre of a woman who had birthed at least two daughters. Why two? No one knew! They would laugh if you asked, joke at how superstitious the ancients were, and how no one believed this nonsense, and yet...

This was where Umiko was going. And why?

It was madness. Every step along the way took her away from the safety and security of court, family, structure, and predictability. From the refuge of ritual and formality. Closer to mystery, doubt, the chaos of gods and spirits and magic not constrained by offerings and plaintive chants.

Wide, well-traveled lanes gave way to twisting, ancient pathways. Endowed shrines tended by fat, contented monks were replaced by the frames of crumbling, silvered poles over worn statues with distinct features. From time to time, the Lady General called for a halt, and offerings were placed before these rustic gods. One night, Umiko walked along the bank of a tiny stream, gazing at the moon hiding behind the peaks above them and found a surprisingly elegant looking Jizo, recognizable in the chubby, childish features of the face, discernible even through a ragged coating of lichen. It was tilted askew by the roots of a willow, its proper shelter long gone. But it was so lonely and beautiful in its isolation. Without thinking, she took the stone in her hands and righted it, finding a more level setting for the base.

I don't have a child's bib or bonnet for you, Umiko thought, reaching into her sleeve. But here is a lovely kerchief. Wear it in the dark lands and know we mortals have not abandoned you. She tied it around the figure's head, making a handsome knot. Please, Old Jizo, she prayed. See my desire for a child. I would cherish them, care for them as I have cared for you.

By the time she returned to the camp, her maids clucking nervously behind her, she almost felt foolish. But that did not stop her from taking the most beautiful rice ball from her morning meal and placing it on the ground before the Jizo as the soldiers and porters prepared to leave the following morning. She sprinkled a little salt over it, the way she enjoyed them when she was a child. But once again, she felt foolish as she turned back to see a fox steal away the rice ball and leap behind the willow tree with its prize.

Despair nearly conquered her. When they were finally on their way again, it took Chiyo a long time to get her to describe what happened. "How can this pilgrimage help?" she cried, leaning her head against Chiyo's shoulder. "Even forgotten, rustic gods reject my offerings!"

"Or perhaps they sent a kami who would appreciate it more," Chiyo suggested. "Surely, stones do not eat rice, but a kitsune… how often do they get such a treat? I have a sudden craving for one myself!"

Umiko thought back to her wedding night and the shadow she'd seen for a flickering moment of time. "A fox spirit? What would one want with me?"

"More rice balls! I will tell the cook to make more later."

Umiko could tell her friend was trying to cheer her. So, she locked her worries inside and put on a brave mask.

* * *

On the second day into the ascent of the mountain, the Lady General called a halt alongside a rushing stream. Across a narrow bridge, a man was fishing, his head covered with an amigasa, a straw hat large enough to hide his face completely. He was the first man they had seen close by since they left the major roads. The Lady General's horse shied before the bridge and stamped furiously, his hooves ringing against the flat stones at the stream's edge.

The fisherman's head turned slightly toward the party. Umiko, puzzled by the pause in movement, slid her window aside to see better and got the impression he was an old man, his posture stooped and his movements slow. He neither hailed them nor attempted to bow low at such an august assemblage. Instead, he carefully drew his fishing line from the water, stuck the pole into the earth—quite rudely!—and bent to retrieve a bundle that had been laid beneath an enormous cedar back from the water's edge. Two swords came from the bundle, and he unhurriedly thrust their scabbards into his wide sash.

Umiko gasped. She could hear the angry hisses of the young samurai around her.

The Lady General spurred her mount onto the bridge. The horse snorted and tossed his head, but she was firm and he leapt forward, landing with all four hooves against the planks, echoes rebounding.

"We seek the sacred waters!" the General announced. "Let us pass in peace."

The old warrior walked slowly to the other side of the bridge, still not raising the hat to reveal his face. He was wearing outlandishly voluminous hakama, so wide one might take them for some theatrical costume, and his gait was odd. It seemed almost as though he walked by placing his toes down first, and then his heels. When he reached the other side of the small bridge, he rested one hand upon the hilt of his battle sword—a perfectly clear challenge.

"Honored General! Allow me to kill him!"

"No, me!"

"He has insulted our lady!"

"I beg for permission to take his head!"

"No, allow me, please!"

The General tightened the reins and stilled her dancing stallion. She dismounted.

"General, I am the least worthy! Please let me take this ronin, he does not merit the favor of death by your swords!" The youngest of her guards, barely into his 16th winter, sprang forward on his equally eager mount. The mare bugled as her hooves touched the bridge. But the General merely tossed him the reins of her own horse. Obediently, he took them and drew her mount away.

She stood at the center of the bridge. "I am Hagane Masako, general! Special Retainer to the glorious Prince Yoshinake. His lady wishes to ascend the mountain and visit the ancient springs. Stand aside or die, old man."

Umiko tapped urgently on the side of the palanquin to be let out. Instantly, the bearers lowered her and her maids rushed to her side as she emerged.

Across the stream, the old man's voice came, weedy and tremulous. "No man may pass," he called out.

"Raise your hat and see that I am no man," the Lady General replied. Her samurai laughed and slapped their chest armor in glee.

"I see you well, lady warrior. I know much of you, more perhaps than you might wish. You may come. Your lady may come. Her maids may come. But no man shall pass." When he spoke, the sibilant sounds were long and slow.

The Lady General stood in silence for a moment. "We mean no insult to the mountain or to the waters or the gods," she finally said. "But the lady may not be unguarded. You say you know of me? Then you know if you impede my way, you will surely die."

In answer, the ancient warrior drew less than a hand-span of his sword.

To the low growling of her guards, the general took the scabbard of her killing sword in one hand and strode forward.

Umiko gasped and clutched Chiyo's arm. Instantly, one of her guards was by her side. "Don't worry, Princess," he said with a bow. "The General will brush this insolent ronin aside like a flea! You are in no danger."

"But... but... look!" Umiko pointed across the stream, as the warrior in his wide hat stepped back to allow the General to join him on level ground. Their

57

shadows were long and as he moved, his flickered and rippled across the bank, showing a profile not at all human! The peak of the amigasa was elongated and pointed like the sharp beak of a crow, and instead of a wide half-moon about his head, there was a tall crest of feathers!

The young samurai beside her frowned in confusion, and Chiyo gripped her back in excitement.

"Tengu!" she cried, her eyes wide.

But before anyone could shout a warning to the Lady General, the two combatants were face to face, and their swords sang free from the scabbards in arcs of silver! They clashed high, and then low, and then each one swept empty air before the two warriors leapt apart.

Or, so it seemed. The general held her sword erect, her arm extended and stance wide. Her opponent held his sword in a two-handed grip, forward and ready to advance... and then the front of his hat fell away, sliced cleanly, revealing his face.

It was the face of a raptor, sharp, large eyes facing forward over a hooked beak, now considerably shortened by the general's sword. Along what would be a hairline on a man was an array of snowy feathers, slicked back and then up like a samurai's queue, and then cascading in an array down his neck. His jacket, which had appeared padded only moments before, was revealed to be rippling with layers of more feathering down his arms and back; a spray of tail feathers poked up through the split back.

"My nose!" he cried, seeing the tip of his beak falling away with his hat. "My beautiful nose!"

"Submit or die, Grandfather Tengu!" the general

said, shifting her stance to match his. "I would not shed your blood on this sacred mountain!"

"The kami shall drink yours this night!" he cawed, and leapt. His hunched form, so ungainly and ancient-seeming on the earth unfolded somehow and his spring was stupendous! What had appeared to be human feet in wooden and straw sandals were instead thick, clawed talons, each toe curling as he flew. He soared up into the air, his arms coming apart to bear him past the crest of her helmet. When he swept down, his sword screeched edges with hers and sliced through the shoulder panel of her armor. It would have taken her arm had she not whirled and then ducked. As he landed behind her, she finished her turn with both of her swords out, the longer in her right hand, the shorter in the left. He screamed again, a raw and ragged thing, the cry of a falcon mixed with the harsh cackle of a crow, and he swept his sword up.

But the general met his attack with crossed blades and thrust down. As the tip of his sword touched the earth, he retreated and then launched a new attack, swinging so furiously the general had to use both blades again to counter his strike. Again and again, the swords met and steel rang.

The young samurai gathered along the bank, not one taking even a step onto the bridge. But they called out their praise and encouragement like youths at a competition. "Kill him, great General! Take his head! Well struck, well struck!" Umiko, barely able to breathe, had never heard men calling so enthusiastically in favor of a woman before.

"She is magnificent," Chiyo sighed, still clutching Umiko's arm. "Fierce as a goddess!"

It could not be denied. The tengu sword-master—for what else could he be, but some yamabushi who had chosen this spot to practice his challenges—tried several attacks unique to his kind. A low, swift rush like a diving raptor; a sudden dart forward like a swallow snaring an insect. But though he could press her back, never did his blade catch her flesh. She deflected and turned his attacks every time, swords clashing or her body dancing around and past him. She whirled like autumn leaves in the wind, swift and graceful, her legs firm and stances wide. Then, in a move so fast Umiko could not follow it, the general's short blade caught a descending sweep from the tengu and the long, killing blade stabbed in like a lance, taking him right in the center of his broad chest, curving up and out his back in an explosion of white feathers stained with crimson.

Blood frothed around the tengu's beak, and he blew out a fine stream of it when the general drew her blade back.

"Taught... you... well," he gasped out. "Honor... and... let... no man... pass." Slowly, he sank to his knees and then toppled over. The escort samurai cheered and slapped each other's shoulders in glee; behind her, Umiko could hear her maids sighing in admiration.

The Lady General slid her short blade into its sheath and drew a cloth from her sleeve to clean the killing blade before sliding it home. She stood over the tengu sword-master and then bent to retrieve his blade and its scabbard. Silently, she took it to where the fishing pole stood erect in the earth, and thrust the sword beside it. When her aide made to cross to the bridge, she held up one hand, and crossed back over the stream herself.

"You will stay," she said, removing her helmet. Her face was resigned, not filled with glee or bloodlust. "The Princess and her ladies shall continue and I shall be their guardian."

"But… General!" cried the captain of her guards. "You have defeated the tengu!"

"He was but the guardian of this bridge. Every step along the way, there will be more."

"We can slay them easily, honored General! Do not order us to leave you and our lady unguarded, I beg you."

"Yes, we may slay them, one by one. And then we would taint the very purpose of this journey with their blood and ours. Make camp here; light fires every night and keep them well-tended. You and you," she pointed at two of them. "Return to my troops and send back the Yumi sisters. If all goes well, they may at least arrive to escort us all home. If I have not returned, they may ascend to follow us."

The Captain bowed, his obedience perfect. "And the tengu, General? Shall we leave it for carrion eaters?"

"No. Gather wood. I shall build him a pyre myself."

They left him burning alongside the river, his fishing pole and katana standing watch over the pyre, rigid as two sticks of incense. Umiko glanced back from the back of her new horse, chosen from among the least spirited of the remounts. With the General before her, Chiyo to her side and two maids behind, she realized she had never before been so far from home without a protective and guiding ring of men around her. Even the servants, although the bearers wailed and the cook packed more food than she and her ladies could possibly eat. There they stood, arrayed along the bank, growing smaller and less distinct with every step her horse took.

It was both unnerving and exhilarating.

Despite the Lady General's prediction, they were not challenged again. Not when they crossed other bridges, or where the twisting, ascending path they rode along crossed with another. Trees grew to astounding heights along the ridges of the mountains, and when the general stopped and dismounted before one, even Chiyo ceased her light chatter to gaze at the massive trunk of such an ancient and sacred sugi. They could easily see it was sacred, for it was bound 'round with a beautifully braided shimenawa, a ritual rope. But instead of being made of strands of rice straw, this rope was clearly silk, and fine silk indeed. It was knotted in an intricate pattern just at the height of the general's broad shoulders, the knot long and shaped like a raindrop. Hanging from the sacred rope were many streamers, usually formed of paper. But these seemed to flutter with the sensual undulation of silk, some of them showing faded stitching or writing.

The general reached into her sleeve and pulled out a similar streamer, a panel of raw, sand-colored silk, rough and unrefined. She bowed toward the tree and then carefully tied the streamer alongside the others. And without a word, she remounted and waved her female party onward.

"Pardon me, General," Umiko called, tapping her mount forward to ride with her strange companion. "What was that for?"

"We shall pass several places where the kami of this mountain have made their marks," Masako said, looking around. "I do not know which one will find her way to you. So, I have brought offerings and prayers for them all. Since the guardian yamabushi have allowed us to travel without further challenge, we shall be at the sacred pool tomorrow, even if we stop at every shrine and hallowed ground along the way."

That night, they made camp beneath the sheltering boughs of ancient trees. The rush of distant waters echoed against the mountainside, heralding the streams and pools awaiting them the following day. But as the shadows grew, the freedom of riding in the crisp open air and the excitement of travel without having to be ever watchful for the fragile nature of men's vanity and sexual confusion gave way to a sense of foreboding.

"Aren't you frightened?" she whispered to Chiyo, while the maids tittered and fussed over tea. The general was pacing the perimeter of the camp she had chosen, seemingly tireless.

"No! What can harm us when we have the greatest of warriors guarding us?" Chiyo asked. Her voice was merry, her eyes bright in the light of their lanterns. "She is so frightening, even to me! If I were just a little more courageous, I would seek her in the night for pleasure. And were she a man, I would do so ten times and burn incense in prayer for a strong son!"

"Not a strong daughter?" Umiko asked.

"Ah, all daughters are strong," Chiyo said. "That is how they can stand becoming mothers." She raised a hand to her mouth with a gasp. "Oh, my lady! You know I did not mean to hurt you! I am so terribly sorry! Please forgive my mouth—it runs like a blind mouse!"

Umiko tried to smile and knew she was doing it very badly. "Of course, Chiyo-chan, of course. But you spoke only the truth. Were I strong enough, surely the gods would have granted me a child for my lord."

"You are strong," said the low voice of the general. She came from under the boughs, brushing sakaki leaves from her hair. "It is not your strength which is in doubt, but your power."

"Power, strength, what is the difference?"

The general sighed and folded her knees to join them upon the mats by the lanterns. The planes of her face were stark in the golden glow, her storm grey eyes eerily lambent. "It is as your handmaid says, my lady. All women are strong, or must be strong, in this world where they are born, live, strive, and carry forth the next generation. But strength is... like a tool. Power is how you wield it."

She looked almost ready to rise again, but Chiyo produced a flask of sake and poured a cup. "Oh, wait, please do not go! Please, tell me more, General, I am a poor woman who doesn't know of such complicated things!"

Masako gave a harsh, low grunt that was almost a laugh, but relaxed back down and accepted the drink. Umiko gave a slight smile to Chiyo for the face-saving question.

"Your lady is more than strong enough for our lord," the general said, after a sip. "But like any good samurai wife, she seeks first and always to please him. To be a proper wife for him. This is laudable and worthy. But it is not what he needs to bring forth the spark of life within him and bind it with hers. He must be mastered by his lady, taken by more than affection or lust. I was mistaken to believe her desire for him would be more than enough for such a binding. Clearly, it pleases the gods that they find joy in each other. But to make an heir will require our lady to embrace the power within all women which we have forgotten in our modern, civilized world. The power of generation, of the Exalted Primal Lady, She Who Invites. We acknowledge her great, shining daughter, Amaterasu, but in the light of day, the power fades from the kami of those lost times, revealed only in shadows."

Umiko shivered slightly under her quilted coat, remembering the dancing shadows of the general and the old tengu yamabushi.

"In the night, though... in the night, a lady may find the power hiding under her strength. Men whisper their secrets, swear oaths, conceive acts vile and ambitious, all in the arms of some lady whose power weaves around and through them with or without purpose. That is why so many men are helpless in pillowing—the powers they do not understand nor believe in embrace them and take them. But that is not enough for our lord." She looked at Umiko. "You must embrace such power deliberately. Allow it to flow through you and over you like a cascade of water, seep into your bones like the embrace of the hottest bath. And then, with such power, direct your strength."

Umiko felt the pressure of tears and blinked them away. I must ask, she realized. I must.

"Is that... is that what you do with my... with our lord? Are you not better suited to him than I am?"

Chiyo sucked in a breath and turned away to busy herself, pretending she had not heard. Of course, it was no matter who the prince pillowed, or why, so long as he treated his official wife with respect and honor. Indeed, any good wife would be amused by such a question—what did some dalliance or even a lustful, joyful time with a concubine or courtesan have to do with being a wife? Umiko lowered her head, suddenly warm under her layers, ashamed.

"I?" The general laughed—and not like a woman, gentle titters and a hand before her teeth, but bold and loud, like a man, throwing her head back. "Ah, Princess Umiko, I do not laugh at you, but at fools like Lord Okubo back at the court. Yes, I have strength and I have power—but I gave up what little was in me that desires life as a wife or mother so I may devote my poor skills to the service of the Chrysanthemum Throne. That your husband saw in me that flicker of power that attracts his own was fortunate for us both. But even were I better born, still I could not. I knew as a child my duty was to guard, to live a life of steel and blood. This has been the calling of my family since one of my ancestors sheltered a prince from the rain in ages past. In jest, the prince called him One Who Serves Close to Nobility.' Had I a sister or brother to continue our line and pass our legacy forward, I would go to the gods completely content. But…" She shrugged. "It cannot be helped. There is no man fit for me. That is my karma, as it is yours to bear the line that will keep our sacred land safe and united."

She finished her sake and rose in one sure motion. "I have looked into my prince's eyes and yours. You are well-matched. And now, we shall make sure you will be a proper woman, a puissant lady for such a powerful lord." And with a bow, she excused herself to once again walk the perimeter in the darkness, their guard against the night.

Umiko did not think she would be able to sleep, but with Chiyo nestled against her back, she drifted off. She remembered thinking of falling leaves that turned to feathers, the salty taste of her husband's skin like scattered grains across a ball of rice, and sparks rising in the night to become stars...

And then it was morning.

"Today!" the general declared, tightening the reins as her mount stamped and snorted. "Today we shall reach the falls, the pool, and your destiny, my princess!"

* * *

The waterfall started above the clouds and sprayed plumes of water from every jutting branch or rock when the winds shifted. It was slender and focused as an arrow, a silvery line of light leaving trails of scintillating rainbows and puffs of mist as it lost and gained momentum along its downward path. At the base of this plateau was the secondary stream, carrying the water from the vault of the sky into the snake-path leading down into the valley. And within sight of the stream was a worn stone path, clearly etched out among ancient rocks covered with lichen and the undisturbed ground covered with leaves, pine needles and the scruff of dead summer buds and autumn berries. The path looked ancient as the mountains, smooth, rain-washed stones arranged in the style of a rustic garden walkway. Enigmatic old stone lumps were still standing, more or less, along the route, whatever features they once held long lost to time. But the trees...

The great cedars all bore silk shimenawa. Some were mere fragments, caught up in the bark, shredded and gossamer. Others were covered in striated patterns of sap and discolored from the sun and rains.

But as they passed one especially noble tree, Umiko examined the rope and found it looked as pristine as the obi about her waist. She could even smell a hint of the sun-sweetened herbs scattered in the chests where fine kimonos were stored, to keep them smelling fresh and free of damaging insects. Even through the strong scents of pine and cedar, the faint whiff brought to mind the songs and whispers of the maids who brought her fresh garments every day, smelling oh-so-clean...

She gasped as her horse shook its head and jangled the reins. She leaned forward to urge it onward and catch up to the general, who was pointing at the waterfall.

"We must be cleansed before you approach the pool. First the waterfall. The water is icy, my lady, there is no question. It shall be invigorating! Your ladies may start a camp there, prepare a brazier and heat coals for tea. I will scout and make sure we are alone, while you prepare." She spurred away, and Umiko dismounted, feeling suddenly lighter.

Perhaps this will work, she thought, as her ladies giggled and hurried. It was afternoon, but the sun was not quite gone from the sky. She would have time to quiet herself, stand under the waters long enough to be washed ritually clean, and then down to the heated pools by night. Then, to immerse eight times, and rise… powerful.

Oh, kami of the mountains, kami of the stream and the waters… see that I have come to you with the heart of a samurai, ready to serve my husband, my clan, my family, my blood. Grant me what is necessary to bring joy and children to my house, to leave a legacy for the future! Do this and I will cause a shrine to be built to you here, and endow it with income to sustain the prayers and offerings of a hundred monks… no! A hundred nuns. It shall be built by the finest of female artisans, if I must bring them from all corners of the world. And I shall bring my daughters—if they are granted to me—here. And tell them of your might.

There. That was a satisfactory offer. She could do no more. She allowed Chiyo and one of the maids to help her disrobe in preparation for the embrace of the water, and then change into the thin, pure white cotton robe to signal her readiness for purity. Her hair was unbound and let down to fall free; once again, there would be no knots upon her body.

All was going perfectly until the youth arrived.

Chiyo spotted him first. "Mistress!" she cried, and slapped fingers over her lips. Thought it had only been a little time without the company of men, that reflexive gesture caught Umiko's attention faster than the cry itself. She turned to see a strangely tall man—and there was no question this was a man—striding alongside the stream.

He was dressed in chestnut-colored wide trousers with wrappings around his lower legs; on his feet were thick straw sandals. His coat was a paler color, and across his back and over one shoulder was a cloak that looked like the thick fur of a bear in winter. He carried a tall, ornate staff, from which hung a small flask and a large conch shell. Lacking only the little round cap, he was a perfect image of a yamabushi, complete with a short sword stuck into his sash and a longer one in a scabbard across his back.

He walked with a broad and rolling gait, full of arrogance and humor. For a moment, Umiko almost expected her ladies to snap open their fans and start cooing and fluttering at him, except they were all frozen in place.

He came closer, and Chiyo stepped in front of Umiko with a hand on the stiletto in her obi. He stopped and bowed, a low, courtly bow—or perhaps a japing version. When he rose again, Umiko could easily see his wide dark eyes, fairly dancing with the sprightly rhythm of the swirling water at his back. He did not have a shaved crown, but wore his coarse, shaggy hair long and gathered loosely behind him, strands dancing in the wind, framing his head. His face was broad and bronzed, the rough darkness of a man who lived outdoors, further coarsened by a light scruff of a beard. What saved him from looking completely wild, like the men of the northern island, was a merry curve to his lips and a fine, long nose. He pressed his palms together before him to show peaceful intent, the staff tucked under his arm.

But he said nothing.

"What... what are you doing here?" Umiko asked. "Who are you? This is a sacred place for women!"

"Yes, Princess Umiko, it is. But it has lately been defiled, and you may not approach the pools." His voice was low and rough.

The ladies all gasped and Umiko felt slightly faint. But the thum-thum-thum of hooves drowned out their gasps as the general rode past them and stopped before the young man. She didn't bother to draw her blade, but merely turned so her sword arm faced him.

"How dare you approach these ladies? How dare you come near the sacred pools?" she growled. "Be gone, boy, before I make an offering of you to the kami of foolish risks!"

"I cannot go!" he said with a shrug. "I am so sorry, you must believe me. It was not I who defiled this place. Some old woman with blood on her sword slew Grandfather Tengu. Now, the kami here are distressed. Or at least the guardians are. I know this because I am one." His smile faltered, and he planted his staff firmly against the ground. "If you wish to pass to be cleansed, you must kill me as well. And if you kill me, you cannot then cleanse yourself!"

"Since I am not the one seeking the blessing of the gods, why should I care? The blame is mine. Whatever the cost is, I shall bear it. But the lady shall seek the pools."

The youth lifted a hand and slowly tugged the cord holding his fur cape. It slipped from his back to crumple at his feet, leaving the ornate hilt of his sword completely exposed, catching the rays of the setting sun. The general leapt from her saddle, giving her mount a slap. He trumpeted and trotted toward the tree line and the other horses.

"Wait! Please wait!" Umiko cried, stepping

forward. "We do not wish to spill blood on this sacred ground! You know this, Brother Yamabushi. You must understand. Grandfather Tengu made a challenge, and the general had to answer it! The fault is mine. Can we not... make an offering? To appease the spirits here?"

He smiled broadly, his teeth showing. "The princess is kind and generous! We would accept an offering, yes. The first born of your loins, when the seed is grown. We do not even need the first son, a daughter will do. Bring her before the hundred days have passed, and you shall have the blessing of this mountains and all who dwell here."

Umiko felt the blood leave her face, and Chiyo hissed next to her. "Vile creature!" Chiyo snapped. "How dare you? Kill him, General! Kill him for my lady's honor!"

"You have sealed your fate, boy," the general said, drawing her sword. "Your insulting suggestion is an affront."

"Why so, Lady Warrior? My own father was such an offering! And one of my grandmothers, as well. It is a respectable life we live, guarding this source of power you wish to take without an exchange." He slid his sword out of the sheath and held it almost casually. "You know we must always keep the bloodlines enriched by imperial sources. And you know why."

"Enough!"

She snapped her blade forward and instantly, he leapt into a defensive posture. Their swords miraculously passed each other in a rush of movement so fast Umiko and Chiyo both gasped as their hair danced in the passage of wind. The general didn't pause, but drove forward, sweeping her sword up, and was met by the youth's blade at shoulder height for them both.

Chiyo pulled Umiko back and whispered, "Go! Go to the waterfall and be cleansed!" Umiko hesitated, but then Chiyo pushed her. "Go, my lady! Now!"

She dashed. Her light straw sandals slapped against the worn stones of the path, and then sank into the wet banks of the stream. Ayyiii! The water was ice cold indeed! But so clear, she could see the stones and waterlogged leaves as she stepped in, the cold tendrils of water running over her feet and splashing around her ankles.

I am samurai, she reminded herself. Cold is nothing. I will endure and conquer. Behind her, the heavy clang-clang of the swords continued, and she could dimly hear their grunts of exertion as she made her way to the rock face and the trickle of water from the clouds above. She glanced up and saw the bowl of the sky turning violet and azure. Amaterasu, let me feel these sacred waters before you hide your face from us, she briefly prayed, and waded further. Her thighs ached with the cold as water lapped up, soaking the white robe, making it cling to her. Suddenly, it seemed all she could hear was the rush and splashing of the waters.

When she turned to see the shore, she was surprised that both combatants were still as statues, their swords extended toward each other, as frozen as her limbs felt. For a moment, she thought they were taking their measure of each other, like two warriors competing in one of the esoteric contests of skill in drawing their swords, or cutting amusing shapes out of rice paper. But then she realized the maids and Chiyo were motionless, too.

73

The sun dipped more. A line of sky the color of a perfect summer eggplant appeared. Shadows rippled and flickered—her own, on the face of the water. The two maids, clinging to each other, like a statue of twins, or lovers. Chiyo...

Low to the ground, four legged, with two enormous, fluffy tails.

The general, her helm making her appear to be some frightening demon out of a drama, the bulk of her armor making her shadow monstrous...

And the boy. Tall, yes, and broad with muscle, but just as Grandfather Tengu—his grandfather, perhaps?—his shadow revealed him to be tengu as well. At least partly. His legs did not appear to end in claws, and the feathering along his arms was not as huge and extensive as that on the Grandfather. And his crest was a poor thing as well, only a few feathers sticking out, barely worth mentioning.

But he was caught completely still, only the shadow flickering as the sun set, making it longer and longer.

Umiko drew a deep breath and ran under the water. It hit her body in an explosion of pain, needles stabbing her skin from all directions. She couldn't feel her feet, they seemed like huge blocks of stone. As the water cascaded down her back and through her hair, it seemed to weigh her down, dragging the robe with it. And why not? The robe wasn't shielding her from the cold and the pain! She thrust her hands against it and pushed it off, leaving herself naked under the spray.

Oh, this wasn't the way it should have happened! She should have walked slowly, with determination and focus through the water, her mind on nothing. But as the water swept over her, through the screen of water covering her, she saw the figures in combat at the shore shifting positions like puppets, abrupt and staccato, as if they were illuminated by bolts of lightning. She wanted to cry out to them to stop; how ill-omened would it be for her child-of-the-future to come into the world over the blood of a guardian creature?

It never occurred to her that the general might lose.

She gasped with a sudden terrible pain; the water was surely turning her to ice! And then, so swift it made her suck in a harsh breath that also bubbled with the agonizingly perfect water, the torment of the water vanished. It became a light, distant sensation, like the touch of a maid on a summer night when you were foolish with sake and safe in the dark. The water became silk—that soft, sanded silk of her grandmother's favorite shawl. It flowed over her, fingers tapping against the base of her neck and across her shoulders, down the curve of her back and over her bottom, and she thought, ah, it is not so cold after all.

In a moment of perfect clarity, she saw two swords falling, flickering, a glorious steel wall, a thousand swords making the arc as they descended, and as they passed, the curtain of water in front of her eyes seemed to part. The Lady General and the tengu half-breed were now standing apart, and both were folding, bending into the broad, elaborate dancer curls, she could hear the drums…

She stepped forward and time shifted again. There was no cold, there was no slow, over-dramatized show before her. Her toes sank into the earth under the water—where had she lost her sandals?—as she walked toward the two warriors and their whirling, clashing, bloody dance.

For blood had been taken. It colored the lapping edge of the water and then was lost in the crystal clarity. She could feel the heat of invisible droplets, taste the rich salt of sea bream, smell her own body mingled with her husband's, earthy and arousing. Her nipples ached, and not with the cold.

She wanted them to continue their battle, spill more blood for her, blood like what she shed every turning of the moon. Let the blood spilled here be theirs and keep hers to nurture the child-to-come! Surely, the sacrifice of either of these great warriors would be a worthy offering to make a child of great destiny! But as her feet found purchase on the bank of the stream, she realized these were thoughts of destruction, of a dark, demonic lust that would issue forth nothing but curses and loss. She had to stop this pointless battle!

To the horrified shrieks of the maids and Chiyo's desperate warning call, she stepped between the swords.

Two lesser warriors would have cut through her body instantly. But the general dropped her left hand from a two-handed grip and threw her right hand and the sword in it away from her lady's body. At the same time, the hairy mountain youth threw himself forward, passing Umiko by a hair's breadth and tumbling, falling, no, diving and rolling through the half-frozen mud to scamper inelegantly to his feet.

"My lady!" the General growled, turning and taking her sword into two hands again. "You must not put yourself in danger like this! Step away!"

Umiko drew her head up. "I am Fujiwara Umiko,

wife to Takeuchi no Yoshinake Shinno! I command you to cease this battle, General Masako."

Instant, unquestioning obedience was the soul of any samurai, and the general served. But her sword arm shook as she forced the blade down. Blood soaked her left sleeve and dripped from her fingers. There was a dark shadow on her blade, and with a snarl, she snapped it off to one side and sent more droplets of blood flying into the pristine waters.

"I thank you for making my task easier," the youth purred. He was well-splattered with mud and his coat was sliced open, revealing a long slash across his broad and firm chest. Blood trailed down along his muscles, whipped by movement into stripes crossing a startling array of enigmatic black markings etched into his skin. A smile still played upon his sensuous lips as he bent his long legs and then launched himself up, higher than Grandfather Tengu had flown, to plummet down at the general. Cursing, she stepped sideways into the water and retreated before him, dodging his landing blow while sheathing her sword. He tried to turn in mid-flight, but she was too fast and he landed badly, coming down on one knee. The general drew her sword, still in the scabbard, and held it in both hands to block the deadly upward sweep he tried.

Remarkably, he laughed. "You are good!" he cried, scampering backward through the water. "Truly, you gave Grandfather an excellent fight. But be reasonable! You cannot win by running and defending. I am better with a sword anyway. Admit you have failed and die with dignity."

"While I live I have not failed," Masako said, her teeth set.

"Please, please stop!" Umiko pleaded. Chiyo had rushed over to her with a blanket, but incredibly, she still didn't feel the cold. "You are both wounded, you have both drawn blood…"

"Not enough!" laughed the half-breed. He swept his sword across his body and grunted as more blood trickled from his wound. The general knocked the blade aside with her scabbard, but her left arm bent under the impact and she was driven back again.

"Fight on then!" Umiko spat. "I will go to the pool while you court death and anger the kami of the stream." She gave them her back and started toward the ancient path. Chiyo hurried after her, still holding the blanket.

The half-breed turned in shock and started to run after her. But the water was up to his knees, and behind him, General Masako grinned fiercely.

"Fight on," she echoed. "As my lady commands." The youth barely turned in time. The arc of her sword as it came up through the water was almost impossible to track. He gave a sharp cry as blood and feathers burst from his arm. Light from the last rays of the sun danced from his blade as he tossed it from one hand to the other. The general pressed her attacks in a flurry, also one handed, and he could only defend, his eyes shifting to try to follow the path of the princess.

Finally, he held his sword away from him in the point-forward stance of a warrior at bay. The general had hers out as well, and both of them had their off-arms sheathed and gloved in blood.

"We are too evenly matched," he grunted, sounding reluctant as a spoiled child.

The general panted and drew long breaths.

Keeping her eyes on him, she backed to the dry land, away from the icy water soaking her armor and sapping her strength. "I… regret slaying your grandfather," she admitted. "If that is what taints my presence here, I would offer to make recompense. But my lady has gone to what is her right, and I will keep you from interfering!" She circled, putting her back to the path leading to the pools.

"Her right? She has no rights here. She doesn't even know the guardians around her, the strong magic made on her behalf! Truly, warrior maid, she is not worthy of you. Let us put our blades aside and sport, and let the kitsune attend to her needs." He licked his lips and widened his eyes suggestively.

"I serve," the general said. But she smiled, just a little. "And I am no maid, boy. You cannot stand against me in combat or in the pillow arts. In the end, I shall win." She glanced up at the darkening sky, stars gleaming as they pierced the mantle of night. "Even now, my lady receives the blessing she sought. Submit and retreat, and I will make recompense for my errors here. I swear it."

He lowered his sword just a little and cocked his head, waiting. Their blood dripped upon the stones.

The general sighed. "I swear it upon the sword of my ancestors."

The youth stepped out of the water with a skeptical shrug. "Perhaps I will accept your oath. But three things will be required, oh general."

"Name them."

"You burned my grandsire but left his sword and fishing pole in a rude array. Bring him proper grave offerings so he may be reborn properly."

"It will be done."

"The silk robe. You know it. We require a piece of that silk, brought here and offered to one of our great trees. It must be braided as a shimenawa."

"The silk is not mine to give. But I shall ask for it. And explain why it is needed."

"It must be offered, or you shall not be released from our vengeance!"

She shrugged. "I accept my fate. What is your third requirement?"

"Your firstborn child." He grinned at her coarse laughter and used one side of his coat to press against the wound on his chest. "Yes, I know! You have no child and you have no man. But I will be your man, if you wish!"

"A half tengu mountain boy? Are you mad?"

He kept his grin. "You do not wish to think of it because you fear I would defeat you! My sword or my lust, we must determine a winner!" He laughed and then sighed. "Or, you may find some dull flat-lander, take his unworthy essence and give me what comes of it. But you must admit you want to test yourself against me." He looked at the mess he'd made of his clothing and stripped to the waist, using the rags to wipe his sword. The black wings etched into his skin glistened under the starlight with the ink-black trails of blood.

The general sheathed her own sword without taking her eyes from him. "Very well. I shall bring offerings for your grandfather. I shall do all I can to have a shimenawa delivered here, or bring it myself. And should I ever have a first born, it shall be brought here and dedicated to the maintenance or protection of the mountain and all its sacred places. But you are cheated already, since I will bear no child."

"Then you will never know what it is to defeat me, whether with steel or lust. Like your prince, I too have given no lady a child. Perhaps my seed awaits a female strong enough to take it." The youth picked up his staff and bearskin cloak and gave her an insouciant bow.

The general watched him leave, then ground her teeth and went to bind her wounds. She was chilled to the bone, aching, and could feel the hot blood under her armor even while the rest of her skin felt icy. But she did not even approach the path leading to the sacred pools and, in fact, didn't look in that direction. She coaxed a fire in the brazier the maids had assembled and lit the lanterns and held her fingers to the warmth of the flames. And it was a sudden, languid warmth against her back that informed her of the return of the Lady Umiko and her tiny retinue.

Masako raised her scarred eyebrow and chuckled.

Umiko was still naked, but now her body radiated humid waves; the heat arrived even before the excited chattering of the maids.

"Guard us," Umiko said, her voice low and alluring. General Masako rose and stepped away from the small camp, not turning to look directly at her lady. But the sounds behind her as she began a slow, guardian walk around them rapidly became even more amusing. Or arousing.

"Please me," the princess groaned. Kisses and sighs followed, with slow, soft hisses, whispers and murmurs.

Best not to look into the eyes of one who has

gained the blessing of powerful, lustful kami. Or goddess. Whatever lingered here, waiting for women to come with their desires and hungers, wishes and curses. The general only hoped the two maids would be sufficient. If Chiyo also joined them at the pillows, ah, well. The kitsune would need to be addressed later.

A long and ragged cry of ecstasy split the air, and the general allowed herself a brief moment of self-pity. It was going to be a long night.

* * *

The Yumi sisters, armed with bows, swords and their matching naginatas, met them almost at the base of the mountain. The journey back was uneventful, the princess quiet within her palanquin and less so in the night. The Lady General sent her youthful male guards to sentry positions as far as safety would allow.

When they returned to the palace, Yoshinake came out in person to greet his wife. Light snow had fallen all morning, and servants had swept each lane with diligence, scattering pine needles to crackle and release their sweet scent into the crisp winter air. Courtiers and guards all stood back from the young lord and his returned lady, watching them bow, greet each other formally, and then walk together back to their private wing.

And very few noticed that when they trod upon the light dusting of snow, the lady left much broader circles of bare stone in her path.

* * *

"My lady!" Yoshinake exclaimed, as she drew away from his kiss-swollen lips. His eyes were vast and dark with shock and lust, his entire body giving off such a delicious fragrance, Umiko had no patience for her maids and their ministrations, no time for even something as civilized as a bath and a massage.

"My man," she whispered, kissing him again. "Mine. My pet, my husband, my own, you must give yourself to me. Now."

"Now—and always!"

Never had the layers of court dress been so annoying and cumbersome. Umiko pushed and pulled, smiling with every shifting glimpse of shock on her husband's face. He tried to help, and she slapped his hands away. She needed her hot hands on his bare skin, yes, yes, pushing against the beating of his heart, marking his shoulders with her nails drawn like talons as she bit him and licked the bite marks.

He did manage to untie his sash, and in a moment was bare for her. The ring on his erect shaft glistened with moisture, and Umiko smiled as she ran her thumb along the edges and then around the head. "This, too, is mine."

He raised his hands to embrace her and she slapped them down again. "No!" she snapped, and in that instant, the shadows of the room grew sharper. "No," she repeated, this time in a softer voice. "Oh, no, my sweet lord. I have no need of those today."

They had gorgeous ropes, softened hemp, braided silk. But it wasn't rope she needed. "Bring me the robe," she ordered, and watched him as he scurried to the small chest where it was kept. Her kimonos fell in drifts of silk at her feet and she stepped from them as warm as she'd felt when rising from that icy stream. He knelt before her, offering the garment, and she felt something… deep inside, something so hard to catch and name, slippery as an eel. She… wanted him. She needed him, his beautiful body, yes, oh, yes. But she… she…

Shaking the thoughts aside, she took the folded belt from where it lay across the robe. "This shall be your binding. And you will not tear it, as you ruined my obi."

He looked at it in despair but lowered his head. "I shall obey my lady."

Truly, her fingers wove magic as she wrapped the pale and delicate silk around his strong wrists. It was almost comical, the contrast between his sinewy body and the delicate ribbon, the warm brown of his flesh and the ethereal translucence of the peach color. But she could only admire it for so long. He needed to be on his back, yes, with his arms stretched above his head and his mighty shaft curving up in its horn guise, dark with blood and slick with his own moisture. She could strike him, use any of the clever toys and instruments they kept for their pleasure, but she had been with her maids for too many nights and wanted this special, living toy now.

Inside her. So smooth and so fat and sweet and hot, yes, he was hot beneath her… no! She was heat herself, as though coals burned within her and warmed his body as well. She sank onto him and threw her head back in sudden rapture, little realizing she'd drawn her nails down his chest. He arched against her, hands knotted into fists, arms so taut she could see the paths and lanes of his blood in stark relief, like the narrow and twisting path leading to the sacred pool…

And she rose and rocked back again, and it was like when she stepped into the dark and noisome waters, letting the heat rise along her legs until it reached her belly and covered her womb and then she felt immediately... lustful.

Like now. Like this. Her nipples tightly knotted, her thighs drenched, every pore and every hair alive with desire. She pounded on her husband's chest, and he pulled his lips back in a curl of pain-and-pleasure and thumped his bound hands against the futon.

When she sank into the water the first time, her mind had been on the sight of her husband baring himself for the first time, the awe and wonder of it. When she ducked her head under and came up, steam rose from around her and a climax shook her body so hard she thought she might drown in the spasms. And so it happened again, only now she had her beautiful husband inside her, under her, his eyes upon her...

The second and third and fourth times she immersed herself, each time made her reflect on the pleasures of the body, the taste of his skin, his mouth on her aching nipples or between her legs. The tender heat of his sack when she slapped it over and over again with the narrow bamboo rod, and the way he became undone when her fingers found that secret spot inside him...

She wished she'd had the patience to make sure he had pleasure beads in him now, but no, no, her need for this was too great. She leaned forward and braced herself on his chest. He was burning, his heart like a great war drum, his hips bucking up with all his strength.

The fifth time she immersed, the pleasures of the body faded and her mind turned to the pleasures not so easily spoken of. Her pride in him when he listened and made judgments in court, always measured and reasoned. The way he would place a tiny flowering branch on a tray for her or leave little gifts where she would discover them. And in the sixth and seventh times, her body seemed impossibly warm, ready to join Amaterasu in the sky and summon spring. His quiet breath on the back of her neck when they were both weary of pleasure, drifting in a moment of oblivion. The way he would make up a poem and recite it to her in the darkness, showing her one of his hidden hearts.

I love him, she thought in the pool.

I love him, she thought, and again, the pleasure built to impossible levels, and she stretched out as far as she could, and when he looped his bound wrists about her neck, they both found nirvana in a thunderous, torrential wave.

When they awoke and laughed shyly at the scattered clothing and rumpled quilts, Umiko found the sash for the robe. She remembered needing to use a hairpin to help undo the knots, which had constricted so much as he struggled, they were like tiny silk pearls.

It was, like the robe had been on their wedding night, pristine. No wrinkles. No tears. It was as though it had just come from the chest.

Her skin was cool again. Beside her, Yoshinake gazed at the sash in wonder. "Perhaps this offering was also acceptable," he ventured.

"If not, we shall have to try again, my husband," Umiko said, leaning back. "And again and again."

* * *

The first child was a daughter. A tiny, delicate babe, perhaps a little early, but healthy nonetheless. Celebrations were ordered throughout the provinces; shrines were endowed and even His Imperial Majesty sent a gift. The Lady General went on some secret mission, accompanied only by her female warriors, and it was said she had gone to make the same magical pilgrimage she'd taken with the princess. Some courtiers made rude jests that she would return also pregnant or perhaps not at all. But return she did, limping from some injury, but otherwise hale. Though it took some time for her to heal and take to the fields of battle again, there was no doubt she remained quite clearly in Prince Yoshinake's favor.

She was also clearly favored by his wife, the glowing, serene Princess Umiko. Indeed, the princess had commanded her own personal guards be all female from the day the general returned, and only women tutored by the general herself. Of course, this led to a remarkable rise in second and third daughters taking up blades and bows with the full support of their families.

In slightly over another year, the court exploded with the news that the princess had been delivered of not one, but two sons. Two sons at once! It was almost unheard of! Rumors and spite aimed at the Lady General faded away, for even though she still held the highest rank among the Prince's warriors, it was clear her loyalty was complete, her vassalage impeccable, and whatever that strange pilgrimage had been, it was obviously successful. That year, she made another journey to the mountain after escorting the princess to her family home for a visit.

But this time, when she returned, she had a bandage covering her right eye. When she rose from convalescence, she wore a patch. A scar duplicated an old wound bisecting the eyebrow, and extended below the patch and across one cheek.

"He has improved... somewhat," the general said, when the Princess asked after her health. And she would say no more.

* * *

When the miraculous twin sons had passed a full turn of the seasons, the summons came from the Chrysanthemum Throne.

Takeuchi no Yoshinake Shinno, Lord of the Five Provinces, Protector of the Shrines, Bearer of the Sacred Kinumora Fan and Prince of the Blood was now Crown Prince of the Blood.

* * *

Several courtiers were watching from the third story of the palace, Umiko could almost hear the bile in their discussion. "Lord Okubo is wroth. He will tell people you are abandoning your lord when he needs you the most."

"Lord Okubo may fling himself off the battlements into a mound of excrement," Masako said, kneeing her stallion in the stomach. The mighty horse blew out a heavy breath and she jerked the girth tighter. "Foul beast," she said, with clear affection.

The general turned to her lady and glanced at the courtiers with her remaining, storm colored eye. "If I stayed, they would say I am abusing my position. If I go, I am abandoning my lord. They are like crows, cawk, cawk, cawk."

Umiko smiled, just a little, raising her fan. "Not like some crows."

The general nodded, squinted at the sky. "No. Not like some. You have proven yourself blessed and my prince's line is secure. I have fulfilled two of the half-breed's requirements in our bargain."

"Will you... must you stay?" Umiko knew all the details of the arrangement, had even helped braid the shimenawa offering.

"Most likely not. If I defeat him, perhaps I will not want him. If he defeats me, I will hardly think kindly of him. But we were too evenly matched. My blade hungers to cross his again. Perhaps I may pay my debt by becoming a guardian of the mountain instead of bedding that arrogant mountain boy. I am still not sure I want to give this land any more of my line. We are a perverse and sad people, those of my blood. Compelled to guard and serve, ever watching over those who do not even seek shelter from the rain." Her rough voice took on the gentle, teasing sound Umiko had come to treasure.

"If you do not return, we shall miss your wisdom as well as your guardianship," Umiko said. "Our thanks will never be sufficient. You say it is your debt, but it is truly mine. Ask anything of me and you shall have it."

"You have given me more than enough, my lady." The general mounted easily, her lacquered armor no encumbrance. The stallion pawed at the dirt, tassels shaking on his panoply. "I was honored to serve you and the prince. If I do not return, toss some incense on the flames for me. And never forget the secrets of the mountain. Take all your daughters there."

As she spurred the mount away, riding through the gates as soldiers and courtiers hailed her, bowed to her and called out wishes and blessings, Umiko stood quietly, thinking of those final words.

All my daughters? And felt a small spot of heat, right at the curve of her belly. Smiling, she fanned herself as she began her walk back to her chambers and her husband, lord and love.

For just as he was truly, truly hers now, so she was his.

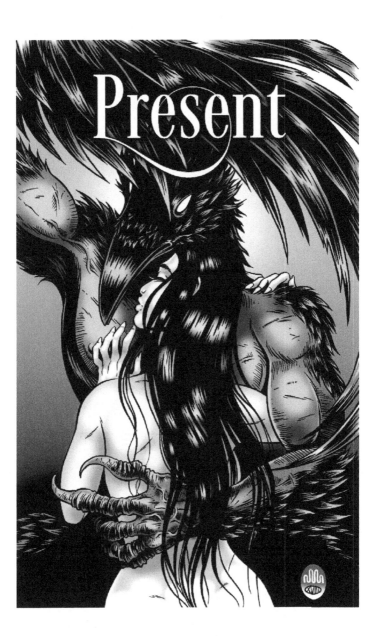

The Secret of Silk

Midori

Kansaburo grinned, all broad-mouthed and narrow-eyed, as Dr. Ami Sato prodded the strips of rags tightly wrapped around his torso. Just beneath the ribs of his left flank the homemade bandages oozed a purplish brown sap, tinged with a bit of dark dried blood. Small hands clad in exam gloves, she unwrapped each sticky strip. Earthy odors of decaying flowers wafted up. She frowned at the exposed wound packed with layers of gummy leaves and matted yellow flowers.

The old examination table creaked under his mass. Usually it supported frail little grannies and gramps—not a heavily muscled young laborer. She sat back on her stool, looked at his shirtless torso and then met his bemused gaze.

"You're an idiot," she said, with an exasperated shrug. "You're risking a nasty infection. Why do you insist on all these weird leaves and berries to cure your injuries?" She continued to peel off the foliage and petals, slowly cleaning the small jagged wound. "What's the point of having my practice here if you insist on your musty old folk remedies?" Her words prodded him as the antiseptic swab prodded the wound.

"But it's not infected, is it?" Kansaburo said. "Have you ever seen any of my wounds infected?"

Ami paused from dressing the injury and glared at him. "No. But I'm sure that's just your dumb luck." But she knew he was right. The wound was surprisingly clean and healing unusually fast. All his wounds were like that. Since he seemed to get hurt frequently, she had more than ample evidence to support his claim.

With a long backward arc, he stretched into a slow yawn. His arms spread with fingers outstretched, like some giant bird about to take flight. His movement and form filled the stillness of the tiny infirmary. As he inhaled into a yawning groan, pectorals flared and abs rippled just centimeters from Ami's face. A bead of sweat trickled down his deeply tanned skin. Faint scent of salt and male musk invaded her mind. She held her breath, and the scent coalesced into a flavor. Salt and sun and leather. The urge to taste from the source swelled up within her, threatening to override the professional medical decorum she had so carefully constructed. Before he could look down, and before she might actually lean in and lick him, she spun on her stool and hurriedly searched for something, anything, in a supply drawer. Her cheeks burned. Then her brows furrowed. It irritated her to no end this yokel farm worker aroused her as much as he did.

"What's your problem with all the 'weird' leaves and berries anyway? It's good medicine, you know." Kansaburo clucked his tongue at her.

"It's not medicine. It's folklore and rubbish. Why else would the federal program stick me out in this backwater village?" Ami said.

"The government just wants to pretend like they're doing something good for a change—and you took the program to pay off your school loan." He laughed.

She glowered at him as she finished dressing his wound. Merrily ignoring her glare, he wiggled back into the white tank top, grease-stained and fitting just a bit too snugly across his vast back. Strange scars crept out from underneath the cotton. Some were jagged and ripped; others were long, thin, and sharp. Others still came in multiple arcing stripes of ghastly claw marks. Latticing his skin, overlapping and varied in age, they marked his skin like some unknown hieroglyphics.

They worried her.

Turning back to her, he smiled softly. Something jagged slipped away within her, and her brow unknotted.

"Do you have any more patients today?" he asked.

She shook her head. He was her only charge today. In truth, she had been bored to tears when she saw him through the diminutive window of the clinic. He was standing on a neighbor's roof, adjusting the rag bandages while laying down new thatch. She yelled out the door at him. After a bit of grousing, he had scrambled off the roof and strolled over to her office. Perhaps he too was bored with his duties.

"Honestly, have you known this village to be a place of sickness?" he asked. She shook her head. He was right. In the year she'd been assigned here, the villagers were significantly healthier than the patients she saw during her internship in Nagasaki and Tokyo. Other than the occasional farming accidents, snakebites, or aching backs, they suffered no ailments and lived well past 90, even boasting several centenarians.

"Would you at least let me show you some of our

'weird leaves and berries?'" he pleaded with charming insolence. Ami rolled her eyes at him but put away the stethoscope and tools of her trade, closing up shop. It was highly unlikely anyone would need her for the rest of the day. Should there be an emergency, someone would clang the firehouse bell, audible well into the deep woods and mountaintops surrounding the hamlet. She slipped off the white consultation coat and hung it up on the rusting hook, secretly grateful for an excuse to leave the stiflingly hot and musty office.

They walked past the emerald green rice paddies, quarreling as they often did. The sun, just past its zenith, beat down on the hunched backs of elderly farmers wearing conical woven hats. Half a dozen or so of these bamboo hats bobbed among the knee-high blades of rice, as their owners weeded and trimmed in the water-filled plots. As the two walked past on raised levee paths, the farmers continued their backbreaking work, paying no mind to the chatter of youth.

Though still only early into summer, the air dripped thick with heat. The white blouse clung to her perspiring back. The breeze was too feeble to offer comfort, much less move her heavy denim wrap skirt. The rice stocks rustled but did not sway. Sweat ran down her inner thigh—and other moisture seeped as well. He ambled slowly, long legs swinging in an easy gait and wooden-toothed geta sandals clanking as they knocked pebbles. She walked swiftly to keep up. She'd abandoned stylish high heels and urban fashion discipline long ago, but she wasn't ready to adopt the locals' antiquated footwear just yet. Rubber flip-flops were hardly authorized hospital wear, but here, no one cared.

She scolded him for lack of immunizations. He

reproached her blind trust in artificial compounds. She extolled the virtue of the scientific method and its rigor. He praised the wisdom of millennia. He tried to explain the Chinese foundation for diagnosis of imbalance. She scoffed and compared it to medieval European bloodlettings and exorcisms. He said maybe she needed an exorcism herself. She ignored that. She elucidated research and inspection standards. He reminded her of thalidomide babies and the recent surge of diabetes. She cited the exceptional education and research of her medical school. He quoted his grandmother.

On and on, round and round, they squabbled through the orchards of plums, peaches, and cherries, past the silk makers' mulberry grove and across the pungent wasabi fields. They crossed the stone bridge straddling Kiyoi River bordering the eastern edge of the village. Water flowed clear and strong. Dark forms of fish undulated just beneath, occasionally slicing the surface with shimmering fins.

The piercing cry of a hawk close by halted them as they stepped off the bridge. Their chatter faded to silence.

Shielding his face from the sun with a broad hand, Kansaburo gazed up admiringly at the circling hawk, a type of kite common to these mountains. Ami squinted into the moist darkness ahead of them. Even in the thick heat of summer, this place gave her chills. Childish fears from long forgotten nightmares washed over her. She crossed her arms snugly and leaned imperceptibly toward him.

The forest trail began where the bridge, and the village, ended. A massive weeping willow hung heavily across the path, branches laden with some unspoken grief. At the base stood a small moss-encrusted stone Jizo, protector bodhisattva of travelers, children, and the dwellers of hell. Serenely smiling with downcast eyes, its gentle head sat atop a body encased in layers of tattered babies' bibs, the tributes of generations of parents praying for the comfort of the souls of their lost or stolen children. At its feet lay fresh flowers and a bowl of rice.

By the time she looked up, Kansaburo was already far along the steep stone trail snaking into the primordial cedar grove. She shook off the gaze of the Jizo and bounded up the steps to catch up to him. The narrow trail forced them closer. The canopy high above shut out the sun, encasing them in a chilled verdant darkness. Occasionally his arm would brush her skin, or her hand would brush his leg. His body radiated heat. Faint curls of steam rose from his bare shoulders and dissipated into the coolness. She found his warmth comforting. Every surface in the forest dripped with moisture. Moss laden stone oozed fluids. Amber drops trickled down the crevices and folds of cedar bark. Thickly curled heads of warabi ferns thrust out from fertile black soil.

They traveled deeper into the woods. Kansaburo effortlessly led them up the labyrinthine trails winding and splitting through the hushed grove. Occasionally he would pluck a leaf, a flower, or a mushroom, call it by some old folksy name, and rattle off its uses. Some were edible. Some soothed wounds, warded off colds, or cleared hangovers. One was for male virility. He chewed nonchalantly on that root while offering her a woolly looking lichen for women's fertility and abundance of children. She rolled her eyes and tossed it off to the side. He looked askance at her. A few of the plants he only pointed out and stayed far and well clear of. One of them caused a terrible rash and blindness, while another could stop the heart.

The steep climb silenced her as she labored for breath. After a while, she merely grunted or nodded acknowledgement to his merry recitation of country herbology. She was actually grateful when he'd stop and make her eat some bitter herb or vile-tasting berry. She didn't believe one word of his education and wondered how ill she'll be later.

She'd never traveled this far into the woods. He bounded steps ahead of her, taking no note of her struggling gait.

Fatigued, she faltered on an uneven stone and slipped. Mud splattered beneath her feet, a flip-flop strap snapped. She tried to stand up, but she just fell backward. Shrieking, she clenched her eyes and fists, limbs flailing out, and braced for the crash and pain to follow.

Which never came.

She landed into the scooping strong arm of Kansaburo.

How?

She opened her eyes and found his eyes, darkest of black, staring into hers.

"You're a klutz!" He laughed, still holding her in one arm, her body halted in mid-fall and head hovering just centimeters above the ground. His breath warmed her chilled cheeks. His scent was maddeningly intoxicating.

She hit him on his chest with her still clenched fist. His body didn't budge as her hand bounced off of him.

"Ow." He feigned mock distress. She hated to be made fun of. "Oh, would you like me to let you go?"

She reconsidered the rocks under her head.

"No! Help me up. Right now," she snapped.

"That's what I thought I was doing." He chuckled and righted her body with the one arm around her waist. Although she was vertical now, her feet dangled free, and she was pressed into his body. One foot bare and muddy—another with a helpless flip-flop dangling. His grip was firm and her body safe as her waist and pelvis pressed into his torso. He hoisted her up, face to face with him.

"You'd better let me down, right now!" she barked.

"Or what? You'll beat me with your only sandal? Oh that's scary. Doc, unless you want to walk barefoot on these rocks, I'm going to carry you. You're just a tiny gal." He turned up the path and began walking with her still pressed into his chest like a child's doll.

"Don't call me a girl!" she declared and hit him in the chest again.

"Tell you what, if you can hit me hard enough for me to notice, I'll let you down." He winked at her. She arched her back, pulled her arm back like a cartoon baseball pitcher and hit him as hard as she could. He laughed and continued up the hill.

The path began to level and brighten as the old growth forest thinned. The moist stillness shifted to dry rustling. Brightness and pale green enveloped them as they entered a sun drenched bamboo grove.

"I'll make you pay for this!" She cracked playfully. At first she beat his chest and shoulders like a trapped kitten. The more she arched her back to strike him, the more her pelvis pressed into his belly. She kept arching. He continued laughing, so she built up a rhythm as she pummeled his hard-muscled torso. It was exhilarating.

Kansaburo came to a stop among the bamboo and relaxed his grip ever so slightly. Her body shifted down his torso and felt heat and mounting stiffness press into her. He regrasped her firmly into his body. She didn't so much hear as felt a guttural sound from deep within him.

Startled by his arousal, she looked up. His eyes were narrowed and lips slacked. His groin swelled.

So she hit him again.

Massive hands moved from waist to cup her ass cheeks.

She hit him, yet again.

He began to rock back and forth, rocking her harder into his crotch.

She swung her legs around his hips—and decked him again. His swelling now pressed against her aroused sex.

He growled low and gripped her ass harder.

She struck him again, and he fell back onto soft dry bamboo leaves, pulling her onto the straining crotch of his work pants.

She pummeled him, her eyes growing wide with excitement.

He began to buck his hips into her, pulling her hips harder onto him. Her hair flew wildly. Strands clung to her sweat-drenched brow and neck.

A gust of hot wind shot around them, making the bamboo knock, sway, and rustle. Crows gathered on branches above and cawed wildly.

Stunned by her own violence, she paused and looked down at his ecstatic face. He looked up with glazed eyes. He managed a grin and sassed, "I haven't noticed anything yet." With that, he reached up and tore his tank top, exposing sweat streaked and faintly flushed chest, challenging her.

She heard a wild howl, only to realize it came from her own gaping mouth. Ripping the remnants of his shirt out of his grasp, she grabbed his insolent hands and bound them crudely together. He cackled and threw them over her head as if to pull her into a kiss. She ducked his embrace, dismounted his hard crotch, and wrapped the shredded tails of the shirt, wrists and all, to a thick bamboo stalk just above his head.

He tugged at the bonds but did not escape. He pulled at them repeatedly as a horse might do to feel the rider's command.

She straddled back atop him and stared in wonder at her newly captured mount.

Black feathered forms agitated above.

He inhaled deeply, swelling and pushing his chest toward her. Taking the cue, she hit him hard with a flat hand. He groaned and bucked against her. She reached to stroke his face and saw ecstasy. She needed to drink from that well—so she leaned in and kissed him. His lips felt strangely cold and hard, though his soft cheeks burned as hot as hers. He whipped his face away from hers. Weird, she thought, but figured it was part of this strange little game he'd tricked her into. She kissed his neck and enjoyed the roughness of stubble. Inhaling his musk she slid a hand down his taut stomach and then into his trouser waist. Immediately an enormous mass met her searching hand.

He gasped sharply as she stroked down the smooth shaft, then they both emitted soft sighs. She repeated a few gentle strokes, just to hear his quivering sighs tickle her ear. His chest heaved. She throbbed within.

Leaning back, she unzipped and peeled back his pants, exposing a thick, rigid rod. It sprang out of its confines. It strained toward her from a frame of jet-black straight hair, pressed down and glistening like wet feathers.

She stared at his cock in rapt attention laced with bewilderment. A year of exile had left her feeling shut out from her own desires. She wanted everything in the moment, yet hesitated from a sudden surge of inadequacy.

He thrust his hips into hers, pressing his cock into her inner thigh. Urgency pressed at them everywhere. Her dripping sex just centimeters from him, the invitation was clear. She looked up and found him looking directly at her, eyes darker than ever. He seemed to challenge her as impudently as ever.

She wasn't prepared and felt ambushed by her own lust. She wanted him inside her—desperately— but she couldn't. This wasn't like her internship days in the city. Frequent staff hook-ups in spare patient beds kept her more alert than any energy drinks. She could always slip a hand into the pocket of her scrubs and find a rubber or two.

Frenzied and flustered, she grabbed his hard-on, a bit too brusquely, making him wince and groan. Pressing her sopping sex against the shaft, she kissed him urgently. His lips felt colder and harder still. Grasping his biceps, she braced herself against him and ground her hips into him. Her wet lips spread onto his length as the swelling clitoris mashed into his hard knob. He bucked back into her, and she dug her fingers into his arms. His arm hair began to prickle and stab at her palms. He seemed to grow in every way beneath her. All her senses fired up wildly. Breathing ragged and growling, they heaved into each other. Wild cawing of crows mixed with their cries and filled the grove.

He grew dark as if a great shadow had fallen over them. The wind whipped at the bamboo, clattering the trunk and churning the heat. Green sliver leaves and black feathers swirled around them. They pounded in unison. A massive ball of heat knotted within her, just above the clit, where it grew and grew. Kansaburo bucked in a frenzy. Ami's legs stiffened, and fire shot up into her gut, making her scream. With her scream his bucking peaked into a fury. Growling he arched his back, lifting her shuddering body, and shot white and hot onto his sweat-drenched belly.

The grove now silent, they sank into the soft leaves. The crows flew away one by one. His gaze followed the arc of their flight. One swooped down and flew so close its wing nearly brushed Ami's brow. Its breeze fanned her face. He smiled.

They lay there in silence as the shadows slowly lengthened.

For the first time, she thought, she heard the forest truly.

The leaves swayed slowly above them.

Feeling a chill, Ami got up, straightened her disheveled skirt and brushed off the leaves clinging everywhere. She was vaguely contemplating her single remaining sandal in her hand when she heard his deliberate cough.

She looked back to find him still bound to the bamboo stalk. He cocked his head toward his wrists and coughed again. Letting out a small shriek, she scrambled down onto her knees and tugged at the threads and strips of shirt remnant around his wrists.

"I'm so sorry. I completely forgot," she said. "This is being really uncooperative." Her face reddened as she struggled with the improvised bonds.

He snickered.

She raised her hand to slap his chest but stopped mid-stroke. The stinging tenderness of her reddened palm crept up her arm and enveloped her mind. All that just transpired flooded back into the moment. She turned a deeper shade of crimson.

Gently now, she lowered the raised hand to caress his chest where she had been hitting him. She leaned in to inspect the damage. The skin was warm and flushed, but there was not a single sign of contusions or welts. Remarkable, she thought. Then she wondered if his flesh was so tough or if she was all that weak. Her finger traced the line of his sternum to solar plexus. Her wondering finger halted at the sticky edge of still warm fluid. She painted through it onto his belly. She felt another surge of reddening.

He coughed. And then laughed in a resonating voice that filled the space around them.

"Doc, you've got me. I promise not to run away if you let me go. I promise to show you more folk remedies for you to scoff at," he said.

"Was that what we just had? A folk remedy?" She parodied her own usual tone of derision.

"Yes indeed! Don't you feel better already? I feel positively cured!" he said.

She grinned as she finished untying him. Finally freed, he cleaned himself off the best he could. Glancing over to her solitary sandal, he turned his back to her, crouched down and patted his shoulder.

"Hop aboard, Doc," he said.

She was about to decline on the principle of independence, but then she remembered the trail they came up through. She hopped on his naked back and wrapped her arms around his neck. She laid her head down on his shoulder and savored his scent. He hoisted her up by her thighs, pressing her naked and sticky sex into his spine. Ever so slightly, she curled her pelvis into him for a little better rub. She ran a hand down his arm—smooth and hairless. Not a prickle.

Odd, she thought.

Night sucked the light out of the forest. He strode swiftly through the encroaching darkness, unencumbered by his passenger. She felt weightless, as if in flight. She closed her eyes and dreamt of flying.

Crows cawed somewhere far away.

A full moon peered over the jagged ridgeline.

She woke in darkness. The sweet smoke of herbal incense wafted around her, warding off mosquitoes and, supposedly, evil spirits. As her eyes adjusted, her room came into form. Shadows of bowing figures loomed on the shoji paper doors, cast by branches of bushy-headed pine trees. The sound of crickets and other creatures reverberated in the humidity. She lay there a while in dreamy confusion.

Had she?

Had they?

Her finger wandered to her lips. She tasted the sweetness of his juice. The other hand crept between her thighs. She stroked her sex lazily, recalling his sounds, skin and the ride. Slow heat crept over her. She arched and let out a small cry of pleasure.

Making her way through the soft darkness, she

stood on the packed dirt floor of the ancient kitchen. An enormous ceramic pot sat in the corner. It sweated condensation, keeping the pristine well water chilled. She ladled herself a large glass and gulped it, feeling the cool water seep to the far reaches of her feverish flesh.

She strolled out to the open-sided bathhouse off the kitchen. The embers and stones glowed bright under the century-old cedar and metal tub. Steam coiled up gently. Curled fronds of fern and deep blue flowers floated on the black surface, perfuming the air. Kansaburo had stoked the bath for her.

She never saw him the next day. He didn't show up to finish thatching the neighbor's roof. Typical of life in the village, the elderly couple living there seemed unconcerned. She glanced out the window frequently, searching for his strong body laboring in the sun.

She struggled to maintain focus all day. A dormant fire had been lit.

The day crawled along.

In the morning, old man Kinsuke came in for a simple cavity. He brought her fresh sugar canes and a bottle of shochu from his backyard still.

Later Mr. Jinki, the jovial old mayor, came in to shoot the breeze and check in on her. Portly with a balding head framed with a comb-over of thinning hair, he'd stare a wee bit too long at her. Then he'd catch himself and blush and giggle. If Sayaka, his equally portly wife, were here, she'd slap him and make him bow. They were a funny couple, so obsessed with politeness yet bumbling. He left her with a basket of cucumbers from their farm.

Just after midday, Dowager Tsuru arrived with a centipede bite, but mostly she just wanted company.

Ami gladly saw them all, for as long as they wanted. Even after all their visits, still the day loomed long ahead of her. She decided to make the rounds and focus on her charges; however unnecessary they considered her visits, they were always hospitable. She packed her medical bag, strapped it on the back rack of her red bicycle, and took off down the packed-dirt road. The rice swayed as if to greet her, and the sun cheered her.

A large crow watched from a power line.

She pedaled toward the silk maker's compound at the northern edge of the valley. The Kinugasa family gave her great concern as of late. Dowager Ito, the sturdy matriarch of the Kinugasa clan, had been taken ill just at the end of the monsoon season. Two weeks since the initial visit, and no news. The family members had been unusually reserved, even by the stoic standards of these mountain people.

She dismounted her bike at the broad, formal entrance gate. Wide and high enough to drive two trucks through, the monumental gate, topped with a formidable sculpted thatch roof and bordered with carved latticing of moths and chrysanthemums, seemed entirely too extravagant among the humble homesteads of the hamlet. Yet there it stood for hundreds of years, imperial service crests carved into various reliefs. Once upon a time, this was the Emperor's private silk source, protected and secluded by imperial decree. Rumor had it they were still retained by the royal house, though that seemed a bit too romantic. Ami figured that tale to be just a nice bit of history and local pride, which did no harm for a dwindling village.

She walked the bike into the large courtyard. In

front of her was the sprawling residence, still elegant in the style of Edo period mercantile wealth, with sliding paper doors, glossy tatami mats, and even a hidden tearoom. To her right was the vast growing shed where rows upon rows of trays nurtured fat white silkworms eating their way through tons of mulberry leaves. Even from this distance, she could hear the cumulative sound of thousands of worms munching leaves. It still unnerved her. To her left was the boiling and spinning house. There, vats of boiling water cooked the snow-white cocoons, with sleeping worms dying within them. Further down, elderly spinners sat in neat rows, chatting while their withered, bony fingers pulled out the thinnest silvery strands. Meter after meter, their hands twisted the finest and rarest silk threads in Japan. From here the precious fibers would travel to centuries-old kimono makers and merchants in Kyoto. Some shipped as far as Tokyo, though many in this village still quaintly called the capital by its old name—Edo.

She waited in the courtyard for some time. Normally the smiling dowager would already be there to greet her and invite her in for tea and crackers.

Silence—except for the hungry murmurs of worms munching.

She smelled prayer incense and burning cypress wood.

Observing country manners, she continued to wait. Her mind wondered, replaying last night's passions.

A long wailing prayer song interrupted her private reverie. Soon Ami caught a glimpse of a minute woman, dressed in crimson hakama pants, a monstrous demon mask covering her face and wildly waving a huge nusa, a ritual purification wand of wood and streamers of paper.

Chanting, the small old woman walked along the veranda circling the house. Trailing her floor-length silver hair, woven wildly with branches and reeds, she disappeared around the corner. The strange apparition had to be Kuroyama Azusa, the mountain-dwelling Shinto priestess—and Kansaburo's grandmother.

Ami stood with her mouth gaping open. Even a city girl like her knew this was a major purification ritual or an exorcism—not a good sign.

Shortly thereafter, the dowager's granddaughter appeared. Kaede was a plump and cheerful middle-aged woman who always sent homemade sweets and pickles to Ami. Kaede bowed repeatedly and apologized profusely. She spoke so quickly with great agitation that Ami could hardly make out what she was saying. Ami tried to calm her and extract information about dowager Ito.

"Thank you, Doctor, for your visit today. Everything is fine. My grandmother is resting. We're having a blessing. Nothing unusual. Just our country ways. We are quite busy. Please, if you don't mind, please take your leave. I will visit you in the morrow. We are always grateful for your consideration. I am sorry we can't serve you properly today. Please. I'm sorry. I deeply apologize," Kaede jabbered on.

Ami wasn't going to get anywhere with Kaede or any of the Kinugasa clan today. She bowed in return, apologized for her intrusion, and bid farewell. As she rode out of the compound, she spotted a large crow atop the entrance gate. It stared at her and cocked its head, as if to ask her a question.

The sun was beginning to dip toward the western ranges already. The pale blue sky showed indigo around the edges and clouds of pink and gold streaked the sky. Stars began to twinkle. She pedaled faster. She wanted to return to the infirmary and close it properly before it became too dark. Her headlight flickered and glowed in time to her rhythmic pedaling. Farmers walking home from the fields waved. She rang the little red bell back at them.

Once she properly closed the office, she decided to head to the local watering hole for a nightcap. A bit of chilled sake seemed just what the doctor should order for herself after a strange couple of days. Flashlight in hand, she strolled down to what passed as the main street of the hamlet. Lightning bugs rose around her. She turned off her flashlight and let their glow illuminate her walk. She imagined Kansaburo walking along with her, telling folksy tales about the summer nights here. The thought made her blush and giddy. Silly, she thought, but she enjoyed the giddiness anyway.

Inehana's red lanterns were the only thing that glowed on the main street. The few remaining little shops were shuttered tight for the day. The smell of grilled chicken wafted from the bar. Inehana was the closest thing to vice and entertainment the village had. Its owner, Inari Chiyo, kept it stocked with good beer, fine local sake, and a few bottles of imported whiskey. In winter she prepared soul-warming oden stew, and in summer she grilled skewered meats and served homemade wasabi noodles, chilled to perfection. What little gossip there was could be swapped there, as many of the regulars, ancient widowers most of them, were more than happy to voice their opinions on just about anything. Chiyo herself was an ageless beauty with flawless white skin, who could keep the conversation flowing all night. She seemed to know anything and everything about the village. Ami didn't know much about her, despite what she believed were clever big-city conversational tricks.

Ami parted the noren curtains and entered the warm, cozy bar. Chiyo signaled her to the corner barstool, farthest from Tanuta, the village drunk and a bit of a letch. A chilled glass of sake awaited Ami. Chiyo was uncanny in her foresight of orders. Everyone joked it was her magical powers.

The sake and conversation flowed. They speculated on the year's crop and betted on how hot the summer was going to get. They moaned about various governmental policies and the price of rice. Many of them lamented the next imperial succession. Ami was surprised to discover all the old men firmly believed Princess Toshi to be the rightful successor and next Empress. The village elders were indignant at what they felt were political moves by foolish Meiji modernists. They made it sound as if the Meiji Era was ever so recent, not 150 years ago.

A few years back the Imperial Court assigned the succession of the Chrysanthemum Throne to the younger royal male cousin and not to Princess Toshi, the only child of the Emperor. She vaguely remembered her grandpa in Nagoya talking about that, but she and her cohorts hadn't given it much mind. When she asked why it mattered, she got an earful on Japanese patriotism and ancient history. One of them broke into a tearful drunken rendition of the national anthem while the others nodded in approval. Chiyo smiled and egged on the singer for another sentimental patriotic performance and inebriated toasts.

As Ami enjoyed the booze-fueled exchange of the

old men, she saw headlights, set low and wide, leisurely cruise down the main street. Through the open bar windows she saw a sleek black sedan with tinted windows. A silver Mercedes emblem on the hood came into view as it drove slowly by, like a shark in still waters. The men kept singing, noticing nothing. Ami saw Chiyo's face harden as her long-cut eyes trailed the unknown car until it was long out of sight.

That night passed as so many did. Rounds of drinks with the village geezers, followed by a quiet stroll home with the packed dirt road lit by dancing fireflies. She crawled into the thick futon alone and fell quickly and deeply asleep.

By the time Ami, dull-headed and dry-mouthed, crawled out from under the sheet and mosquito netting, the sun was well up, and the house was already bright and warm. Today, yet another Sunday, would be spent cleaning the vast farmhouse, airing out its musty corners, and putting away her laundry, finished and delivered to her by the village laundress, Dowager Chimiko.

The wood and mud daub house was ancient but well-suited for the changing seasons. In the winter, as snow buried the steep roof line, with all the sliding doors and the storm shutters shut, the central room glowed and baked with the heat from the irori open floor hearth.

Now in the summer months, all the sliding paper doors and walls were flung open to let the fresh breeze through. The wood-floored hall, wrapping around the perimeter of the central rooms, became the veranda. There, long balmy evening hours were spent, cold sake in hand, gazing at fireflies and other glowing night creatures drift among the grasses and white moon flowers.

The day was waning already as she swept this veranda along the back garden. Just then, a long shadow crossed the brightly polished wood. It arced like a massive wing, then twisted, faded in the passing cloud cover, and returned again in the slanting light to form the shadow of a man.

She startled up to find Kansaburo's outline against the setting sun. He stood there quietly on the steps, holding a large basket.

"Oh! It's you! Don't startle me like that," she yelped as she shaded her face with a hand and blinked to get a better view of him. "How long were you standing there?"

His great shadowed form spoke: "Not long. But long enough to see you missed a spot."

She wanted to hit him. But she really wanted to…

She blushed and flustered and settled for slapping him on the hand.

"Here!" He thrust the basket at her. She took it, and its weight nearly toppled her. She gingerly set it down on the veranda. It overflowed with perfectly round green watermelons, long eggplants, and black tubers. "It's from Granny. She sends her greetings. She said you saw her the other day." He stood awkwardly, and at a distance, scratching his head.

She stared him as he kicked a rock and watched it roll away.

Neither spoke.

She began to paw through the care package from his quirky priestess granny. She'd never seen the black root vegetable before. The length and thickness of her forearm, it looked like a daikon radish, but black as coal.

"Betcha never seen that. It's called a Karasu

Daikon. It'll keep you in the cool humors during the next few days. Granny says it's going to get hot around here."

She patted the floor next to her. He hesitated and then sat carefully down, his torso just a feather's distance away from her. She put down the daikon and reached for the eggplant. It was cool, magnificently thick and smooth to her grip.

He reached over, grasped the watermelon with one big hand and knocked it lightly on the stepping-stone. It cracked open easily, effortlessly, willingly, glistening red flesh and juice dripped down his palm, drenching his wrist. He broke off a smaller section for her while biting eagerly into the flesh of the larger piece. They devoured the crisp flesh hungrily. Sweet summer juices ran from lips, dripped off chins, and trickled down necks.

She tossed her head back to flip her hair off her face when he leaned in. He leaned in and kissed the stream of sweetness flowing down her neck. Her heart leapt into her mouth, and a moan escaped her lips. He kissed and drank his way up her neck to her ear. The pieces of watermelon rind fell out of their hands and tumbled into the dirt.

Her hands shot up to his head and sweet-slicked fingers tangled into his jet-black hair. He pushed her down—or had she pulled him onto her—his arms planted on either side of her as she threw her head back, giving him full access to her flushed throat. He kissed and licked her neck, then brushed her lips with his. She locked her arms around his massive back and pulled herself closer into his juice-soaked shirt. He slid an arm under her and with one quick shift brought them both onto the veranda, stretched fully, his weight and heat bearing down on her. His thigh pressed onto hers, asking a question. She answered with a hip thrust. He moaned.

As he raised his hips before another downward thrust, she giggled and slipped out from beneath him. She skipped into the next room and returned as quickly as she had escaped. As she turned to him, she saw his half-prone form, rising as a black silhouette against the crimson sunset and golden clouds.

A flock of crows silently descended upon the bent maple in the garden.

His silhouette waivered uncertainly. Waited. Waited for her.

She returned to him, reached up and wrapped her arms around his neck and kissed him deeply. His lips were supple, yet chilled, even in this moment of passion. His neck and cheeks burned hot.

She waved at him a little purse in her hand, opened it, and flashed a silver foil packet at him. Then she giggled and ran down the veranda. Stopping to look back at him.

"You bad, bad girl! Come right back here!" he shouted in mock anger.

She giggled back at him and started a sprint around the corner.

He ran to catch her. He'd fly at her with strong arms outstretched to clutch, and she'd duck down and slip out. She threw her blouse at his face. He got down on all fours and ran to her like a hunting dog, and she loped away like a fawn. She slipped out of her skirt and waved it at him like a bullfighter. He charged bull-like at it. She threw that off and skittered away. He leaped slowly at her, and she ever nimbly dodged away. Around and around they laughed and chased as darkness enveloped them.

She dove in the mosquito netting and hid behind her sheet, giggling. He lunged into the netted enclosure, ripped the sheet away. She feigned protest as if to push him away. Her hands pushed down toward his pants. In the dusky room, she fumbled unsuccessfully with the buttons. He kneeled up, stripped his shirt off and tugged his fly open. In rigid full attention his rod sprang forward. It swelled and quivered, anxious for her touch.

She paused.

Leaned in.

Breathed on his enormity.

He inhaled sharply.

She slipped her tongue out.

He watched. Breath held.

She licked the glistening droplet. Tasted the salt.

He groaned.

Her tongue stroked the length of his shaft from the base back up to his knob. She needed this.

He gasped.

She reached behind her and unclasped the white cotton bra, breasts freed and full with hardening pink nipples.

His cock quivered.

She tore open the foil packet. With only a bit of fumbling, she had his sword sheathed in gleaming silvery latex.

His head pulsed.

She sat up onto her knees as well and leaned in to kiss him, but before her lips could touch his, his hands wrapped around the curves of her hip and pulled her up to stand before him. He cupped her breasts in each hand and nuzzled them. His grip was delicate but hinted at force barely contained. His tongue licked her hardening nipple. Now she groaned. He kissed and suckled each nipple. His lips were rough, and they rather pinched, but then she liked that.

She took his hands, slid them down to the waist of her panties. Taking her cue, he began to slide them slowly down her flushed thighs. He gazed up at her. Even in the darkening room, she saw his eyes burned bright but his brows were gentle.

Was it reverence?

She reclined slowly onto the futon. He took her invitation and lay upon her, pressing his face tenderly into her neck and hair.

The crows began to caw.

She spread her legs, tilted her pelvis to meet his swollen head.

Raising his face to her, he gazed with an unspoken query, soft and even hesitant.

She moaned and sank her fingers into his ass cheeks.

Then, with a single violent thrust he entered her.

She cried out and tore at his back. Her legs wrapped around his hips. He pulled out and then thrust long, slow and deeply into her. She pulled him in further. His shaft grew thicker and his mass heavier upon her. His body hair rasped at her but she pulled him in harder anyway. She reached for his face, but he took her hand and pinned it down. "No, not the face."

Before she could speak, he pulled out briefly and rasped, "Roll over."

She spun around in the darkness and pressed her ass into him. He plowed in repeatedly, matching her thrust for thrust.

She heard the rustling of feathers. In the frenzy, she wondered if the crows were so close again.

The tingling began in her toes and shot up into her uterus. Waves of agony and the heat of pleasure washed through her. She needed a breath. She had to slow down. Too intense and too fast. Pressing her palms behind her, she pushed him away. She felt him hesitate, uncertain whether he should continue.

With the moment's space, she rolled onto her back and pulled him into her again.

Her cries gave way to ragged gasps as he resumed pumping. Her heat built again. His hairs stabbed at her skin, hands, breasts and belly. Bright blazing lights in her mind punctuated the pitch darkness of the night. She lost track of the waves of her orgasms. His voice cracked, "I have to… I have to come."

"Yes, now. Please. Now!" she pleaded and commanded.

At that command, he howled and cawed and wailed like every wild animal and pounded deep into her as if to split the ocean with his very will.

Panting, they lay in the darkness under the netting.

He stroked her sweat-drenched brow and kissed her softly, lips now warm and supple.

She didn't ask. Neither spoke.

At some point during the night they made love again.

After that, he gently towel-bathed her sweaty body with a cool wet cloth.

She slept deeply, tucked safely under the vast wingspan of his powerful, gentle arms.

The next morning she woke alone under the netting. Last night's clothes were folded neatly by her head. Hot porridge simmered on the stove. This time he had left a note for her.

I have to get to work. Can I see you again tonight?

She pedaled with a giddy stride as she rode her bike to work.

A crow cawed lightly and followed above.

Later that day she saw him from the infirmary window, finishing the villager's roof. As he waved enthusiastically at her, he slipped and nearly fell off the roof.

That night, as darkness fell, he came to her again.

The nightly visits continued. He eagerly tried any position she desired. They chased each other through the house, laughing. She would pounce on him like a kitten on a tiger and replay the captive game from their first encounter. He granted her every erotic whim. But he refused any illumination during the peaks and orgasmic explosions. He was ready and willing to make love but shy to be seen in his passions. She found that endearing—at first.

He was always gone by the time she woke. She figured he was keeping the quaint country manners of unmarried lovers.

She was grateful her charges did not require much in the way of attention. She often spent her days with her brain in a fog of pleasure. The villagers continued to drop in occasionally for social pleasantries and minor care. All passed sweetly in her distracted state. Even her concern for the Kinugasa elders faded behind the flush of arousal.

Her senses were awakened. Colors around her

seemed brighter and more vibrant. As a doctor she could easily explain it away: regular vigorous sex induced greater oxygenation of the blood, alongside oxytocin and dopamine production—though it seemed more than that. But she didn't really care. She just wanted him, his body and the pleasures he brought out in her. She wanted all of it. Her receptors were fired up. During the daylight hours all her senses reminded her of what the night would bring.

She developed a nostalgic and erotic fondness for long eggplants. It was, as an additional benefit, smooth and conveniently shaped. One evening she confessed this to Kansaburo, which led to some interesting vegetal experimentations later.

At times she thought her lust was making her hallucinate. She was troubled slightly by the wild residual imaginings of her sex-fueled brain. She began to feel like the crows were watching her and talking about her. Perhaps that was simply excessive self-indulgence combined with self-consciousness from trying to hide their affair from the villagers. But the crows were everywhere, and they were watching, intensely.

Kansaburo chuckled at this.

"Silly city mouse! I think you're just finally seeing the nature around you. Crows are everywhere. They watch everything. Don't you know that?" At that, he looked to a plain black crow on the pine above them and cocked his head mockingly at it. The crow cawed and puffed its feathers up. It shat at them. They laughed.

What was more troubling was that shadows began to change shapes around her. Shadows of people would flicker, then sprout tails and wings and other such appendages. First, it was just a shadow or two rippling. Then a few more shadows made odd shapes of blurred outlines. Then, each day, occurrences increased, accompanied by sharper focused shadows of unnatural forms. In particular, the sunrays of dawn and dusk cast the most monstrous shapes.

She wondered if she'd been concussed during one of the wilder rendezvous on a recent night.

They were walking in a bamboo grove one evening when she finally shared this concern with Kansaburo. He was quiet for a long time. It made her nervous. Perhaps she shouldn't have told him this. Finally, he took her hand and spoke softly. "You're fine. This happens around here, especially with special people. And you're special to me. But I will ask Granny. She knows about this stuff. I know you don't believe a lot of our ways, but let me ask. In the meantime, let's keep this between us, okay?"

Then he fell silent again. They walked wordlessly back to her home where he turned the lights off, and they made love gently.

In the fortnight that followed, they spent nearly every night together in passionate embrace. Her senses on fire, she delighted in every touch, before, during, and after making love. Often they'd steal away to the bamboo grove, and meadows farther, where they moaned and gasped, even screamed to their hearts' content. No one to hear, no need to muffle their cries of ecstasy.

Once they even entered an abandoned Shinto altar beneath a great pine. On this occasion, Kansaburo knelt and put his hands together in a quick prayer and requested the permission of the resident kami—the spirit to whom the shrine was built. Ami laughed and followed half-jokingly. He turned to her and winked. They entered the empty prayer hall. Though dusty, it still smelled of cedar and candles. Groping in the darkness, she found on the floor a ragged old shimenawa, a rope meant to purify and mark sacred places. Half-stripped, she slid herself on to his hardness then grasped the rope. She went to bind his wrists together, expecting to be lectured for being disrespectful.

"May I?" she asked. To her surprise, he held up his wrists to her.

"The kami would appreciate this offering." He grinned. She tied his hands roughly. He wrapped his captured arms around her neck, pulled her in to him, and whispered, "You've bound our pleasure as an offering to the kami. And now I'm bound to you."

What a strange thing to say, she thought. Ah, this country boy and his country beliefs. Yet somehow, it seemed right. His lips were cold against her ear. Then her cheek caught fire as he thrust up deeply into her. She held his captive hands and rode until she had no thoughts, only pleasure.

On these nights of wilderness sex, Ami saw the stars above burn brighter than fire. The night sky seemed as bright as day in the peak of orgasm. She welcomed the brightness of her senses, as he refused any light during their passions. In the black night lovemaking, all the strange shadows and forms of wings dancing around her seemed a feverish dream she hungered for.

She came to long for Kansaburo. The scent of his skin haunted her days.

That night, as on other nights of their outdoor erotic adventures, she fell asleep by his side in the

123

wilds—but somehow woke in her own bed, with the morning light streaming onto her. She had no memory of how she returned home.

She reached to caress him but found the futon empty. Instead of his tousled hair and smiling face on the pillow next to her, she found a cobalt blue bellflower.

Freshly cooked rice and miso simmered and waited for her on the old propane stove.

Whether their passions took them indoors or out of doors, he would come to her at night but be gone by the morning. Sometimes he would leave flowers or a pretty leaf, sometimes a bit of hot breakfast, and sometimes a scrawled note.

"Why don't you stay and enjoy the morning with me?" she would often ask.

He'd always shrug those massive shoulders "Can't. Gotta get morning training in," he'd say.

"Training for what?" She'd press.

"Country man stuff. You know. Martial arts while eating weird plants. I like to run and stuff like that. Sometimes I help Granny. It's boring. Don't worry about it." He'd make mock machismo muscle moves and make her laugh. He would not share details beyond that.

After another fortnight of passions, however, she became concerned with his adamant avoidance of light. It was not as if she'd not seen his body, whether on her examination table or half-naked working around the village. She had no complaints of him as a lover. Quite the contrary, he was, even as the farm boy he was, exquisite in the sheets with fantastic endurance. Perhaps manual labor made him a better lover, she thought, than the book smart city doctors.

But there were odd habits. He would not let her

touch his face during sex. She was also convinced something odd happened to his skin during arousal. She didn't know of any such diseases, but perhaps there were recessive traits among the isolated population here. Next time she had access to a full medical database she would have to look into this. Medical concerns aside, it baffled and infuriated her that he would not let her gaze upon his aroused form. She dearly wanted to see his face of ecstasy in the pleasures they shared.

She longed for him.

She hated to admit she was falling for him.

* * *

Her neurological issues persisted. Shadows continued to flutter. Now they came accompanied by a woozy feeling.

She rested. Slept. Drank plenty of fluids. In the absence of proper equipment, she monitored herself the best she could for signs of low-grade head injury or neurological problems. Still the visions of shifting shadows would not cease. As the days went on, they flickered into strange forms more and more. Not everyone seemed to cast these chimera silhouettes. Eventually she learned to avert her gaze from the dusk-time shapes. She thought that sometime soon she ought to return to the city for proper tests and screenings.

With a penlight in hand, she was examining her own eye dilation response when the old doorbell clanged loudly. Startled, she jumped and nearly stabbed herself in the eye with the penlight. In all the time she'd been here, she'd never heard it. Nobody here used the doorbell. They'd just let themselves into the clinic reception room and call out to the doctor in the infirmary.

Ami got a second startle upon opening the door. All angles and bright fluorescence, a young woman waited at the clinic entrance. Just a few years younger than Ami, she was tall and lean with a precisely painted face framed by severely geometric bangs. A suit of asymmetrical neon green lapels and planes of orange panels segmented her lithe frame into a geometrical case study of competitive, urban fashion tribalism.

Ami stepped back, a little woozy from it all.

"Hello, Doctor Sato. My name is Yamada. I'm with the Taira Group. Might you have a moment?" She spoke with a measured voice, while bowing deeply and quite properly.

Ami regained her composure, remembered her manners, and invited Yamada in to the sparse reception area. She cleared off the little table of old magazines and newspapers and offered her one of the rickety green vinyl seated chairs.

Back in the utility kitchen, Ami prepared tea and laid out some rice crackers. She'd heard gossip about some big-city business interest coming around in the last couple of weeks. Normally she'd have all the details and chatty speculation from her patients, the nosy mayor and the denizens of the Inehana bar, especially as outsiders rarely came to this hamlet. Distracted by her nights of passion with Kansaburo, she'd not taken any notice.

Serving tea to the rigidly seated Yamada, Ami looked down at her guest's feet and had another little shock. Yamada's feet teetered dangerously atop 15 centimeters of bright fuchsia plastic platforms, wrapped in an impossibly intricate lattice of laces and a geta-like thong strap in dayglo yellow. It must be the latest trend for women's shoes.

A few years ago, before med school, she cared about such things. A few years ago, she would have marveled at Yamada and her ilk as the gatekeepers of taste. Even just a year ago, when she was new to this village, she would have sat Yamada down to devour all her words as the news of the civilized, urbane, and fashionable.

To Ami today, Yamada didn't seem to be any of that.

"Thank you for your hospitality. My employer is Mr. Taira. As you may know he is the head of the Taira Group." She presented a pristine business card of holographic plastic with embedded chips. Fancy stuff.

Sure, Ami thought, who didn't know about the Taira Group? The descendants of the ancient noble clan, fallen from grace a thousand years ago. Now they'd risen to power in the new millennium, spearheading the economic recovery of faltering Japan through corporate growth and national empowerment. Or, as others would think of them, crawling out of hell to grasp at imperial might through ruthless ravaging of the nation's resources. Whichever camp you were in, everyone had heard of the Taira Group.

Ami poured more tea as Yamada continued.

"Mr. Taira's familial roots are deep in the soils of Nippon. He is very concerned about the preservation of tradition, the traditional land, and the health and well-being of the rural population. As you know, the government has been neglecting villages such as this one, and the population has dwindled. In the long run, this brings ruin to our people and our great country."

Ami nibbled on a cracker. Through the window behind Yamada, she saw a crow on the wall outside, looking at her.

Yamada continued this well-rehearsed speech.

"Mr. Taira believes private citizens such as himself, and private interests, such as the Taira Group, can protect and grow these important places."

Ami stared at her and sipped more tea. What did all this have to do with her?

"Dr. Sato, at this point I'm sure you're wondering what this has to do with you. Mr. Taira feels you represent the new generation, a new vitality, which will bring these regions new rigor. He's very keen on having a meeting with you, to get your perspective on life here in this village. He'd like to meet with you as soon as possible."

Ami nearly spat out her tea.

"The Mr. Taira? Me? Why?" she sputtered.

"Because you are the bridge of change." Yamada smiled thinly. "If you are available later this afternoon, he'd like to invite you to tea and a meeting at his place."

"But how? He's in Tokyo, isn't he?" Ami wiped tea dribble from her lips.

"Oh we have a mobile villa set up outside the village. We can send a car around to you. How's 4:00?" Yamada's thin smile did not move.

Ami agreed. They exchanged stiffly formal farewells. Ami watched Yamada totter off on impossible fuchsia platforms, dodging stones and holes of the dirt road. A black Mercedes pulled up. The back door opened quietly, and she folded herself into the dark interior. The sedan drove off leaving a cloud of dust.

The crow fluttered and flew silently toward the mountain peaks.

* * *

The black Mercedes arrived with impeccable punctuality. A young muscular man of stern features held the back door open for her. He wore a neatly fitted black suit, black shirt, black tie, white gloves and a black chauffeur's cap. She slipped into the darkened back seat. The chauffeur bowed efficiently and closed her door. Classical music played softly. A vase of roses and a bottle of water waited in the center console for her. They drove down the mountain without exchanging a word.

An hour later, they came to a clearing in an abandoned rice field. Three enormous motorhomes, each as wide as train cars and two stories tall, arrayed in a U-formation occupied the entire field. Warm golden light flooded out of the glass encased second levels. Double doors on the side of the units opened onto a shared platform patio and boardwalk. She exited the car directly onto the boardwalk where Yamada greeted her with a deep bow.

"Mr. Taira will see you now, Dr. Sato. Do go in." Ami looked at each of the three units. Yamada nodded toward the center vehicle. "You don't need to knock— just go in." The angular woman smiled thinly as usual.

A few steps up into the main receiving room, cool air enveloped her. Blond wood walls, slate tiles and chrome surrounded her. Densely shagged sheepskin rugs tossed with precise carelessness on sleek leather furniture completed the postmodern Scandinavian chic interior. Seeing no one around, she made herself comfortable on a chrome origami armchair. As she caressed the crisp metallic edge of the chair and breathed deep the machine-purified air, a part of her gave way. A tumble of a pebble above a tectonic shift. This was the air and aesthetics of her previous life— life in the city where she gathered with friends in elegant lounges and glamorous clubs.

A tall man entered from a staircase at the far end. The navy blue linen suit fit handsomely, vaguely suggesting lithe musculature beneath. A pale lavender shirt of subtle print, unbuttoned once, framed his cool complexion and fine features. His eyes, warm brown black, cut long above high cheekbones.

He walked toward her and extended a hand Western-style as he cocked his head slightly to the side. "Dr. Sato, it's a pleasure to meet you." She rose, while awkwardly denying her habit to bow in the country way. They shook hands. He met her eyes directly and beamed a surprisingly gentle smile.

Taira wasn't what Ami expected. She expected him to be more like his notorious father. The elder Taira was a brutish muscular man, fancier of Judo and patron of the Sumo stables. Whispers of political graft and whiffs of the Yakuza always swirled around that elder statesman, even as he led the postwar recovery of a fragile Japan and the Taira companies.

This Taira was sleek and elegant. Western in etiquette, but something about his sculpted features and in his graceful movements seemed regal and almost ancient Heian.

"Mr. Taira. Thank you for this gracious invitation. But I am but a humble country doctor. To what do I owe such kindness?" She slipped into formal protocoled speech. Her grandfather would have been proud of her.

"Oh please, just call me Takahiro. We are both moderns—no need for the old formalities. My closest friends call me Taka—but I hope we'll have time to get better acquainted for you to call me that. May I call you... Ami?"

He beamed that disarming smile again and fell effortlessly into a cloud of sheepskin and leather. He gestured with long fingers to the other end of the sofa. With a deep exhale she pushed the old world formalities out of her body and fell, slightly less elegantly, onto the sofa. She laughed at her awkwardness. He laughed supportively.

The wall opposite them slid away, startling Ami. There stood a young woman with short platinum hair slicked back, wearing a black tuxedo and a bow tie. She stood before a vast wall of bottles while tending to an array of cocktail implements. Her shoulders were square, muscular and masculine, but the lapels emphasized the swell of her ample breasts.

"Hey, boss, what do you fancy? Hello, miss. Care for a cocktail? I'm the best mixologist this side of Honolulu, you know!" She winked at the two of them, struck a muscle-man pose, and laughed easily. Ami soon learned Tachiko's talent for wickedly smooth elixirs.

Taira Takahiro told tales of his travels to far reaches of the globe, of his homesickness while studying at Oxford, his weakness for French pastries and Argentinian beef, and his deep love of Japan. He asked of her research focus and her dreams of travel. She passionately spoke of her early research into biomedicine and surprised herself with her own heated advocacy.

As the libations flowed, they began to speak with blushed cheeks of their nightlife adventures in Tokyo, Nagoya, and other cities. His work association required him to belong to several stuffy private clubs, but he loved the dark dance clubs and other pleasure palaces. She pushed for more details. "You'll have to earn the right to hear those!" he teased. Tipsy, she confessed to her fondness of themed love hotels in Osaka. Then she shrieked and clasped her hand over her mouth. All three of them laughed. More drinks came. He sat closer to her. He put his hand on her leg.

She let him.

It felt good.

Thoughts flitted in the back of her buzzed mind that she ought to be asking questions. But she couldn't remember what they were.

The chrome lights dimmed, and the drinks flowed on perfectly formed ice cubes in stylish glasses.

For all the innuendos, he was a gentleman. His hand stayed on her leg but never traveled further. She wanted more.

She'd lost track of time and a bit of decorum when he offered a ride back home. He helped her up to her unsteady feet and walked her to the front door. Uncertain as to how to bid farewell, she waited for his cues.

"Let's do this French style," he whispered. Not knowing what to expect, she simply giggled. He kissed her cheeks, alternating sides, three times. His lips were warm, supple and full. "I don't know what you had in mind, Ami, but that is French!" He winked. His hands lingered on her waist and slid down, fingers pressing into her muscles. Her hips readied to yield. Was that a barely perceptible pull into his body? She kissed him once on a cheek, turned quickly on her heels and stumbled out to the bright lights and cacophony of the mega city.

Except, it wasn't.

The only bright lights were the stars above. A dozen fireflies flitted in the grass. Beyond the golden glow encircling Taira's compound, deep black darkness crouched, breathing deep its sanguine moist breath.

She had, for a few hours, returned to her libertine ways in the company of a charming rake. Those carefree nights melted from one into another, the endless floating world. Eventually it did all end, of course, as her compatriots were felled one by one— some to respectable marriages, others trapped by the career track, and she to the responsibility as caretaker to her geriatric charges. Ami collapsed into the back of the Mercedes and stared at the ceiling.

Kansaburo did not come to, or with, Ami that night.

Restless, she let her hands take her to jagged edges of fitful pleasures. In her mind, they were hands of others, shifting from the calloused hands of a laborer to strokes of fine fingers. They were surrendering arms in rag-made bonds, then linen-sheathed muscle. They were supple warm lips, then hard cool lips. The scent of rich fertile soil mixed with fine French cologne. Her hand drenched in confusion, she fell into a strange sleep full of weird beastly passions.

* * *

The next day passed in dullness. Dull weather. Dull head. Dull work.

Ami made her late afternoon rounds reluctantly.

Dowager Ito still refused to be seen. Once again, Kaede shooed her away. This time she seemed more emphatic and frazzled. The Ito compound was unusually busy. Workers rushed hither and fro. Some adding mulberry branches to a massive pile, the size of a small house, while others tended to the spinning wheels. A small group of elderly men and women in formal black kimonos and white pilgrimage garb sat on the veranda drinking tea. Their faces were unfamiliar to Ami, but they all wore the moth and chrysanthemum crest of the Kinugasa clan. They sat silently and did not acknowledge the young doctor. Ami bowed at Kaede and turned back toward the infirmary.

As she walked through their central courtyard toward the entrance gate, she heard a bellowing sound and turned to see where it came from. That was when she caught sight of the private residential wing in the back of the estate. The wide shoji doors slid open, and a group of elders clutching mulberry branches streamed in and disappeared into the darkness of the room beyond. Toward the end of this procession was Priestess Azusa, hair wild as ever and waving a Nusa. After her, a tall man blew on a conch shell the size of a watermelon. Its low mournful bellowing continued. He wore a white and saffron jacket with billowing hakama pants tucked into shin guards, an animal skin across the back, and a small black lacquer hat on the forehead. A long rosary hung from his other hand that held a long silver staff. Even as a city girl, Ami recognized the ritual garb of the Yamabushi—these were ascetic monks, the mountain warrior priests, and a rarely seen people of a bygone era of spiritual rigor. She was quite surprised to see such a figure even in this backwater village. She was even more

134

surprised as he turned to enter the room and she saw his face.

It was Kansaburo.

What? Why? Why was he in ritual garb? Weren't Yamabushi supposed to be celibate mind or something?

The door closed behind him, and all went silent.

Except for the cumulative sound of thousands of worms munching leaves.

And a crow cawed in the distance.

Ami hurried out of the gate.

As the sun dipped toward the mulberry orchard, Ami saw Chiyo walking toward her. Loosely clad in a cotton yukata of morning glory print, she let her long hair hang damp down her back. She must have just taken a dip in the natural hot springs in the cliff-side caves. Chiyo called to Ami and waved. As Ami was about to wave back, she stopped dead in her tracks. Chiyo's long swaying form cast a longer swaying shadow, with small pointed ears, thin muzzle, and a distinct thickly tapered tail. It was clear and crisp as everything else. Suddenly nauseated, she clasped her clammy hand on quivering lips and ran back to the infirmary, where she retched for quite some time.

That was the final straw. She had to schedule an MRI for herself soon. She had picked up the old rotary phone to call her former research hospital when the doorbell clanged again. She shrieked and dropped the handset. The dial tone went dead.

At the door was Takahiro's crisply dressed chauffeur, bowing deeply and presenting an ornate envelope, carefully held in white glove-clad hands. In the unintended gap between glove and shirt cuff, Ami spied brilliantly inked skin. The crimson envelope was sealed with one giant butterfly crest. She opened it to find a single page note, elegantly handwritten in classic script and addressed to Ami in familiar terms.

To the delightful Ami,

> *I hope you don't think me crass for my behavior with you last night. Your charm caught me off guard, and I completely forgot the reason for our meeting. I hope you'll allow me to apologize to you in person tonight. If you should accept, please come for dinner tonight. My chauffeur will bring you to my place.*

> *Humbly,*
> *Takahiro*

The driver stood ramrod straight, holding the car door open. Obviously, declining the invitation was not an actual option.

They drove silently into the fast approaching night.

Once again she stepped into his cool oasis where he greeted her French style. His fingers brushed the nape of her neck, making her shudder. He wore a dark blue linen shirt, relaxed with sleeves loosely rolled up, and perfectly cut designer jeans. The lounge was converted into a crystalline dining room, flooded with flickering candlelight. The large table was set sumptuously for two. Tachiko waited in the back, tuxedo-clad with a long black apron. At one seat was a large red box wrapped in gold ribbon. He handed it to her.

"Oh I couldn't. It's not necessary." She pushed it away.

"Please accept this from me. It really would give

me pleasure for you to have this." After a few rounds of ritual refusal, she finally surrendered and accepted the gift.

The box opened up to a cloud of fragrant paper. From it, Ami pulled out a delicate length of fabric, peach and purple with sumptuous embroidery of peonies and butterflies. A signature Hanae Mori slip dress. The finest silk flowed through her fingers like cool water. The sensation took Ami's breath away.

"If it doesn't displease you, I hope you'll try it on. I'd love for you to wear it for our dinner." Takahiro gestured toward the back of the room where Tachiko held open a door. She entered the room, a private lounge and dressing area full of amenities and toiletries. Ami was baffled as to why such a room existed. Perhaps it was for his staff. She looked in the mirror and was a bit mortified. She came wearing her country doctor work clothes—utilitarian white blouse and even more utilitarian khaki pants with cargo pockets. She swiftly stripped out of her clothes. How could she come dressed like that? Why hadn't she bothered to put something nice on? Did she even have anything nice for such an occasion anymore?

The dress draped and caressed Ami perfectly. She looked to the woman in the mirror. She was beautiful. She was still elegant. A bit more tanned than in the city days, but she still had it. Her posture shifted and spine elongated. She raised her breasts and breathed deeply. She shifted her weight onto one leg and curved a hip out. She had missed her own sophistication. Running her hands along her thigh, she enjoyed the feel of the silk and then the curve of her mound and the arch of her back.

As she emerged of the dressing room, she heard Tachiko audibly inhale. "Miss, you're breathtakingly stunning!" She cooed and handed Ami a small box. "This is also part of your ensemble, miss."

In it Ami found a pair of bracelets, perfectly matched bands of twisted gold and silver, lined in white kidskin.

"Let me help you with that," said Takahiro. He unlocked the clasp and placed each around her wrists. A hinge mechanism allowed the small circles to fit delicately around Ami's wrists. He clicked them shut.

They matched the silk gracefully, felt soft against her skin, but substantial and laid heavily. They brought her arms down gently, as if to ground fluttering wings.

He took her hands and gazed at her with a sly grin. His gaze bore into her.

"Beautiful," he whispered.

She blushed and turned nervously away. Then, feeling silly for acting like some schoolgirl, she took a breath, and turned to gaze directly back at him.

At that, his eyes narrowed slightly and the edges of his mouth curled up imperceptibly. He stepped back and bowed crisply at the waist in the European manner, then led her to the sumptuous table.

A luscious French feast followed. Tachiko made sure the wine flowed. Takahiro gazed admiringly at Ami. His fingers stroked her wrists and bracelets. Talk turned to his dream of Japan's once and future glory. His breath was hot on her neck as he whispered visions of a new mighty Edo period. Her pulse raced as his breath quickened. Ancient villages would wither no more, they'd be new destinations of Nippon pride and grand development, he declared. More courses of divine dishes came. His hand stroked her silk-clad thigh.

"New vigor spreading to every corner of Japan!" His firm grip gently pulled apart her thighs, now moist. "Timid no more and beholden not to foreign powers," he crooned. More wine flowed. His hand stroked slowly up her thigh. She was getting light-headed. He led her to the chaise.

Dessert of absinthe-infused strawberries and molten chocolate cream arrived. "Take your gorgeous village for one." He took her hand and turned her toward him. "It's slowly dying, don't you think?" She nodded.

He wrapped an arm around her waist and brought her in closely. "Should this once beautiful historic village fade away like a ghost and the villagers die in indignity?" He frowned. She shook her head. With his free hand, he dipped a plump strawberry into the thick chocolate sauce. He brought the dripping fruit toward her. Her lips parted, wanting.

"Wouldn't you want this village to thrive again, drinking full the sweet nectar of abundance?" She could hardly nod as he brought the fruit to her lips and pressed, filling her mouth with tart sweetness of summer and rich dark chocolate. She sucked greedily as he laid her back.

"I want to bring riches to this village and area. Would you like that?" He brought to her mouth another swollen berry dripping in chocolate, breathing hot onto her neck. She nodded. His weight pressed down onto her.

"I want to make this part of Japan a destination of Nippon pride. I want your help in this." Her thighs slacked and parted as his hips fell between them.

"I will preserve the dignity…" His hand slid up her dress.

"Remake the village into recreation of its grand glory. An exquisite Old Japan resort of such sophistication! It'll be the most desired destination. People will want to come in droves." His hand traveled to her sex, as the other hand slipped between her strawberry-filled lips. A shudder wracked her frame.

"So many people will come. The riches will explode into this valley." His fingers parted her labia and played her. Heat shot through her, and her hips arched forward, wanting desperately to feel his fingers in her.

"I need the villagers to understand my desire. It's for all our happiness. I want what I know they want. I want them to desire what I am offering. I want you to desire what I'm offering. We can all soar together. Please, please help me. I can't do this without you. Help me in." He slid his fingers out of her mouth and encircled her wrists. The other hand played and taunted her vulva.

Unable to bear the sweet torment, she cried, "Yes, for god's sake, yes!" She thrust her hip forward, chasing his teasing fingers and swallowed them with her sex. He graciously obliged and began a rhythmic hand thrusting, with the other hand never letting go of her metal-encircled wrists. She shrieked, shuddered, and climaxed to his expert handling.

She lay on the chaise panting, damp silk gathered around her waist, chocolate-smeared cheeks, and a flood between her thighs. He leaned back and surveyed the room with a satisfied smile.

Tachiko bowed and offered them each flutes of Champagne.

Ami had forgotten all about her. She must have been there the whole time. She made a half-modest attempt at covering herself up, but the silk clung to her sweat and sex-drenched skin. She gave up. Tachiko silently stood, holding up a silk dressing gown, while tastefully turning her head away. As Ami accepted the robe, Tachiko seemed entirely unaffected by what had transpired before her.

Takahiro sat back and studied Ami silently.

"Did you mean all that?" she said to him.

"Yes, I find you irresistibly erotic and attractive."

She blushed. "Well, thank you..." Her cheeks began to burn again, and she felt a sexual power welling up deep within her.

"Though I meant if you were serious about the village development project." She spoke slowly to bring down her racing heart rate to a dignified level.

"Yes, completely." He took a long slow drink of Champagne. "It would bring progress, employment, and youthful vigor back to this area."

"You have a point there," she said. "But what do I have to do with this?"

"Beyond making me love this area more with your sensual beauty?" He slyly smiled at her from above the glass flute.

"Yes—and thank you. Yes, beyond my amazing country doctor sex appeal. What do I have to do with this?"

"Do you think your elderly charges will accept the sort of change we are proposing?"

"Well, no. They're traditionalists."

"In many ways, I am a traditionalist too, but it's about a stronger, proud Japan. I firmly believe the rest of Japan ought to experience the ways of this village. But that won't happen unless the area is developed into an accessible and convenient resort destination."

He raised the freshly filled glass to toast her. "To you." He raised the glass and blew a kiss at her. She blew a kiss back at him and took a drink herself.

He raised his glass again. "To Japan." His gaze drifted off somewhere far away.

After a long sip, he looked back at her.

"You have a unique view of what the outside life is like. You are the future of Japan. You understand the benefit of progress. Your elderly charges, on the other hand... many have never left this village. I fear they are saddled with the old post-War spirit of defeat and inevitability. They think small and are bound by fear. They trust you and would listen to you. Why should they continue with backbreaking work when they should be enjoying their golden years? You can share the truth of the modern Japan. I just want you to talk to the villagers about our vision. You are the ambassador of a new generation!"

She accepted another glass and toasted him back. "Well, thank you. It does seem an attractive concept— as are you. Can I sleep on it?"

"Of course! And I hope you'll join me for dinner again. I'm sure Tachiko would enjoy lavishing you with more of her culinary and service delights!" Takahiro shot a sly glance at Tachiko, who rocked back on her heel and grinned a crooked grin.

Later that night, the chauffeur delivered Ami back to her home. It was dark and musty. The house creaked, and a draft came through thin paper walls. The first chill of autumn whistled past her. She hugged herself tightly. Propane was low so she couldn't make tea. She'd have to order a tank tomorrow. The dirt floor of the old kitchen needed sweeping. Something skittered across the pane window. It all seemed so shabby.

She found the bed made but unoccupied.

A perfectly formed scarlet maple leaf lay on her pillow. She winced. Was she a fool?

She slept an uncertain sleep.

Once, during the night, the house shook violently. She woke with a start, thinking it was a typhoon. When she rushed to close the storm shutters she saw the waning moon disappear behind a vast black cloud of silent wings. They flew north toward the mountains, stirring the night into a dark storm.

The next day she buried herself in work at the clinic. It had been neglected from all the recent distractions. She cleared the cabinets and storage room of all clutter but could not clear her mind. The supply drawers got organized, but her heart did not. The floors, gowns, and linens were clean and dry, but she wasn't. The various cables and cords were untangled and detached, but not her.

She saw the few patients who dropped in.

Mayor Jinki came in with a basket of early autumn pears. He hesitated at the entrance.

"Mr. Jinki, would you like to sit for tea with me? I could use a break." Ami pointed at the waiting room. He bowed gratefully, sighed, and sat heavily down. The chair sagged under his round body. She sliced the pears on a plate and made some tea.

Uncharacteristically quiet, he nibbled absentmindedly on the fruit.

"Doctor, should I be worried about the future of this village?" he said, pensively.

"What do you mean?"

"Well, it's just us oldsters now, except for you and Kansaburo." He looked at her sideways.

"Uh, yes. Kansaburo... Hey, Mayor, if this is about me and him..." She put a palm up and waved away at an imaginary thought bubble.

"Oh no, I'm sorry. I surely didn't mean it like that. Though the two of you would make a lovely couple... but I don't mean to be presumptuous. Well, are you two...? Oh, that's impolite of me. I'm sorry." He babbled and blushed.

Ami had half a sense of the mayor's dirty mind. It wasn't that much a surprise.

The mayor's face sagged into worry again.

"We're getting older. The village is dying. It's the hard truth. Those of us who have kids, they're not coming home to care for us. Take our two kids. My daughter's in Tokyo, she's an important woman now, engineering massive water projects. I'm so proud of her. And our son? He's trying to get through college. I don't expect them back here, and we certainly don't want to be a burden to them." He faded off in thought.

"What about the Kinugasas? They seem to be taking care of Dowager Ito. Do you know how she's doing?" she asked.

He winced and looked away.

"Oh yes, the Kinugasas. Well, they're a special family, an important lineage. Dowager Ito is... Well, I'm sure she'll be fine. She has Kaede to take care of matters. It's probably best to leave them be. They know what they are d-doing," he stammered.

After a bit of awkward silence, he continued. "But about this village. Maybe it's time we thought about future. Bring in young blood and grow the economy. We could use better services. No offense, Doc. But you could run a little hospital. Make this beautiful place a destination… Maybe he's right…"

"Who's right?" She had an idea, but she had to ask.

"Well…" He hesitated. "Please keep this between us. It is a gossipy town," said the village gossip. "An important man. It's a young master of the Taira clan." He spoke of the corporation as if they were still the Daimyo overlords of the feudal past. He fretted to Ami about loss of tradition. He confided that Taira wanted to buy the village and give it a viable future. Taira's muscular corporate buzzwords spilled from the mouth of the meek Mr. Jinki.

"They promised to take care of us villagers in every way. We just need to sell them the land, and they'll make it all good. What do you think?" He peered into Ami's face.

"Hmmm. The village could use help in many ways. In the years to come I'm not sure who'll harvest the rice and care for infirm," she mused.

"Exactly! And I could be the mayor to usher in progress!" He smiled for the first time in this visit. His eyes twinkled. Ami noticed Mr. Jinki's irises seemed more yellow than brown or black, an odd light shade of yellow. She leaned in and stared at him as if studying a specimen. The mayor flustered and looked away.

"So what's the down side?" she asked, resuming a more polite posture.

"My wife is dead set against it, for one. See, we live on her family's land." He scratched his head in embarrassment. "And the Kinugasas won't budge. They own most of the valley. And the other half is owned by… Well, that's complicated.

"Kaede refuses to discuss this. Ah! Women. So set in their ways." He rolled his eyes. "Of course I must understand. It's not a good time with what's ahead for Dowager Ito."

Ami raised a finger and cut in quickly. "What exactly is ahead for Dowager Ito?"

"Oh nothing, nothing at all! Just that she has to watch her health… and all those relatives to entertain… and the spinning season is upon us and… It's nothing. I'm sorry." He flustered. "I'm glad you also think progress is a good idea. Thank you. Thank you for your time. Thank you for the tea." Bowing vigorously, he scooted hurriedly out of the clinic, leaving Ami with her mouth hanging open, teacup still to her lips.

Later, she gathered her house-call bag, mounted her bicycle, and headed out to the Kinugasas once again. As she rounded the last corner, a hundred meters from their gate, a tall white-clad figure shot out and ran down the road in the other direction. Without a doubt, it was Kansaburo. She tried to call to him, but he was already far down the road. He moved at an uncanny clip. She rode after him, pedaling as fast as she could. He moved faster ahead still, rapidly becoming smaller and smaller. She had never seen anyone move like that. Soon he crossed the Kiyoi River and disappeared into the dark woods. When she finally arrived at the bridge, he was nowhere to be seen. She listened for the clacking of wooden geta on stone, but she only heard rustling leaves and the chirping of birds.

At the bridge, she hesitated. Should she let him go and confront him later for all the questions? But she needed to see him. There were so many mysteries. What was he doing at the Kinugasas? Why wouldn't he stay with her through the night? Why all the hang-ups about being seen in the midst of sex? What did he mean by her being special? Why was he not surprised at her troubling hallucinations of late? Most importantly, why had he not come to her bed in the last few nights? She longed to touch him. Her desire now awakened, she'd let herself become emotionally attached.

She cared for him despite her best efforts. A relationship would be foolish. What kind of future would that be for her? A life as a handyman's partner and a country doc? That was certain career suicide. In another year, she would return to the cities, the hospitals, and someday onto leading international research facilities. Men like Taira should be fawning over her.

Her mind churned full of frustrating questions. Uncertainty overwhelmed her. Unmoored. Ungrounded.

She needed the firmness of his embrace.

She leaned the bicycle on the weeping willow, squared her shoulders, and headed across the small stone bridge.

Ami did not notice a fin cut the surface of the flowing water—nor did she see the pair of yellow eyes floating up from the dark, watching her hesitations, and then disappearing in the shadow of the bridge.

Determined, she struggled up the rocky trail.

Quickly it became steep and slippery. The narrow paths twisted and split off. As best as she could, she tried to remember the way that Kansaburo had led them up in previous trysts. Often the paths became little animal trails and disappeared into the thick underbrush. Branches and blades of grass cut at her ankles. Mud coated her shoes. The chill of the forest seeped into her bones.

Eventually the trail leveled, and the dark grove gave way to pale verdant hues of giant bamboos. Pools of sunshine dappled the ground in gold and green. With ragged breath she stopped and bent over, leaning on her knees trying to recover. The bamboo clattered and creaked in the breeze.

For all this effort, he had better be up here. She steeled herself for a serious conversation. She should come clean about her night with Taira. Kansaburo was a country boy of old ways, so he might not take the news well. She didn't like that she was likely going to hurt his feelings. Would he be angry? Could he accept it? It crossed her mind briefly: what might Granny Azusa do about it? Honestly, she dreaded any chance of upsetting that strange little crone. This might be dropping a bomb on him, but she had to be the grown-up of the two if there was any hope for some sort of relationship moving forward.

A sharp metallic clap jarred her out of her contemplations. She heard the clanging again. The sound grew like metallic rain with whooshing wind. It came from deeper in the grove. Screams or shouts, or perhaps they were animal cries, punctuated it in short bursts. Then silence. Motionless, she listened. The cycle repeated. The grove grew completely still except for these sounds bursting through the air. Cautiously, she crept toward its source.

Something moved ahead of her. She froze. Another motion. She crouched low under a clutch of young bamboo growth. Ahead of her, a thick old bamboo stalk sprang up. Then another swung down, and back up again, creaking. It hit another with a loud pop. Then another to the left, and then to the right. Clanging and screeching came from overhead. Dark shadows were cast across the grove floor and disappeared, then cast dark again. Slowly she turned her head skyward.

Far above her, at the very tops of the bamboo, vast black wings beat the air violently. Darkest black feathers gleamed on wings easily five meters across. They swooped and collided, deafening shrieks piercing the atmosphere. She counted two of these massive birds, perhaps, or were there more? Squinting into the blinding sun, she tried to get a better view. It was too bright, and they moved too fast. Her heart beat so loud she feared they'd hear her. Falling feathers and leaves swirled wildly in the air.

As the birds dove into each other, sparks flew. Monstrous talons gleamed, clawing at one another. A naginata blade clanged against a pair of crossed katana.

Katana? Naginata?

Ami fell back.

Human arms sprouted from the base of the wings and wielded weapons, slashing at each other. They plummeted toward the forest floor, locked in combat. They landed on a bamboo stalk just above her. The blades locked, neither yielded. Their wings so wide

149

they blocked out the sky above. Raptor legs thick as tree trunks sprouted razor sharp talons. The silvery black monster wore a crimson hakama and kimono. The other, blue-black-winged and beastly, clad in white Yamabushi garb and bare-chested, exposed a sweat-drenched human male torso. Each of their massive black wingspans was topped by giant raven heads, black eyes gleamed as thick hooked beaks split open with mind-shattering screeching.

She covered her mouth, but it was too late. She'd shrieked loudly in reflexive terror.

The monsters snapped their heads toward her in unison. Their eyes burned bright.

Cowering, Ami inched back, scooting backward on her seat and trying to avert their raptor gaze. She looked for something to hide behind, to disappear. There was no place to hide. Staring unwaveringly, the monsters relaxed their locked weapons from one another, letting their human arms drop to the sides. They turned to look at one another, cocked their heads. Beaks cracked open, and they cawed with strange staccato cries at each other. Ami inched back some more. The hakama-clad one with the naginata spread her wings, turning to her companion. She cawed again, reached out with one wing and slapped the male monster across the back of his head. Then she flew up, disappearing into the sky beyond the bamboo leaves.

Now alone, the male monster stared directly at Ami. He dropped his wings down slowly, lifted the double katanas in the air. Ami trembled.

He raised the swords up and back, then slipped them into sheaths strapped to his feathered back. Ami still trembled. He dropped his head and turned away, a wing reached over, hiding his face. His human shoulders trembled. He looked toward her again with that horrible bird head. The beak opened. Instead of shrieks and caws, it spoke—oddly resonant and hollow, but still a human voice and clearly Japanese.

"Ami... I'm sorry... I..."

He leapt toward her.

She let out a sharp wail, "No!" scrambled up, and stepped away from him. "No! You can't be! You can't really be... No..."

"Ami... I'm..." With those horrible talons, he stepped toward her on the leaf-covered ground.

"Oh god, no. No! Leave me alone..." She stepped back, turned and ran.

She ran and ran and ran through the grove.

His frightful wings beat the air just behind her.

She fell and tumbled. She heard him approach behind. Without looking back, she crawled until she regained her feet again.

Down the mountainside she ran, breath ragged, heart pounding, legs mud-splattered, slashed, and torn from branches and cutting blades of grass.

By the time she reached the willow at the bridge, the tree already cast a long dark shadow in the scarlet light of the setting sun. She let the tree hold up her quivering body. Through gasping breath she listened— without turning or looking—listened for him—for it.

Nothing.

Just the evening melodies of songbirds, crickets chirping, and splashing fins from the river.

She did not bother to close the clinic that night. She didn't care. She went directly home and curled up under the covers. Horrifying images invaded her mind.

Claws and beaks ripped her thoughts. The shrieking and cawing echoed in her head. Sleep would not come, but she lay in the darkness wrapped in nightmares.

"Ami…" His gentle voice called to her through the darkness. She came to from a wretched sleep she didn't realize she was in. Tears soaked her pillow. Her head ached. Her body ached. She tried to shake the bad dreams she had.

"Ami…" he called to her again.

"Hmmmm, what are you doing out there?" she mumbled, half asleep. "Come in already." She moved the cover aside and reached for the lamp switch. The austere room glowed yellow from the tiny incandescent bulb. Her mind began to clear. Weird shadows of hunched trees danced on the paper walls. As the shoji screen began to slide open, she remembered. The claws, the shrieks, the wings, and monstrous visions flooded back to her mind. Her heart raced as she clutched the covers and cowered into a corner. She saw his fingers and hand, human in form, on the edge of the shoji. It opened further. His other hand came in, holding a lit kerosene lantern. Shadows danced wickedly on the walls.

He entered the room. She clenched her eyes and began to scream. She screamed until she lost her breath. She gasped like a fish on the boat floor.

"I'm sorry…" he whispered in his soft, low and very human voice.

Then there was nothing.

She did not hear wings or clacks of claws.

Slowly she opened her eyes. He sat a few meters away lit by the flicker of the lantern. He was as he always had been. Human legs clad in workers trousers, worn with a white tank top on a very muscular but very human body. Cautiously she looked up from his legs to his head. Human. His was a human face, through his brows knitted in grief and torment. It wasn't the terrible black eyes and beak of earlier. As their gaze met, quickly he averted his.

Still she did not move out of her corner nor unclench the blanket. He made no attempt to approach her either.

A long silence passed between them.

Finally, he put his hands on the tatami before him and bowed deeply. He waited. She struggled for breath and calm.

"We are truly sorry. This one did not mean to terrify thee. This one did not mean for thee to discover in this manner." With head still bowed to the floor, he spoke with the archaic formality of the Imperial Court. How had this country bumpkin learn to speak this way?

"What... what are you?" she blurted out. "That was you, wasn't it?"

He raised his head and sat up. He looked directly at her for the first time.

"Yes, that was I."

"You're... you're not human... What are you?"

"Well, I'm mostly human. My ancestry is mixed."

"Mostly... human?"

"I'd like to explain all this to you. But I don't want to frighten you any more than you are. I promise you, what you see is really me. I'm not faking this body. We're not that kind. We're not the sort to hurt you or harm you."

"'We?' You mean there are more of you?"

153

"Um, yes… we've been around for thousands and thousands of years."

"But that can't be. I've never heard of creatures like you."

He winced at the word creatures.

"Actually you have. But you think we're just characters in children's stories."

She stared at him while running through a mental inventory of children's tales. The memory and stories seemed so far away. When she was little, her grandfather used to tell her strange tales of mythical creatures and gods of Japan. He knew them well and often acted them out, overacted pantomime of a doting old man, making her laugh and squeal. There were the powerful gods, the trickster foxes, the drunken badger, the rescued crane lady, the kind fishermen lost in time, and the crow men called tengu. She blurted out, "Tengu?"

"Yes. That's one name."

The kerosene lantern flickered, and his shadow danced on the wall and ceiling. Ami screamed, pointing at the ceiling behind him. He sprang up onto his feet and turned to look behind him, clenched fists ready for battle. Kansaburo's shadow sprouted wings that spread across the room. The shadow raised its fist as well.

Seeing nothing but his own shadow, he relaxed and sat back down.

"You saw my wings in my shadow, didn't you?"

"Yes…" she whimpered. "I'm seeing things that aren't there."

"You're not—you're not imagining it at all. You're seeing our real shadows. Ordinary people don't have this subtle perception. Like I said, you're special." He hesitated, looked at his hands and blushed. "And you're really special to me." His voice dropped to a whisper. "I don't know if I can bear to be without you anymore—so I didn't want to scare you."

"Why didn't you just tell me?" she snapped at him. While shocked from the shadowy apparition, she was equally stunned to hear him confess tender affections to her.

"Would you have believed me?" He gazed up at her with brows furrowed in pain and anguish. "Would you have just accepted me had I told you I sprout wings? I have claws and a beak? Could you have embraced that I'm of a race of beings told in stories to frighten children? You don't even believe the medicine I show you. You're always so certain you know more about this world than I do. So how was I going to tell you? Do you know how badly I've wanted to share this with you?"

He turned away from her. His face hidden in the shadow, his shoulders shook quietly. Was he crying?

She softened her voice slightly and asked, "Do the villagers know?"

He answered, still looking away, "Those from the old families do. We've lived side by side for a thousand years. We all keep the secrets of this village. My family's been protecting this area for eons."

"Protecting? From what?"

"Yes, protecting. My clan is sworn to protect this valley and the mountains. We guard the sacred places and the people who worship them. We provide medicine. We are the priests, priestesses, soothsayers, and mediums. My ancient ancestors once served the gods directly and came here from far, far away. We are warriors above all." His back straightened as he spoke, and he looked directly at her. Great pride emanated from his steady gaze. He seemed to speak of a timeframe far greater than she'd ever given thought to.

"Warriors? Protecting? What on earth against? And in this little village? Who uses swords anyway?" She cocked her head, baffled.

"You are infuriatingly modern, Ami." He rolled his eyes. "You do remember Japan was a land of swords and blood longer than it's been peaceful. And we are peaceable today only because we were crushed in The War." He spoke as if World War II was still recent history. "Back a couple hundred years ago, this was an important town and a significant stop on the Eastern Trade Road."

"It was?"

He sighed heavily. "It was… Of course we don't teach our own history anymore. It's all been altered and redacted to be entirely inoffensive. Gods forbid we realize we've choked the life out of our own spirit and soul. After all, the sun did once rise from these islands." He drifted off to a far away gaze, falling silent. His sat in seiza pose with shoulders squared and straight back. His jaw set firm and proud. An uncanny stillness came over him, and Ami felt a wave of something powerful wash over her. If the ghosts of great samurais past could become flesh, could this be it? Where was her bumbling country boy lover? His thoughts were now entirely foreign to her. His entire being was now fully alien to her.

Caught back into the present, he looked back at

her. No longer the reminiscing warrior, he glanced up at her like a frightened little boy.

"You must think me a monster now. I am so, so very sorry." His head dropped.

She sat silent.

Time passed. He stared down at his fingers.

Shyly he broke the silence. "I'm sorry. I'm not much good at this. I don't have much practice with this."

"With what?" she asked.

"With telling people who I am—who we are. Granny's been at me for a while now to tell you. She gave me what for today after you saw us."

"Your granny? How does she deal with your… um… condition."

He winced again as she said condition.

"It's not a condition. It's not a disease. For god's sake, please, it's who we are." He bit into his lip. "Yes, of course she knows and deals with it. You saw her too."

"That was Granny Azusa? She's a tengu too?" Ami shouted.

Kansaburo winced again. "Of course she is. She is my grandmother after all."

Ami head began to spin again with visions of claws and screaming.

"Then why were you trying to kill each other?"

"Kill each other?" He blinked uncomprehendingly.

"Yes! The swords and the naginata and all the fighting! You were trying to kill each other!"

He muffled a chuckle. "That? That's just the daily training, though it was harder than usual, given the situation now… She really is something. She's got me

157

on a heck of a regimen. You know, I've yet to win a match against her? One day!" When he stopped chuckling, he finally saw Ami's terrified and confused face.

"I'm sorry. I'm sorry... Yes, of course, it must look like we're trying to kill each other. I would never hurt her, and she's not going to kill me. It's just practice. We're okay. We scared you so much today. I'm so very sorry."

After another bout of silence she asked, "So you can fly too?"

"Yes."

"Does it hurt?"

"What, flying? No, it's the most amazing feeling."

"No, I mean when your body changes. Does it hurt when the wings and beak come out?" She asked with measured curious tone that surprised both of them.

"Do you really want to know?"

"Yes."

"No. It doesn't hurt anymore. The first few years, when I was a teenager, it was miserable and really painful. I wasn't much good at it, and practicing was hard. Now it feels like an itch under the skin before ecstasy."

"You weren't always able to change? You have to practice?"

"It starts in puberty. It's really awkward. Puberty's bad enough for regular boys with whiskers and hard-ons sprouting, and voice changing and stuff. For us we have to deal with the feathers and beaks and raven songs. Getting the hang of it is really tricky."

"I want to see," Ami blurted.

"Now?"

"Yes, now." She clenched her teeth with determination. "I want to see you change."

"Um. I'm not sure I'm ready for that. I've never..."

"Never what?"

"I've never shared this with anyone outside of our kind. By custom it's shared only with our mate-consorts."

"Mate-consort? Is there someone else other than me?"

"No! No!" He waved his hand wildly. "I don't have a mate-consort. If anyone you'd... I mean, you're my only... Yes, you're my lover. But mate-consort is like a betrothal. It's a committed union with responsibility. It's a lot to ask of you, and I hadn't even told you about me and..."

"I want to see. Now."

"Now?" He waffled.

"Yes, now. I want to know I'm not imagining this. I want to know you're telling the truth." She stared at him.

"Will you lay with me then?"

"What? Sex, now? I just want to see you change."

"Yes. It's through sex. Or more precisely through a special process of sex."

Ami suddenly remembered their past lovemaking, how his hairs became stiff and his lips cold and hard. How he wanted to make love in the darkness and rarely in the light.

She stared at him suspiciously.

"Of course. That's rude of me to ask. I can change myself. It's most effective in union with a partner, but we're trained for singular transformation. Are you sure you want to see this? You will see me like that again." He waved toward his winged shadow still dancing over him.

"Yes. I want to see."

He nodded gravely and stood up, stripping off his tank top. His abs rippled with his movement.

"What do you mean it's 'more effective in union?'" she asked.

He stopped in the middle of unbuttoning his trousers. "It means that the transformation is deeper. My form is larger and my wings are bigger. With a joined transformation, I am stronger and I can be in wings longer. It helps me heal faster too." He waited for her to ask further. She stared at him in disbelief. After a moment he tentatively continued to undress.

Naked, he stood before her but did not approach her.

Under her unwavering gaze, his untouched cock began to stiffen.

She stared unblinking at him, but her cheeks began to redden. Fear, curiosity, and lust gripped her.

He sat down and folded his legs into a lotus position. He entwined his fingers into a complicated mudra prayer position above his loin. He looked deeply into her eyes and waited.

She didn't move.

Soon he closed his eyes, and his breath became long, slow, and deep as a low murmur emanated from his throat. He began to chant in a tongue Ami had never heard. It sounded as though a dozen voices whispered songs at once.

The hair on the back of her neck stood on end.

The black shadow wings behind him slowly beat

in an unseen sky. His cock began to swell. He shifted his hands and laced his fingers in another mudra around his enlarged cock. Slowly the interlaced hands stroked the hard shaft. The strokes quickened, but his breathing stayed steady. If anything his breathing became deeper, and the chants dropped to an even lower pitch. His cock swelled larger than Ami had ever seen it before. It throbbed and swelled, as thick as her arm. Against reason and fear, her sex throbbed at the sight of his arousal.

His figure was getting darker, as if a shadow was cast over him. She blinked and squinted to clear her vision. It wasn't a shadow, nor was her sight failing her. He was getting darker as feathers sprouted along legs and arms. Black feathers covered his face where it was a faint five-o-clock shadow. His lips became black and thick, thrusting out into a peaked point.

He stroked faster, and the chants came rapidly. His breathing mixed gutturally with the foreign words. The veins on his shaft pulsed, and his chest flushed. She knew what would come soon. As the head swelled even larger in anticipation of climax it suddenly turned a shade of blue black she'd never seen before. His glans wasn't the reddish purple of aroused skin. Rather it turned a metallic sheen like darkly polished steel. As he chanted he suddenly arched his back and threw his head back in a massive spasm. He slammed his mudra hands down on his steel club shaft. She leaned in for the magnificent eruption of his hot fountain.

But none came.

The rod was dry as bone; the strokes slowed but did not cease. And his rod and balls were shining blue black like his gleaming feathers. His hands slipped away, and his rod disappeared amid a riot of feathers from thick raptor legs.

She looked up and met not the gaze of Kansaburo but the blackest eyes of the tengu. Black wings unfolded behind him and stretched across the width of the room.

Sitting before her was a mythical being made flesh. And it was her lover. She began to shake in confusion and shock visited anew.

The resonant voice came from the open beak.

"Ami... it's still me. Please say something."

She gasped for air as her heart beat wildly somewhere in her throat.

She struggled for words between fear, wonder, lust and awe.

"You are... you are..."

He shifted nervously and looked away. With one bird eye, he glanced at her. Black eyes blinked tentatively. "I'm afraid I'm scaring you. I'm sorry. Please, please don't find me ugly. I must be hideous to you."

She choked for breath.

"You're... amazing," she gasped.

He blinked. "What? Really?" His raven head picked up, and the wings quivered upward.

She realized then that birds couldn't smile—not with their hard beaks. He couldn't smile! Something about that realization made her laugh. She wasn't sure why. The whole situation was simply strange and surreal. She wanted to burst out laughing hysterically. Perhaps she was on the verge of cracking.

Before her was her lover.

Before her sat a giant raven man.

The raven was her lover.

He blinked.

Tentatively she leaned forward. The blanket fell away revealing her nakedness. He did not move.

Cautiously, she crawled over toward him. His wings quivered.

Hesitatingly, she sat an arm's reach before his massive alien form. He inhaled sharply and held his breath.

Curiously, she reached out toward his thick black beak. He closed his bird eyes.

She was surprised how smooth it was. It wasn't cold like stone or metal, but somehow subtly warm, like polished mahogany or oak. He exhaled a thin nervous stream of breath.

She stroked the smooth onyx surface of his beak, itself as large as her head. She stood before him, close. He didn't move. She stood utterly naked, with the curiosity of a child. His tensed wings quivered quickly and relaxed ever so slightly. She stroked his feathered head. She played with individual feathers. He sighed and leaned into her caress. Engrossed in the details, she became lost in the beauty of this being, her lover.

The storm window rattled in the autumn winds, and a piercing cold draft shot through the room. She shivered. He arched his wings forward, encircling her in a cloister of warm black feathers. She continued to explore his most curious body. Where feathers grew the skin shone steel blue-black. Where no feathers sprouted, his chest and belly were a leathery tan, much like his usual skin in color but thicker in texture. He sat silently, breath quivering, the subject of her intense scrutiny and focused study. She could not read nor understand his avian expression. Once she must have pulled a feather too hard as he blinked quickly and twitched a muscle. She wondered if she ever could learn to read this bird's emotion. She marveled at his eyes, black, smooth, and large as saucers. She stared directly at him, and he gazed back with preternatural intensity. The gaze was distinctly other, beyond anything human. He did not blink under her scrutiny. A primordial shiver wracked her body. She wondered of the terror that prey must feel.

Then she remembered exactly how that felt. Pure terror had gripped her in a state of incoherence and paralysis. She stopped stroking his feathers—remembering.

He cocked his head, fully raven, like those damned crows all over the village.

But the mysterious feathers drew her in again. She stepped closer into him to stroke the feathers from his shoulder to chest. Heat radiated intensely off his skin and feathers. She liked the warmth—comforting and strangely safe. The black winged circle grew close around her.

* * *

Kraaaangg! Kraaaang! Kraaaaang!

The incendiary sound of metal striking metal ripped the gentle night as the village fire bell shattered the silence. Torn from the moment by the jagged sound, they rushed to the front door, she grabbing a blanket for cover while his massive body and wings barely fit through the hallway. His taloned feet clacked and gouged the polished wood floor.

Kraaaangg! Kraaaang! Kraaaaang!

Stepping out into the cold night, she shuddered on the icy stone steps and wrapped the blanket tightly around her shoulders. A black wing gently draped around her, fending off the frosty air. Warm, soft feathers comforted her. She let the blanket fall, just to feel him on her naked flesh.

The inky sky glittered with a riot of stars, and the Milky Way flowed wide with a thousand diamonds and pearls.

Kraaaangg! Kraaaang! Kraaaaang!

They turned toward the clanging and saw the sky blazing red and orange. Brown smoke rose heavily around the edges.

"What the—!" she shrieked.

"Damn! That's toward the Kinugasa estate!" he shouted. The end of the sentence punctuated by an odd screeching caw. He looked down to her with that strange avian face and cawed, "I'm sorry. I have to go." He spread his wings and, with one massive wing stroke, lifted into the air. The gale of his beating wings knocked her off balance. When she opened her eyes, he was gone.

Naked and stunned, Ami stumbled back into the house, quickly tossed on jeans, sweater, and a pair of sneakers, grabbed Kansaburo's lantern, and rushed down the dirt roads to the silk-maker's home.

A crowd gathered outside the main gate as smoke billowed out and over it. More came running. Soot filled the air choking everyone. Her eyes burned and teared wildly. Shouting everywhere, people screaming and crying. Cries came from within the walls. Balls of flame danced across the thatched roofs, jumping to new roofs and spreading across the compound. Dowager Chimiko, the laundress, came running barefoot and shouting in her night kimono, pulling a farm cart full of buckets, tubs, and pots. The villagers swarmed, grabbing containers and ran to the irrigation stream. Mayor Jinki jumped into in the stream and began scooping bucket after bucket. Chiyo, Kinsuke, even the drunkard Tanuta carried and hurled water onto the raging flames.

Ami stepped out of their way to look for the source of the fire. Squinting, Ami's gaze searched above the wall, above the burning thatch, into the smoke-filled dark sky. A ball of fire arced across and landed on a dry roof, touching off another fire swirl. Another fireball arced and then another, each setting off a new blaze of panic.

More red demons scarred the night sky.

She traced their arc back to a single point on a branch of an ancient cedar tree behind the estate. The shadows birthed a spark, popping into a fireball that bobbed up, drew back, and then shot through the sky. An arrow! Somebody was shooting flaming arrows into the estate.

Before she could shout out an alarm, she saw the black outline of a massive winged being descending upon the old cedar. Blocked by the smoke and blazing brightness of the fire she couldn't fathom the details except that the massive tree shook and shuddered wildly.

A searing sharp wailing of a woman sliced through her thoughts.

"Dear gods, there are more trapped inside!"

A collective gasp rose from the villagers. Then the bucket brigade of aged men and women shuffled faster with desperate urgency. Someone threw a wooden rice pail to Ami, who caught it before it struck her head. She ran to the creek, filled the pail and rushed to join the frantic bucket line, the sloshing water soaking her through. Pail after bucket, pot after tub, they threw water onto the blaze devouring the gate and walls. The fire drank it up and blazed even stronger. Sweat streaked the soot- and ash-covered faces as tears ran into furrows of distress.

The wind changed briefly, pushing the thick curtain of smoke aside. They saw clearly into the great courtyard. The growing shed had already succumbed to the flames, collapsed into a heap of burning timber, thousands of silk worms scorched in a living hell. The spinning house stood like a fiery phantom, held upright only by the upward thrusting flames, turning to ash before their eyes. The wind blew again, clearing another curtain of smoke beyond that, bringing to view the great residential hall of Dowager Ito. There they saw the entire Kinugasa clan, their visiting elders from far away, spinners, workers, and even the servants encircling the dowager's residence. Their backs were turned to the bucket brigade. The villagers shouted at them, but none turned. No one rushed to the exit gate. Instead they ran their own bucket line from the courtyard well, dousing the walls and roof of the dowager's quarters. They poured water on nothing else, oblivious to the rest of the estate burning down around them. The villagers shouted louder.

"Come out!"

"Save yourselves!"

"You're going to die. Please!"

No one turned to the would-be rescuers' frantic calls.

A large piece of burning debris flew onto the thatch roof of the residence. As the fire erupted, a vast wing descended, beating the flames violently, extinguishing it. The Kinugasa clan members looked up and cheered. Then they returned dutifully to fending off the encroaching inferno. The massive silver-black tengu hovered above then circled swiftly around the structure, wings beating to squelch series of small ignitions.

Stunned, Ami looked around for others and their shock, for another witness to this bizarre vision. But none of the villagers showed signs of bafflement or disbelief.

Did they not see it?

With a gust, the wind changed directions again, blowing blinding smoke, soot and burning ash into their faces. The view and access to the courtyard disappeared behind the billowing curtain of smoke and flames. Coughing and gagging, they retreated to the creek, beginning the bucket brigade all over again.

Ami stumbled to the side, choking. Bewildered and frightened for the Kinugasa clan, she decided to run to the rear of the compound to search out another escape route for them. The thatch tops of the perimeter walls were all ablaze. The mud and straw surface radiated intense heat, reddening her face as she ran alongside it. She tried to run faster, but the heat scorched her lungs and smoke filled her mouth and nostrils. She stopped several times to cough and sputter.

She was about to turn off the dirt road to a side alley around the compound when she saw a limo parked across the road. It was hidden partially by the thinly leaved branches of cherry trees. The black car shimmered, cool red and twisted orange reflecting the blazes. Taira leaned against it with arms loosely crossed and head lazily cocked to the side. The fire danced across his mirrored aviator glasses. Dressed in a black turtleneck, blue jeans, and snakeskin cowboy boots, he studied the pandemonium like an artist stepping back from his canvas. He turned toward Yamada, standing stiffly a short distance away in a floor-length black knit dress. Wrapped across her face and one shoulder, she wore a voluminous hood and shawl of teal and purple feathers trimmed with red fibers. It looked like a peacock died gruesomely on her head while she was swallowing it whole. She leaned in to Taira, who said something that made them both laugh. The dead bird thing quivered as they chuckled.

Ami turned her stride toward them and tried to call out to Taira. But her smoke-filled lungs got the better of her, and she had to stop before making it across to them. Nausea overwhelmed her, and she buckled over. Tastes of burning straw and kerosene churned in her mouth.

Tachiko stepped out from behind a tree where she was having a smoke. Tossing the butt into the rice paddy, she trotted over.

"Hey, miss? Are you okay? Can I get you some water?" Tachiko offered with consummate hospitality while the inferno roared behind them. It was shortly followed by a loud bang. Another structure collapsed in the Kinugasa estate.

Taira stepped in and wrapped one arm around her, supporting her and gently assisting her up.

Ami sputtered for breath as she clung to his embrace. Her chest was tight and her lungs burned.

"The fire... they're in the... trapped... please!"

169

Taira signaled to the chauffeur, who opened the car door. The sweet, clean air of the interior bathed her soot-stained face. Taira carefully sat her down and knelt on the ground next to her. With one hand he held hers, and with the other he caressed her hair. He made soothing sounds to her. The drowning gasps gave way to deep gulps of air, then to ragged but regular breathing.

"People are still trapped in there! Please do something!" She clutched at him and pleaded.

"Yes, yes. Don't worry. We've called the regional fire department. We managed to reach them with my satellite phone. They should be able to get up the mountains in a couple of hours." He smiled and patted her hair.

"A couple of hours! But—"

"And the villagers are working hard. I'm sure it'll all be fine. It's a straw and mud structure. Let the blazes die down, or it'll just be more dangerous."

She looked at Taira, then to Tachiko, Yamada, and the chauffeur. They were all calm and collected. Was she overreacting? Was she becoming so provincial?

"But…"

"It's all right. Just sit here with us. Let the rescue workers do their bit. There will be plenty for you to do tomorrow to care for their burns and injuries." He continued to stroke her hair. As he soothed her, exhaustion washed over Ami. Tears began to flow silently from eyes bloodshot from smoke and fire.

"I will arrange personally to help the Kinugasas to get back on their feet. They're an important family to this…"

A violent burst of wind shot across them and drowned out the rest of Taira's words. The gust beat at them fiercely. Shielding their faces with their hands, they squinted into the night sky. Above them hovered a massive tengu, blacker than the night sky, framed by the smoke and red flames behind it. It let out a brain-piercing shriek. Ami's mind burned at the ragged ratcheting sound. It beat its wings fiercely and screamed in pure fury. Its gleaming talons gripped a man, writhing and struggling against its monstrous captor. A talon tore through a thigh and another impaled a shoulder. Blood splattered from the thrashing man, raining down on the horrified witnesses.

The tengu looked down. Ami met its onyx-eyed gaze. The tengu cocked its head weirdly.

Though she wondered, was there a way a giant-winged man-beast could cock its head that wasn't weird?

She could not read his expression, though she knew it was he.

With no hint or prelude, the tengu spread its claws and dropped the man. Screaming, he fell several meters and landed on the ground before them. He landed with a wet squidgy thump and cracks.

The bleeding and broken man groaned. Dressed in all black, his face was covered in a hood showing only his pain-dilated eyes. Strapped across his back was a black lacquer quiver, still holding one arrow.

With one unnaturally bent arm he reached feebly to Taira. "Boss... I..."

Taira stared at the tengu. His expression settled in an enigmatic half smile. The billowing fires glinted off his mirror shades. He did not look at the wounded man on the road but looked directly at the giant man-bird hovering just above them.

171

The crow spoke with its eerie hollow voice, resonating from all the trees around them.

"Here's your minion! I should have figured you were behind this."

Taira leaned back slowly against the limousine and crossed his arm. "You accuse me falsely. In fact we've just called the provincial fire department to come to the rescue."

The broken ninja groaned. A pool of black arterial blood seeped out on ground around him. Seeing no one come to his aid, Ami rushed and knelt over him. She ripped away his garb, exposing the deep wounds and bones thrusting from torn flesh. His whole body, even to his scalp, was covered in elaborate irezumi—traditional tattoos of the outlaws and denizens of the underworld. Letting her training take over, she began a desperate regimen of first aid. He mumbled something. She leaned her ear to his mouth and heard sutras chanted in an unfamiliar ancient Japanese tongue.

"Set the fire and call the rescuers. That's just sweet. A fine way to be a hero and win the hearts of these villagers. That's going to happen over my dead body." The crow screeched an avian expletive.

"I certainly hope it doesn't have come to that." Taira spoke calmly.

Keeping pressure on a spurting wound, Ami glanced over her shoulder to the young oligarch and his retinue. Taira was calm, almost bemused. Tachiko, a new cigarette already hanging from her lips, stepped back a few meters with hands hidden behind her back. She studied the tengu's every move. Yamada merely looked annoyed with feathers ruffled. The chauffeur sat placidly in the driver's seat.

No one seemed particularly shocked by the midair monster, the dying man, or the blazing inferno. No one, other than Ami.

The tengu alighted next to Ami and the bleeding ninja. He kneeled down, folded in the giant wings, and gently placed his very human hand on her arm.

"Ami. There's a war going on around us." His black eyes looked into hers. She glanced toward the burning Kinugasa compound.

"No, it's not just the fire. There's more to it. It's about the survival of our village, our peoples, and the treasures here."

"Treasures?" she implored.

"I can't explain it now. Not here. Not now." He cocked his head to Taira, who was whispering to his secretary.

"I know about you and Taira."

Ami recoiled. How did he know? How long had he known? She opened her mouth to explain, but he squelched that with a finger on her lips.

"I've known. The crows told me. I... never mind. Now isn't the time. You are your own woman. You have to do what you believe is right."

"But... what..." She tried to speak, but he waved a wing tip and continued in a whisper.

"Taira will have his way with this village... and with you. I am fighting for the village. I will fight for you if you will it." He fell silent and bowed his head.

He stood and expanded his wings, preparing to take flight. As he rose into the air, he shouted over the roar of the fire.

"Dr. Ami, you have three choices. You can stay and fight alongside me. Or you can go with that monster"—pointing at a yawning Taira—"and destroy the root of Nippon. Or better still, just leave. Go back to the city and forget all about us. Save your skin." He cried another avian curse and flew back into the smoke and fire.

"Me, a monster. He's got some nerve." Taira chided. "Miss Ami. I believe your friend is overly dramatic and backward in his ways." He signaled to the chauffeur who hustled over and picked up the wounded and now unconscious man.

"Here I am trying to save the village and give it economic viability and sustainability. Some people are simply fearful of change. The only thing he's protecting is the certain death of this village."

The chauffeur laid the bleeding man in the back the car and took his place back in the driver's seat.

"Ami, can I offer you a ride back to our encampment? You need to rest. You'll have so much to do tomorrow to aid your charges. Please, come with us." Taira extended a hand to her. Tachiko came over and wrapped her own jacket around Ami's shoulder.

Ami stood for a while, stunned, staring at each of them and back at the fires.

She heard faint screams between the roar of the blazes.

Tossing the jacket back to Tachiko, she blurted out, "I can't. I have to go." She turned on her heel and ran back to the bucket brigade and the villagers.

Just once she looked back, only to see the limo driving slowly away.

It was a long, long, horrible night.

It was almost dawn by the time the provincial fire truck finally arrived. By then, the villagers had managed to extinguish most of the blaze. The estate walls were crumbled and the spinning shack obliterated, the growing shed charred beyond recognition. Many of the central structures sustained minor to moderate damage. Miraculously, the Dowager Ito's residential building, beyond being soaking wet, was perfectly intact.

The exhausted villagers let the firemen tamp out the final embers and remaining pockets of fire. Mostly the firemen helped Ami tend to the villagers' burns, wounds, and smoke inhalation injuries. Once they set up a temporary hospital tent, they packed up their gear and left.

The uninjured cleared out the debris and charred aftermath. Just once Ami caught sight of Kansaburo among the ruins, now fully returned to his human form, removing chunks of burned lumber. She worked through the day tending to the villagers. A few wailed in grief and pain, but most were stoic, even as tracks of tears showed on their dirty faces.

A chill autumnal breeze swept through the valley, blowing away the acrid stench of damp charred wood and rotting silkworm carcasses.

Quiet returned to the village.

It was already midafternoon when Ami finally took a break. She returned to her clinic, closed the door, and sat down in the ancient office chair.

She fell deeply asleep, enveloped in a heavy exhaustion she'd never known before. She slept so deeply no fitful dreams of horrific visions touched her.

In darkness she awoke. Her neck and back ached from sleeping awkwardly. Stillness surrounded her, punctuated only by the ticking of the pendulum clock.

She yawned and stretched, glad to be alone in the quiet.

A large shape stirred in the darkness.

A flame flickered on and a face emerged in the darkness.

"What the—!" she shrieked and fell out of the chair.

"Boo," said Kansaburo. He was sticking his tongue out. He finished lighting the lantern, and the room came into view, bathed in the warm flickering kerosene light.

She grabbed for something, anything, on the desk, and threw it at him—a stapler. He caught it precisely.

"You jerk," she yelled and began chuckling.

"Yeah, guilty as charged! Sorry 'bout that. I just didn't want to turn the lights on while you were sleeping."

Ami's chuckle turned into rolling giggles and then to hysterical laughter. Her body racked and shook as the laugh turned to crying. Gingerly, Kansaburo knelt before her and put a hand on her shoulder. She threw her arms around his neck and collapsed into him, sobbing uncontrollably. He wrapped his arms around and held her and all her emotions tightly. She sobbed and sobbed and sobbed until her voice gave out. She clutched at him like a woman drowning in an ocean of tears. He sat on the floor holding her firmly, burying his face into her tangled, smoke-filled hair. He breathed long and slow as if to breathe life and light into her very soul.

The silent night marched on, and he would not let her go.

She woke, this time to the morning light warming her smudged cheeks. She could see the sun rising through the small clinic window. Birds chirped somewhere nearby. She looked up and saw Kansaburo smiling and gazing down at her. His eyes were bloodshot and face as dirty as hers. He was still sitting on the floor holding her in his arms.

"Were you up all night with me?" She reached up and caressed his tired face.

"Oh maybe. But you were so pretty and comfortable, I couldn't just dump you on the ground. You want me to?" He sassed. She playfully slapped his sooty cheek. They both let out an exhausted half-laugh.

"Oh no! My patients!" She tried to leap up, but Kansaburo's embrace wouldn't let her go.

"Don't worry Ami. Granny's got that covered," he said. Ami looked sidelong at him. "Oh you know she'll have them fixed up and in fighting shape by the time you get up. If I let you go back to work now Granny's gonna kick my butt. Now you know exactly how mean she can get, right?" He laughed as Ami's face contorted in recollection of the granny as the naginata-wielding crow-beast.

"Doc, you did great with treating us in the tent. Thanks to you, everyone's fine. Relax right now." He half-scolded and half-soothed her.

She sat a while longer, savoring the warmth and safety of his embrace.

With a heavy sigh, she broke the silence. "Kansaburo, you know there's a lot of answers I need." She waited for his smart-assed retort. None came. Instead he met her gaze directly and nodded solemnly.

"Yes, of course. I didn't want it to be this way, all

177

so sudden and violent. I'd planned for a nicer way, but it wasn't meant to be. There's so much to go over... I'll share as much as I can. As much as I know. I've never shared any of this with someone from outside the village. But now you are of the village... hey, you are, aren't you? Are you staying? You are staying, right?" He pulled back nervously and looked hard at her. She smiled and nodded.

"Okay, good. To be honest I was worried. I frightened you. And you probably are still in some way... I'm pretty weird looking when I'm..." He trailed off, voice fading in nervousness. She stroked his face and kissed his neck. He giggled.

Her mind filled with a thousand questions all fighting for immediate resolution.

"Kansaburo, tell me first what's going on with Dowager Ito and the Kinugasas. Is she all right? Then there's all those relatives suddenly in town... and none of them leaving her quarters and risking their lives through the fire. Then there's the fire itself. It has something to do with her, right?"

"That's your first question? You want to know how Old Lady Ito is doing?" he rolled his eyes dramatically at her. "I thought you'd want to know more about my prowess." He laughed. Now it was her turn to roll her eyes.

"Actually, Ami, you've nailed it. It's one of the big secrets here. The Kinugasas are very important. Not just because they were some rich Edo period merchant family. No, they're really significant—and part of the reason why this village is so secluded."

Ami cut in before he could go into a long-winded history lesson.

"How ill is the dowager?"

"She's, um, not exactly ill. In fact she's really fat and happy right now. In a way. But she's got some changes she's going through."

Ami looked at him suspiciously.

"Okay, I realize I'm not making any sense to you. Let's just go and see her." He helped Ami up onto her feet. He closed up the clinic while she blinked in the bright morning light. He straddled her bicycle and patted the back rack. She hopped aboard and wrapped her arms around his waist. As he pedaled down the road, she pressed her face into his muscular back. The wind through her hair eased her tangled thoughts.

They left the bike at the cherry trees and walked the last hundred meters to the Kinugasa estate. Mountains of burned rubble dotted the property. Here and there black-charred skeletal columns of former buildings thrust to the sky. They had managed to clear the entry area, allowing them access onto the property.

The monumental gate of carved moths and chrysanthemums was no more. Instead, a hastily assembled gate of giant bamboo stood bound together with gardening rope.

"Ami, right now I really need you to follow my instructions." His tone shifted to grave seriousness. "I know these aren't rituals and ways you're comfortable with. You probably want to scoff at them. But in order to get the answer you seek, we have to go through these." As he spoke his posture became more formal with a regal set to his brows. She nodded. He pulled out from his pocket a necklace made of white silk threads and pale green jade stones shaped like a curving tusk. He closed his eyes and slipped it on, while making incantations and strange ritual hand symbols.

When he opened his eyes, he met her baffled stare.

"Oh this? I guess I never told you. I'm being trained to be the Protector Priest—that is, if Granny doesn't kill me in the process." He laughed.

Ami made a mental note of several more questions to ask—later.

They passed beneath this temporary gate, under the shimenawa and paper purification streamers, and stepped over symbols drawn on the earth with thick lines of pure white salt. Kansaburo took care not to disturb the salt, and Ami followed suit.

The central courtyard was surprisingly busy. Many of the extended Kinugasa family gathered in groups. A group of old men to the right tinkered and fixed salvageable silk spinners. A clutch of old women next to them sewed white ritual kimonos and cleaned odd objects. To the left, the loyal workers piled fresh mulberry branches and firewood. Beyond them a group of men struggled to assemble a large cedar and metal vat. The middle of the courtyard was occupied by a series of makeshift tables full of jars, bowls and bottles. Kansaburo tugged at her sleeve and brought her over to a table. He brushed himself with a leafy branch. Then he stepped to a large stone bowl of water where, using a ladle, he carefully washed his left hand, then right, then rinsed each foot, and his mouth. She followed each procedure carefully. After that, there was a terracotta bowl billowing aloe wood and sandalwood incense. He smudged himself and then wafted the smoke all around her. More incantations followed.

She wasn't religious by any means. But somehow this felt familiar. Something from long ago that she vaguely remembered. Something about her grandfather stirred in the back of her mind.

Finished with the ritual cleansing, they stepped away from the table and started toward the dowager's quarters.

As they walked the path to the dowager's building, passing among the Kinugasa elders, each turned and bowed deeply to him. He bowed back in return, chanting to each one.

She walked behind him, dumbfounded. She didn't expect all this of her country beau.

Dowager Ito's residence stood intact and in perfect calm amid the rubble. Purification streamers hung from every part of the eaves and the surrounding veranda.

They stopped at the steps leading up to the residence.

They waited.

Eventually a door opened in the central room and a small figure wearing a crimson hakama emerged. Granny Azusa's usually wild silver hair was pulled tightly into a precise long braid down her back. She glided across the veranda toward them at an unnatural speed.

Azusa stopped directly before Ami and stared straight into her. Though her face was a wrinkled as last year's apple left on the tree, her eyes were clear and full of life and power.

Truth be told, Ami had never been this close to the Priestess. She was the one person who refused a check-up. Ami, flustered, blushed and looked down with a hasty bow. Granny chuckled and patted her shoulder. A raspy voice came from the ancient lips.

"Ahh, young lass, don't worry. I'm not going to scold ye or smack ye. I reserve that for my silly grandbaby boy there."

When Ami finally raised her head Azusa smiled broadly, rearranging her deep wrinkles into new patterns.

"I'm sorry I scared ye so bad when we last met. My lad's cute, but he can be an idiot. And he was surely a fool for not preparing ye." Granny shot a playful look of disapproval to Kansaburo, who was still holding a deep formal bow to her. "I like ye, city girl. I'm glad yer're sticking around. But don't go coming near me with them strange medicine of yer city ways, all right?" She chuckled again. Ami saw where Kansaburo got some of his quirks.

"Well, yer're here to pay respects to the great dowager. I'll get her ready for an audience. In the meantime, make sure Kansaburo explains a few things to ye." She was about to turn away when she paused and asked. "Now, yer're not squeamish about bugs and crawlies, are ye?" Azusa didn't wait for Ami's answer. She just chuckled, turned around, and glided back into the building.

Kansaburo sat down on the steps and invited her next to him. He held her hand and began to talk.

"The Kinugasas are an ancient family. They are part of what my people protect here in these parts. You know they make some of the finest silks of Nippon. But it's more than that. They're special. Legend tells us this... When gods roamed this land, they began as the loyal attendants to Amaterasu Omikami, the sun goddess and weaver of the world and sister to Susanoo, the god of storms. The first Kinugasa took the shape of a silk moth at will. The moth died defending the goddess

182

from her rageful brother god. As reward for its loyalty and sacrifice, Amaterasu made a race of humans from the trampled wings of her attendant. They can no longer shift to moth form at will, but when duty calls, they change. In their blood they know when the next true ruler, the next Emperor or Empress, will rise.

"The head of the Kinugasa clan will then take to darkness and shun the company of common man. Every fiber of their being called to duty, their flesh begins to change. Their limbs shrink and torsos elongate. They transform into giant silkworms. Soon this elder will weave a silver white cocoon around them. The silk harvested from the elder possesses not only unnatural strength, but harbors a deep protective power. It is impenetrable to swords and blades of all types. We've learned in this era that it repels bullets and fire. One who wears the threads, or a garment made of this thread, is protected from all manners of ailments, curses, evil, and even assassinations.

"Every Emperor and Empress from the age of the gods has been bestowed with secret garments of protection made by the Kinugasas. The mother, pregnant with the future ruler, may be protected by a Kinugasa sash."

Kansaburo paused to take a drink of sake offered by one of the family members. Ami took that opportunity.

"Then Dowager Ito is going through this now? She's going to make the cocoon for the next emperor?"

Kansaburo nodded and took another sip.

"What happens to the dowager after that? Does she return to her human self?"

He shook his head and offered the sake gourd to her. She took it gladly.

"No. There is no after. You don't know how the silk is harvested, do you? All those little worms that were growing out there, they make a cocoon with a single strand of silk, within which they transform into a moth and fly away. To harvest the silk, you have to boil the whole cocoon. With the worm still in it."

Ami choked on the sake.

"The worm doesn't survive?"

"No."

"Then the dowager as a worm has to be…"

"Boiled."

"Boiled?"

"Yes, boiled. Dead. It's the responsibility of the next in line to do this. It is an honor but, understandably, a difficult one. For this generation, Ms. Kaede will carry out the honor. She's been raised knowing this and has been prepared for some time, but I'm sure it won't be easy. She's very close to her grandmother and deeply devoted. All the clan members gather from far and wide to help, to support, and to ensure the duty is done."

"What if Kaede doesn't? What happens then?"

"Then the Emperor will not be protected." He shrugged at this. "It's happened before. It was… 1920-something, when Emperor Hirohito was about to ascend to the Chrysanthemum Throne… The time had come for the matriarch Kinugasa—Omatsu was her name—to begin her change and her duty to serve. Her son, Gousuke, so loved his mother and was so deeply devoted to her, that when time came for him to… send her on…" Kansaburo faltered in finding the right word.

"Boil her? You mean he couldn't kill his own mother for the good of Japan."

Kansaburo nodded, taking another sip of sake.

"What happened?" Ami nudged him.

"Well, you know how badly the Great War of the Pacific went for Emperor Hirohito!" Kansaburo said.

"You mean World War Two. It's called World War Two now. You are such a geezer," she teased him.

"Yeah, yeah. Whatever. Well, Emperor Hirohito, the one without the talismanic protection of the Kinugasa silk threads, not only led the country into a devastating war, but fell in with a set of corrupt generals, was nearly assassinated, let the country be occupied by foreign forces, and then was dethroned from his place as the living-god of our islands.

"He was a nice guy, I'm told, smart and gentle with a supernatural gift of horticulture. His line's known for that, I think. Yeah, helps to come from the Rice God, you know. Granny did his birth ritual and coming-of-age cleansing. She liked him a lot. She thinks he never deserved all that.

"Everyone around here thinks it would have gone down differently, and Japan wouldn't be in this mess, if Gousuke'd had the gumption to do what had to be done."

Ami did a quick bit of math in her head.

"How old is your granny?"

"She never says, but I think she's about 150 years old. She still kicks my ass." Kansaburo scratched his head apologetically.

"Is this a literal transformation or just metaphorical?" Ami pressed on.

"Literal! Yes, they turn into a giant worm that makes silk! You don't think we'd just boil a person out of some stupid superstition?" Kansaburo spat out the words.

"Okay, okay, calm down. This is all sudden and really strange for me, you know." Ami patted him on the chest. "What happened to Omatsu? If her son couldn't do the deed, how did she return to human form? What happens if the duty isn't done? Beyond the Emperor and Japan falling into bad times, that is," Ami asked, trying hard not to sound disbelieving.

"Omatsu didn't change back. Gousuke stole her in her cocoon and hid in the deep mountains. He was never heard from again. I guess he couldn't show his face for the shame to the family. Sometime after that, a gigantic moth was seen flying around the night sky. Granny said it was larger than a baseball field, and its eyes glowed blue. It cast off a silver shimmer. It stayed around for a moon cycle and then flew off. It's not been seen since. After the tragedy of Omatsu and Emperor Hirohito, the Kinugasas are taking their duty really seriously. But it's also been challenging to keep them protected in this modern world." Kansaburo paused and sighed heavily. For the first time, Ami noticed the darkness around his eyes.

"Is this power what Taira is after?" Ami peered into his tired face.

"Maybe. I really don't know. We really need to reach the Imperial Onmyouji about this, but he's been missing." He sighed again. "That's the official court shaman and astrologer. Mostly he's the head bureaucrat and liaison for these matters. No? You've never heard of this post? Of course not!" Kansaburo chuckled. "There's a lot more of this island, my city girl, than you learn in your fancy, fancy schools." He winced mocking as she smacked his shoulder. "But I suspect Taira and his clan are behind this. All is not well."

"Kansaburo, I'm sorry about Taira. I've meant to..."

Kansaburo stopped her with a quick kiss on the lips. She returned his kiss.

"Don't. I don't want to talk about him now. I don't think this is the last we'll see of him. And we have a lot more to worry about right now."

She dropped the topic.

"Ahem," came a raspy voice from behind them.

Granny Azusa stood over them, grinning.

"Aren't ye cute li'l love birds! I remember when I was a lass... There was this one handsome rogue tengu. Well, he was something with his, ah, sword, especially midflight..."

"Granny! No, not now, please. It's embarrassing. Let's not shock her, all right?" Kansaburo blushed and flustered. Granny Azusa grinned even broader, and her wrinkles furrowed deeper.

"Ah well, that's a story for another time! So ye ready to pay respects to the good and brave Dowager Ito? Her mind is fading, but she's good-natured as ever. Of course she don't look like she used to. No sudden moves or loud sounds. Speak soft. I'd take a branch of mulberry in with ye."

With that, she turned on her heel. They followed closely behind.

They entered a dark room pungent with vegetal decay and chokingly humid air. Someone sang a strange melody in an even stranger tongue. Rhythmic munching sound filled the room. As their eyes adjusted, they saw Kaede sitting before a vast saffron curtain, crying, and singing from a bronze tablet of cuneiform writing. She bowed to the guests but did not stop the chanting.

Granny bade them to sit before the curtain, and they obeyed.

She slowly drew the curtain back.

At the sight of what had become of the dowager, Ami gasped and fell back into Kansaburo's embrace.

* * *

The first frost came early, just a few days after that strange night. The coming winter promised to be long and hard. The Kinugasas busily prepared for their strange Imperial duty under the watchful guardianship of Granny Azusa. The rest of the villagers divided their time between rebuilding the fire-damaged structures and bringing in the fall harvest of rice, millet and yams. Ami made extra rounds of house calls to cheer the injured. Kansaburo spent the days rethatching everyone's homes and farm sheds.

He finally started to return to her bed each night. The crows on branches eavesdropped on sounds of their spats and quarrels, which eventually turned to moans and gasps. The black-feathered gossips cawed in delight and beat their wings excitedly.

But each night, as the villagers slept soundly, he'd creep out of her bed.

From the Hour of the Rat until the faint glow of dawn, the lone crow-beast circled far overhead, counting each of the black-clad ninjas creeping into the surrounding hills.

Granny Azusa took up her post on the old fire watchtower on the southern edge of the village, by day as woman and by night as tengu. She glared into the forests, watching and sensing all movements. Her brows were knitted so tightly her wrinkles nearly realigned to form an entirely new map of her face.

On the fifth day, Kansaburo and Granny swapped guard duties. She took to the sky, and he kept watch from the old tower. He set up camp in the observation deck high above all the residences. The watch post had a clear view of the entire valley and surrounding ridgeline. Steep switchbacks of rickety wooden steps led up to the hatch door that opened into the small room. The roof shielded him from the sun and rain, but the half-height walls and pane-less windows left him exposed to the elements. A wooden stool, a small desk, the giant bronze alarm bell and binoculars were all that were provided. Kansaburo kept watch day and night, not returning to Ami's bed. Each night he focused, hoping to hear her breathing shift into the slow, deep pace of sleep.

* * *

Three nights later, Ami could not bear her solitary bed anymore. She hadn't slept much without him. She would wake to the slightest sound. The drafty old house creaked, bumped and wheezed all night in the late autumn winds. She would rise several times a night to look out the window, searching for fires, smelling for smoke, and casting glances for dark-winged figures in the sky. When she managed to drift off, she tossed in fitful dreams of orange blazes, dark blood, and flesh churning into beasts and worms.

Tonight, she did not want to sleep alone, only to be wracked by anxiety in the cold night. She made some rice balls and packed it in a basket with natto, sticky fermented soybeans, wrapped in bamboo leaves, and a large Thermos of piping hot green tea. She rode her bicycle over to the fire watch. Basket in hand, she labored up the creaking steps in a dizzying ascent. When she opened the hatch into the room, it was empty except for his satchel and a bedroll. A feeble lantern lit the drafty space.

Where had he gone?

She looked down out of each of the four windows. There was no sign of Kansaburo.

She turned to look out one more time when she came face to beak, into his inverted giant feathery crow face.

She screamed.

He cackled.

He was looking into the room. He stood on the roof and craned himself down into the observation deck.

She slapped his beak hard. "Jerk!"

A squeaky little chicken peep came out of his massive mandibles.

"What are you doing up there?"

"What else? Watching for attacks. Listening for creeps. Anyway I can see better up here. It's too cramped in there."

She looked around and realized how small the room must be with him in it. Three steps in any direction and she'd hit a half wall. How would he even expand his wings or stand to his full height?

"I brought us dinner. Come down and let's eat."

She couldn't quite bring herself to admit how deeply she missed him.

"I can't," he chirped. "I'm still on watch duty. Granny's gone flying the outer perimeter so I'm the only eyes on…" A gust of wind blew his last few words away.

A chill ran up her spine and took hold of her brain. She shivered.

"Do you mind if I hang out here? Do you have something to read?"

She couldn't bring herself to admit that waves of anxiety gripped her late at night as she slept alone.

Peering at him on the roof, she watched Kansaburo cock his head. He fluffed his feathers against the cold and refocused his attention to scanning the dark woods beyond.

"I think there's a copy of my Kojiki and a magazine down there. Help yourself."

In the desk drawer, she found a firewatch's journal of tedious notations, a greasy copy of a year-old Mechanics Monthly, and a well-thumbed reproduction of the Kojiki, the oldest known chronicle of the origin of Japan. She found his jacket and, wrapping herself in it and his bedroll, breathed deep of his scent. She sat on the floor to try to read the Kojiki's arcane words. If he could understand this, surely she could! Pouring herself a steaming cup of tea, she buckled down into the dense document. Written in nothing but ancient Sino-Japanese alphabet, she struggled to even recognize every fifth word or so. He read this for fun?

Soon her head grew heavy, and the book fell to the floor.

* * *

The tower shook violently. She woke to a start in deep darkness.

The lantern had gone out. Blinking, she strained to adjust to the night. The new moon blackness shrouded all. The tower became still.

A gust of wind, perhaps, hoped Ami.

She rose to her feet and looked out of the enclosure toward the center of the village.

The sky churned bleak and twisted. Then the twisting form coalesced and shot down toward the ground. Her heart thumped into her throat.

Was it he?

Cold blue sparks shot from the rooftop of a farmhouse nearby. The flash followed by sharp clanks of metal striking metal. Dark forms tumbled, and the sparks and clanks repeated.

She saw a crow rise into the air, followed by another. Then both dove straight back down. Below, dark forms split, ran, merged, and flew apart again as the tengus flew back in, swallowed by the black swarm and then shot back up again. The two pairs of wings sounded like a hurricane. Angry shrieking caws obliterated the sound of muffled human voices.

What the…

The roof shook and thumped with his weight, and she heard him scream at her from above.

"Ami. Get out of the tower. Now!" He flew off and then struck at the sides of the tower below her. Soft, rapid footsteps rushed up the switchback stairs toward her.

They were in the tower. She spun on her heel and felt blindly on the floor until her fingers grasped the handle of the hatch door. It wouldn't budge. As she managed to turn the handle, the hatch flew open, throwing her back on the floor. Stunned, she rose onto her hands and knees to stand, when a searing pain exploded through her flank. The man in black kicked her again and again. Gasping, she clawed at the floor, pulling away from the ninja.

"Go ahead, lady, you're just wasting your energy. You're coming with us, one way or another." He growled with a deep, guttural Kansai accent.

Her clawing fingers touched the woven bamboo of the basket. Overturned in the commotion, the contents spilled out on the floor.

Coughing, she spat out, "You piece of—"

The assassin laughed over her stammered words. "Your feathered freak boyfriend's not coming to your rescue, sweetheart. He's busy fighting the good fight elsewhere."

As he laughed, she found the Thermos. His dark figure loomed ever closer.

She wanted to cry.

She wanted to cry out.

She wanted to disappear.

Then red rage rose from somewhere deep within her gut and took over her mind. Suddenly the darkness burned bright in a red glow, and she saw everything. Time slowed down around her.

Sucking in her breath hard, she rolled over. She could see his eyes glinting and glowing catlike in the strangely lit room. At his eyes, she flung the opened Thermos. The scalding green tea sprayed across his face.

He stumbled and scratched at his eyes.

She snatched the leaf-wrapped packet as she scurried to her feet. The room still showed in the red vision.

Cawing and screaming pierced the night outside.

The ninja leapt at her. She ducked, lunged, and pitched the packet at his face. The bamboo leaves split, bursting sticky natto across his face. Wiping at his already burned eyes, the pungent goo matted his hands with long, glue-like threads. An uncanny rage fueled her. Hands outstretched, she dove at his throat. They tumbled back against a half-wall. He swiveled on a foot, tripped her, grabbed her by her throat, and pushed her half out the window. There she dangled. Her rage waged war with her fear. He pressed a blade against her neck.

"One slice, lady, one slice and you're dead. So just shut the hell up and cooperate."

Her animal fear started to win. She clenched her eyes. Her heart beat louder and louder.

Something sharp touched her shoulder. Her ears rang like thunder and storms.

Warm fluid gushed across her face and throat.

Screaming filled her head—a low guttural howl of the hooded stranger.

She opened her eyes just in time to see the man, pierced through the shoulder and arm with a giant black claw, bleeding and tossed into the darkness. Above her hovered the raven Kansaburo, black eyes gleaming and vast wings beating hurricane winds. With his left talon, he gently cradled Ami in midair, with one claw tip lightly grazing her left shoulder. His right stretched out behind him, dripping viscous and dark.

They hovered just above the tower and above the village. He reached out with his human hand and caressed her hair. She let out a slow, long breath and unclenched her fist. Her palm bled from her own nails digging in. Neither spoke. She stared at him. He cocked his avian head, looking closer into her. She gasped a first sob. He cooed gently. Her sobs flooded over her. He held her with his human arms to his chest. She buried her face into his warmth and held on. He embraced her tightly. His wings stroked long and slow. They began to turn and rise into the new moon sky.

Her sobs slowed to a raspy but steady breathing.

Placing her palms against his chest, she felt his deep slow heartbeat. Sliding her hands up, she ran fingers through black down, across the powerful neck, and stroked his beak. He let out a hot breath. She stroked his feathery face. He outstretched his wings to an upward soar.

He held her closer into him. She felt his sex swell against her. Heat washed through her.

"Can we?" she whispered.

"What?" he chirped.

"Can we? While you're flying?" she asked, more firmly.

"Um, yes, but..."

"I need you. Now," she stated, distinctly and firmly.

Then the image of the attacker flashed across her mind. She looked down across the village and its homes getting smaller and smaller beneath them.

"Oh gods, I'm sorry. The ninjas... The village... Of course not," she stammered. "We're in the middle of an attack. Right. You should let me down. I wasn't thinking. It was just so much." She gulped. "They're still down there. Let's go fight."

He cawed his strange laugh at the sky and spun her around in an aerial waltz.

"We're fine. It's all fine. The villagers are safe.

We've fought them off. The villagers are tough. They fought with Granny and me. That guy in the tower with you, he was the last of them." He stroked her worried temples.

"What did he want with me?"

"I reckon they meant to kidnap you for last-ditch leverage. I saw what you did to him. When did you turn into such an amazing fighter? Has Granny been training you?" He gave her a sideways gaze. The beak wouldn't belie mirth or humor.

"No, no. It just all happened. I don't really know. I've never been in a fight. I'm sure it was some fight-or-flight adrenal response…" She stopped when his finger pressed against her lips.

"Yes, yes, Doctor. I'm sure it is. Or maybe there are other mysteries about you that we're discovering. You'd have made the legendary Lady General, Hagane Masako, proud!"

"So the attack is over? We're safe?" She searched his face for any clues otherwise.

"Yes, all's quiet now. We're back to normal. For now, at least. I don't think Taira's given up—but we have peace for now. It's always been like this…" He trailed off and lost his words in gazing at the far edges of the valley.

She punched his chest with a small fist.

"Ow! What did you do that for?" he squawked.

"Well, if I'm your Tomoe Gozen, this noble warrior demands your service. Now!"

"Now?"

"Oh yes, now!"

"But your clothes?"

"You've got talons. Use them!"

He cawed delighted laughter, held her tightly to his chest, and flew up and around. His rod thickened and throbbed against her.

Flying high above the village, he spun her in his arms. She faced the star-filled heaven and black outline of the mountain ridge. He grasped her around the waist and breathed hot on the back of her neck. Hard muscles of his chest heaved against her with every quickening breath. His wings beat the air in a slow throbbing. Raising a long feathered leg before them, he turned the talons nimbly toward her. Four talons loomed at her. The cold black blades grasped her face with shocking tenderness. Under one claw, her jugular vein pulsed. She held her breath and indulged in the sensual fear of her mighty lover. Her heart beat in her throat. Deftly he twisted his claw, turning the smoothly rounded side against her neck and traced it down to her arching breast.

One sharp claw tip slipped under the collar of her sweater.

She waited.

They flew higher into the night. The village grew smaller beneath them.

One swift arc and the sound of ripping fabric filled her head. Cold shocked her exposed body. All her layers of warmth and modesty ripped away, she shuddered in the bracing night air. As frigid as the fall wind was, her skin burned bright. Arching farther, she thrust her ass into his steel-hard shaft.

The wing beats sped up.

He curved his back, meeting hers.

She threw her hands back and wrapped her arms around his neck and tangled her legs around his.

He pressed his thick head. She thrust back. He gave one long hot breath and thrust deeply into her. Her vaginal canal throbbed around him, engulfing him. His human hands grasped her hips harder.

With familiar rhythm, they soared into each other.

Reflexively his wings tucked in.

They tumbled in the air, head over heels and claws. They tumbled toward the ground as they rode each other faster and faster. The canyon cliffs showed ghostly white below them. The tightness wrapping around her womb clenched into a fiery ball and shot up her gut and down her legs. He thrust harder into her. They plummeted closer and closer to a cliff's edge. She screamed as explosion arched deeply and screeched into the night.

Just as they neared a boulder, he spread his wings and soared back into the sky. Ami's body collapsed into his embrace.

His wings beat easily and slowly as they glided high above the rice paddies. Beneath her, she could see the dirt roads and orchards as he flew them toward her cottage.

Tomorrow, they would heal the injured and rebuild the damage.

But tonight, she would sleep in deep peace in her warrior lover's arms.

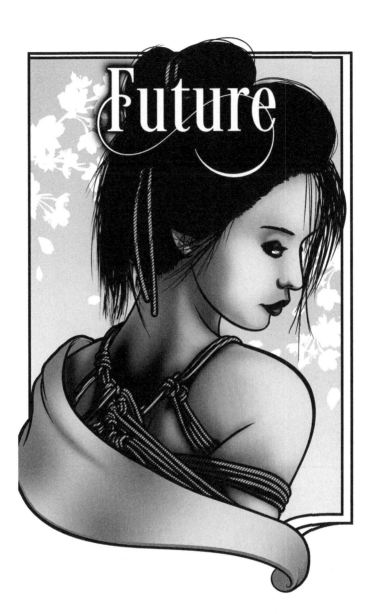

The Bonds of Love

Cecilia Tan

Chapter One

Nagasaki: 1945

What is one person's happiness when measured against the fabric of a nation? This is the question my elders asked in a thousand ways, every time the subject of my marriage came up. I knew, of course, the expected answer. The nation and our society should be far more important than the happiness of one person, or even of two, if you counted me and my miserable bride-to-be. It was four people if you counted her and the man she truly wanted to marry, and me and the woman I truly wanted to marry...

How many of us would it take to change everything? I imagined an unbroken chain, from the man she loved, to the woman his family wanted him to marry, and the man she would have been arranged to...

and on and on. Or was I the only madman who wanted to tear the fragile silk of our so-called society apart?

"Jiro."

I looked up from the sake cup tilted between my fingers. Akio was trying to get my attention.

"No mooning about," my friend said, with a warning look. "I didn't take you out drinking so you could mope."

"I'll be happy when I am with Chiyo and not sooner," I said with a sigh. We were in one of the large establishments on Mirayama Street, where there have been brothels and entertainment houses for hundreds of years. A burst of laughter from the next room washed over us like rain, as someone must have told a hilarious joke.

Quite suddenly a man pushed aside the thin, rice paper door, and slipped inside, shutting it behind him. He wore a disheveled military uniform, his face quite red. He had a jug of sake in his hands.

Akio stood, an imposing presence ready to throw the man out if he had mistakenly stumbled into the wrong room, but then the officer spoke.

"Are you M-Mizushi... are you 'chiro's brother?" he asked drunkenly.

"I am," I answered, too surprised to do anything else. My brother had been killed six years before, in Nanking. I had barely known him, as he had been at military school when I was a child, and then in the army, where I was unfit to follow.

The officer did not so much sit as have his legs collapse under him at our low table, and he leaned on his elbow, proffering the jug. "Here, then. A gift from the general. Let us drink a toast to your departed brother."

Akio and I exchanged glances. "I'll pour," my friend said, taking the jug from the drunken man with his meaty but deft hands, and filling our cups.

We drank in silence. It would be bad luck, I thought, to secretly blame my brother for dying and putting me in the position I was in. I couldn't ever be him, not with my bad foot. I had been treated like a child most of my life, as if because I could not be a warrior I could never be a man. But now, my family had arranged a marriage for me. Now suddenly they wanted me to become the scion of the family they had never treated me like.

And everyone seemed to know it. "Another toast," the officer said, holding out his empty cup for Akio to fill again. "To your impending marriage."

"Thank you," I said, bowing my head. The sake was good. Perhaps there was some truth to the rumors that the military got better provisions than we did, even here in the city.

We drank until the jug was empty and then the officer stood, bowed deeply to us, and left the way he had come.

"Who was that?" Akio whispered, the moment the door had slid shut behind him.

"I have no idea," I answered. "Someone who knew my brother, I guess. He's not even going to remember this in the morning. I've had enough for one night. I'm going to go home."

"But..." Akio hurried to help me up. I didn't need the help, but he felt it was his duty to do all he could for me.

"You stay. Have fun. I'm going home."

"You shouldn't walk alone at night," he said. "There are desperate men."

The shortages brought on by the war had made people suffer. "I'll be fine, Aki." I knew he didn't want to leave. He hadn't seen the girl he liked yet tonight. "Really. You stay. It's not that late. And it's not far to go. Besides, I have this." I slung the coils of rope over my shoulder.

He sat back down with a grumble.

"But don't stay too long. My father expects us in the dojo in the morning."

"Agh, my back hurts already thinking about it. Try not to throw me so hard tomorrow, eh, Jiro?"

I laughed. "All right. See you tomorrow." Akio's trouble was his epilepsy, which had kept him out of the military but not from growing a bullish strength and powerful arms. One blow from him could—and frequently did—knock me across the room.

My father and grandfather had refused to teach me our family martial arts, both sword and fist, when I was growing up, because I was unfit. My grandfather died when I was 10, and my father had maintained the rule. But I still remember when I was 14 years old, after the news that Ichiro had been killed, him calling me into the family dojo, where I had never before been allowed to set foot. I had thought perhaps he had relented, and would teach me the way of the sword after all.

As I limped down the steep alley down to Mirayama Street I recalled my excitement. We are not a rich family, not in money, anyway. We are rich only in tradition. Our lineage is traceable all the way back to Empress Gensho's personal guards. As I stepped into the family dojo for the first time I felt as if the ghosts of our ancestors hung from the rafters, waiting for me.

I will not fail, I told them. I will succeed. I will be a warrior.

Imagine my surprise, then, when my father, who had a limp himself from an old wound to his leg, shuffled into the room and threw down at my feet not a sword, but a coil of rope.

"Pick it up," he said, without preamble.

That day he began teaching me our family's secret rope arts. They included ways to use the rope in self-defense, neutralizing an attacker and then, if desired, to immobilize, humiliate, or torment him as a prisoner. I still do not know why my father decided to do this, other than a guess that he wanted to pass some of his knowledge on, now that the son he had taught the most to was gone. Having forbidden me the sword, he could not change his mind about that, but perhaps he could show me this instead.

And I had promised my ancestors that day I would succeed. I threw myself into learning the art. To my father's surprise, I was good at it. Aki became my training partner. More often than not, he was the one on the receiving end of my most brutal techniques.

But even Aki did not know that some nights when I carried the rope with me to Mirayama Street, it wasn't in case I was jumped by thugs on the way home. It was because of Chiyo.

Chiyo, who was on the receiving end of my most gentle techniques. How can I describe the feeling of turning the one I loved into a work of art, to cherish and admire, while at the same time laying claim to every inch of her skin, making her mine in a way that no other man could, not even the customers that she saw as part of her work?

I could not tell my father about her, and I most certainly could not tell him that I had turned our family's art of war into an act of love.

Now he wanted me to marry a woman I had not even met. And for what? So I could give him a son he could teach the sword to, who could charge off into war and be killed like my brother was? So I could try to restore the standing of a family whose last real honor had been in serving an Empress who ruled over a thousand years ago? Why, then, was it such an issue who I married? Why could I not choose my own wife? We had larger problems, I thought, than who would bear my sons. We were at war, there were shortages, there were sicknesses, who could even think of the fabric of our society when it seemed to me it was already being torn apart?

As I descended a stone staircase, a tug on the rope brought me up short and I looked behind me, up the set of stone stairs carved into the side of the hill. A lucky kitten had pounced on the end, which I had not realized was trailing behind me. She was white with orange and black patches on her back, like a koi fish. I scooped her up with one hand under her belly, scolding her. "Bad kitty. This rope isn't for playing with. This is a samurai's rope."

The kitten began to purr immediately and rubbed her head against my chest. "What do you think, Neko?" I asked her. "Should I do as duty demands? Or what my heart tells me? Do I love my country and my family less than I love a woman?"

The kitten climbed into my yukata, purring all the while, and settled in the pocket made by the loose fabric and my belt.

I was not yet ready to go home. I stopped by a noodle shop, where I discovered the rope-loving kitten also liked to play with, and eat, the long curly noodles. I drank a bit more. And perhaps that is why I found myself in the family dojo in the early hours before dawn, sneaking into the chest where my father kept the sacred rope.

Most families have hereditary swords. Ours also has skeins of silken rope that have been passed down from generation to generation. No less beautiful nor less well-crafted than the finest of samurai weapons, the rope felt like magic flowing through one's fingers, yet so strong nothing less than a katana itself could cut it.

I think I had a crazy idea that I would bind my true love in our sacred rope, and then my father would have to accept her as mine. I am not sure. Or maybe I had made up my mind to propose she run away with me. I'm no longer sure. My memories of that night are quite fragmented. I slept not a wink.

The kitten and the rope were all I carried as dawn broke, as the men who worked in the trading houses of the Nagasaki port made their way down the hill. Our city is built on crags and razor-sharp hills, but our port is deep and the water is as smooth as glass, protected by the hills as it is.

My wanderings took me toward Chiyo's house, but I decided to wait until midday to approach her. I could hear the bells ringing from the cathedral the Christians had built in the valley. Did Christians arrange their marriages as my people did? I wondered. I had watched from the far side of the canal one day as a marriage ceremony had been performed in the church. The bells had rung for a long time. Did they ring longer for a happier marriage?

The sun was high in the sky when I ducked my head into a shop and saw it was 11:00. Nearly time to make my way up the hill to Chiyo's house. I sat under a tree, with the kitten asleep in the crook of my arm, while I pondered my outlandish hopes. Perhaps if I told him what I did, then my father would cast me out of the house, and my choice would be made for me. There were too many things I loved—my country, my family and our traditions, and Chiyo—and I wished for a world where I could love them all equally.

I wished, fervently, that everything could be different.

In the next moment, my world was shattered in a roar of heat and noise and light.

* * *

Tokyo: 2047

"Ami? It's time to go."

I looked at my assistant and sighed. It took a moment for my eyes to adjust from the brightness of staring out the high rise window of the family penthouse to looking at her in the dark-paneled office, in a dark suit, her black hair bound up in a bun and her iWand in her hand. She waved it and a holographic display appeared between us with my schedule.

"Must I?"

She frowned. "Is that any way for the future Empress to talk?"

"Oh, come on, Kumi, enough with the 'future

Empress' line. It was funny when we were at Harvard. It's not so funny now." Especially since the arguments against female succession were cropping up once again in the legislature.

She flicked her wrist and the display winked out. "I'm not trying to be funny," she said, her stance and voice softening. "If you want me to reschedule it, I will..."

I shook my head. "Which thing is this again? The Industrialists Society?"

"No. We told your father you couldn't do it because I'd already scheduled you to do the government hospital. The one you picked, Ami, because of the Kanda Women."

"Ah!" Now I remembered. "I didn't realize you'd pulled that off!"

"Yes," Kumiko said as calmly as a cowboy blowing the smoke off the end of her six-gun. "I had quite the showdown with Ryoko over it, but in the end, I won."

I hid a smile behind my hand. I could imagine her facing off with my father's indomitable assistant. Ryoko had been with him for at least 15 years and she was not to be trifled with.

Neither was my father, but just because he was emperor didn't mean he always got his way. When I had proposed this charity trip to him, he had objected vigorously. Too vigorously. That had only made me dig in my heels. There were many people at this state hospital worthy of help and notice, but the Kanda Women were of particular interest to me and no doubt they were why my father wanted me to pick some other place to visit, though he wouldn't say so out loud.

Fifteen minutes later I climbed into my armored limo with my security team, waving goodbye to Kumi as the door with its tinted windows shut. Honda drove and Taka, the head of our family security, took the seat next to me.

Taka was very professional. So professional I was never even tempted to see what would happen if I ran a toe up the side of his leg in the back seat here.

Well, maybe a little tempted, because Taka was all muscle and menace, which I found kind of sexy. And I wondered maybe, just once, if I could crack that implacable facade of his. But I had never dared.

Flashbulbs nearly blinded me as we emerged at the other end. "Asian Princess Diana" the international tabloids called me. Honestly, I enjoyed the charity work. It was all the press that was tiresome. The photographers vied to get pictures of me, jostling each other, and their remote lenses bumped against each other in the air. I smiled. Honda and Taka, one on either side of me and scanning the flying lenses for any threat, did not.

The medical facility didn't allow the cameras inside, thankfully. It would upset the patients too much. That was fine with me. Instead I was followed by a small gaggle of reporters. First I visited a ward of children with autoimmune diseases that kept them from going to a regular school. Then some survivors of the Roppongi Riots. Finally we came to the Kanda Women, a group of 12 who were blinded in the male supremacist attack on the Kanda train station.

One of the women touched my face and exclaimed, "You can tell she's beautiful! Our princess is beautiful."

"Thank you." They couldn't see me bow, so I held her hand against my cheek as I did. Then I moved on before I could be embarrassed any further. I wanted to see them, but the women made me uncomfortable. Or maybe it was the memory of what happened that day that made me uncomfortable, but it was a discomfort I did not want my country to hide or forget about. A Manpower terrorist had unleashed a biobomb that was intended to kill all the women, but not the men, within the district. His nanotech had been imperfect, though, and he merely blinded these 12.

I never forgave my father for saying his sentence should be lightened because the women had not actually been killed.

I hurried on to the next door down the hall without asking what was there. I entered a room that was completely quiet, where a man was lying in bed as if asleep. Or sedated.

The director of the hospital, a short man in a white doctor's coat, appeared at my elbow. He had an iWand in his hand, but gestured with the other. "Our mystery man," he said. "He has not woken since being found in an alleyway in Nagasaki a month or so ago. He is not in any database, not his fingerprints, nothing. He was wearing very old style clothes, which were a bit singed, as if he'd been in a fire or explosion. But there were no explosions reported in the days before he was found. He had rope sandals on his feet. Quite the mystery."

Odder to me than the man's mysterious identity was the fact that he had a tiny cat asleep on his chest. He had some deep scratches on his forehead, as if he had been in a car accident. "What will happen if he doesn't wake?" I asked.

211

"Like all the cases in our hospital, his care will be paid for," the director said, seeming annoyed that he had to look up at me.

I hadn't been asking about the state of funding. "Will he live?" I asked, more bluntly. The patient was a young man, his face beautiful under the scratches.

"Oh, for a while at least. He swallows if we spoon miso into his mouth, and he moans if any attempt is made to remove the cat or that hank of rope from his presence. We think perhaps he is trapped in a dream. All tests have shown his mind is functioning, but he is unable to wake."

Without thinking, I reached out to pet the little calico cat. She stretched and yawned, digging her claws into the man's chest.

He gasped suddenly and his eyes flew open. He looked right at me and said, "Chiyo!"

No one had called me that in years. Before I could pull back, though, he had seized my wrist.

"Chiyo, where am I? What happened? Why are you here?"

With as much aplomb as I could muster, I patted him on the hand. "The doctor says you were trapped in a dream. It looks like you were in some kind of an accident."

The cat, who I could now see was still a kitten, her broken tail tapering to a point, walked up his chest and nuzzled against his face.

The director finally recovered enough from his shock to speak. "What is your name?" he asked.

"Mizushi Jiro," the man answered. "Son of Mizushi Kaneda." He looked around the room and seemed to recognize that he was not where he had come from. "From Nagasaki," he added, as if that would help us. Then he addressed me again. "Chiyo, is this the Christian hospital?"

He had tears in the corners of his eyes and I reached out and brushed one of them away. I couldn't tell him I wasn't the woman he thought I was. He was disoriented. I didn't think it was a good idea to give him any more shocks, and it was clear to me his heart was in pain. "You should rest now," I said, instead. "You've been through a lot. Let the doctors help you, all right?" I petted the cat again. "Neko will watch over you for me." I smiled my best "benevolent princess" smile at him.

"Yes," he agreed.

A bustle of doctors and nurses took over then, as I stepped back, but as I backed out of the room, his eyes never left me.

The headlines were predictable, with all the takes on Sleeping Beauty and Rip Van Winkle you can name, everything short of giving me magical, angelic powers. Sigh. I couldn't very well tell them that I thought the cat had woken him, not me. All the uproar accomplished was to make my father insist I needed even stronger security around me, as now there would be those who wanted me to touch them to heal them.

"I told you going to that hospital was going to be a disaster!" my father snapped one morning as the holonews that floated in front of him recounted the story once again while he ate his breakfast.

What could I say to that? "Don't be ridiculous. We couldn't have known something like that would happen." I sat across from him on the atrium terrace, an untouched cup of tea in front of me. I was not hungry for breakfast yet but my father expected me there.

Ryoko swept in with light, quick steps and placed a tablet in front of him. He glanced at her and she gave him a short nod before sweeping out of the room again. No wonder he would never get a new assistant, I thought. The two of them had reached the point they could read each other's minds.

"I get mobbed anywhere I go anyway," I insisted. "This won't make a difference. Taka, tell him it's not that big a deal."

"Taka," he said, as if I hadn't even spoken. "Cancel all her upcoming appearances."

Taka merely nodded from where he stood off to one side, his eyes hidden by dark glasses.

"What? Are you going to keep me locked up?"

My father switched abruptly to a smile. "No, no, no, darling. Of course not. Just for a few weeks. Let things calm down."

Taka cleared his throat and made a half bow. "Perhaps now would be the time to start your esteemed daughter's self-defense training."

My father nodded. "Yes, perhaps you're right. You can begin while I am gone this week on my goodwill trip to Australia."

"I've had plenty of self-defense lessons," I said, looking back and forth between them. They were trying to make it sound spontaneous but to me it was obvious this was something they had discussed in advance.

Taka bowed again. "I will be instructing you personally," he said, in the gruff, unemotional tone that I knew my father expected to hear. But as he stepped back where my father could not see, I saw him roll his shoulders slightly, a minute adjustment to his stance that spoke volumes to me: a hint of the cocky swagger he sometimes adopted when he had to take action. That intrigued me. Maybe these lessons wouldn't be as dull as I imagined.

"Fine," I said. "Check with Kumi about any other appointments I had."

"I have already done so, your highness," Taka said.

I narrowed my eyes at my father. The whole conversation had been for show. They had decided between the two of them before I even sat down what was going to happen. I wasn't even sure why they bothered to keep up the charade that I had any say in what I did or when. Well, other than I would go ballistic if they didn't.

I knew to pick my battles. This one wasn't worth fighting. I pushed back in my own way. "Fine. See you in the gym in an hour, then."

"An hour," Taka acknowledged with a bow as I pushed past him out of the room.

* * *

I swaggered down to the private gym in what I would have worn to a workout back in my Harvard days, a black sports bra and yoga pants, my hair in a ponytail.

Taka had removed his heads-up glasses and when he saw me I saw the look blaze through his eyes. I was daring him to say something about how I was dressed. Or maybe I was daring him in general.

He slipped his suit jacket from his shoulders and I

215

took in the sight of his well-built chest and shoulders in his plain black T-shirt. Taka's biceps bulged as he stretched his elbows back. "Remind me what lessons you had before," he said, as he began warming up with light jogging steps in place.

"Two years in the Harvard Karate Club and a couple of personal lessons about escapes from holds taught by your predecessor," I said. "Though honestly he was afraid to grab me very hard so all we did was go through the motions."

I had never seen Taka grin before. The sight was a little unnerving, partly because it revealed how attractive he actually was. "I am not afraid to grab you, princess. Not when it's for your own good."

"Okay, fine, I—" I didn't get to finish what I was saying as he lunged for me. He got an elbow to the chin for his trouble and sat down hard on the mat.

He rubbed it appreciatively. "Good reflexes," he said, with no apparent chagrin that I had bested him.

"Are you all right?" I reached out a hand to help him up.

I should have known not to, I guess. This time I had no chance to strike him as he pulled me down and rolled on top of me, then got a hand over my mouth.

"That's all it would take to kidnap you," he said, even as I kept trying to struggle free. "A little Knockout in a handkerchief, over your nose and mouth, and you'd be helpless." He let my mouth go then, but didn't get off me.

"You think I don't know that already?" I said. "That's why you're there."

"But imagine I'm not. Snipers already took me and the rest of the entourage out, maybe."

"If that happened, I sure wouldn't be giving a hand up to an attacker on the ground," I pointed out, trying to wiggle my hips to the side. All I was succeeding in doing, though, was reminding myself how long it had been since I'd been under a man. Two years since I'd graduated and given up the relative freedom I'd had as a university student.

Taka sprang off me abruptly and I saw him adjust his waistband. Apparently I wasn't the only one affected by the friction. "Let's work on escapes, then."

"All right."

"If you're kidnapped, we can't assume it would be for a ransom. It might be political. They might well want to hurt your father or trigger an incident. They might not want to keep you safe."

"Okay."

"If you have a single captor, you might have your best chance of escape if he attempts to—" Taka cleared his throat rather than speak the unspeakable. The slight blush that tinged his tawny cheeks was sexy as hell.

"If he tries to rape me," I said, unflinching.

He bowed his head and his manner returned to stiff and formal. "Please assume the rape position."

I raised an eyebrow and challenged him. "Which position is that?"

Taka decided to accept that challenge. He narrowed his eyes and kept to the gruff tone. "On your back. Spread your legs."

I did so and he positioned himself between my legs. There was no hiding the telltale bulge I could feel against my most intimate place. "You're making this very realistic," I said.

"I won't make the mistake of your previous teacher," he answered. He trapped my hands against the mat, then. "Now, how will you escape from this?"

I wriggled around as best I could, but all that did was rub my sensitive areas against him. He had to know what an effect that was having on me, but he said nothing.

"Now I will teach you a move that will allow you to escape this," he said.

Before it drives us both insane, I imagined him thinking. That was certainly what I was thinking.

We reversed positions and he showed me how to use the leverage of my legs to pry my hips free, putting the attacker into a vulnerable position long enough for me to launch an attack of my own and then hop up and run.

After repeating that for an hour, we were both sweaty, panting messes. "What about if my attacker tries to kiss me?" I said, as we got back into position once more. "Should I try to bite him?"

I pressed a kiss against Taka's tightly closed lips. He was off me in an instant.

"Princess." He shook himself like a dog while he tried to muster the words to scold me. "There are... lines we cannot cross. Your father would have my testicles if your husband-to-be didn't get to me first."

I hopped up myself. "I'm not a virgin—" I started to argue, then it hit me what he'd said, or maybe the way he'd said it. "Wait. What husband-to-be?"

He backpedaled a little too obviously. "I only meant whoever might be your husband in the future, of course."

"Taka!" My father's sudden swings between

placating and overprotective became clear. "My father's picked someone, hasn't he."

"I am not privy to—"

"Bullshit!" I said in English. The word had a satisfying feeling, like spitting fire, when it was said. "That's why he's been so crazy lately. Worse than usual! Who is it? Tell me."

He bowed deeply. "I do not know. Honestly. If there has been an arrangement I have not been told to whom."

"I don't believe that for a second. You've probably already done a million security checks on the guy." I sat down on the bench, the reality of it hitting me. I'd always known that for the sake of tradition and family politics it was possible a match would be made for me. Somehow I'd held out hope that I'd meet a dashing diplomat or hit it off with someone interesting but powerful in industry and then get my father to approve. But there was no one interesting in industry and who was I kidding, anyway? I wondered if it was even going to be someone I had met.

At that moment I wanted to tempt Taka into having sex with me. Because even though I didn't actually like Taka at least I found him attractive and I knew it would be my own choice. I had a feeling he was probably as good at sex as he was at everything else physical.

Taka bowed again. "Tomorrow, we will work on submission holds."

"I look forward to it," I said, as he left the room.

I hurried to my private quarters, where I picked up my iWand and immediately sent Kumi out to buy a rabbit pearl vibrator. I made an immediate appointment with some of the porno films I had stashed in my private server.

The next day we worked on escapes from various holds. I dressed as I had the day before, making my diamond-hard nipples hard to miss. Taka appeared to be struggling with his conscience internally, but his reserve was not enough to keep him from putting me into compromising positions. My conscience was not enough to keep me from clocking him a couple of times, too, which I felt earned me a smidgen of grudging respect from him. Maybe it was time to take up kendo.

When Taka said, "Let's review what we did yesterday," I lay down immediately and spread my knees, welcoming his erection against my clit. We were fully clothed. Surely no one could impugn what we were doing, even if we were observed, which I doubted we were. Taka no doubt controlled the security monitors himself.

He said nothing as I "struggled to get free," rubbing myself against him brazenly, while he remained stoic. Hard as a rock in every way.

I couldn't come that way, though. It wasn't enough, though I was close.

"What if..." I hesitated, not sure even I could be bold enough to suggest this. Not sure I could give voice to the fantasy that lived deep inside me.

"What if what?"

"What if my kidnapper tied me up," I said.

He reached up and wiped the sweat from his own upper lip. "We... we can work on rope escapes tomorrow."

"All right. Then leave me alone right now."

"As you wish, your highness." He leaped up lightly, slipped his monitor glasses on, and made his exit quickly.

I jammed my hand into my yoga pants without moving from the spot. I wondered if he were watching me with a security camera right now. Probably. I didn't need pornography when I had such vivid images in my mind now, of Taka tying me up and teasing me. I used my fingers to make myself come, arching against the wrestling mat and wondering what my father, or husband to be, would think if he could see me.

* * *

The next day, I felt myself go wet the moment Taka took the rope out of his bag.

"Put your hands behind your back," he said. As he knotted my wrists together, I moved my legs, feeling how slick my lips below had become.

I waited for the practice to begin, wondering what he would tell me about defending myself in this position, or escaping from it. I tested the ropes and couldn't move my arms at all.

He grabbed me from behind, then, one hand under my chin, an inch from a stranglehold. This put his mouth near my ear. "Struggle to get free," he growled.

I struggled as best I could, but I could not twist away from him. He kept a foot between my legs, and nothing I did could free me from his grip.

My heart began to pound suddenly, with equal parts fear and thrill as he said into my ear, "I've seen the pornography you think you have hidden. I've seen the rope bondage."

I gasped and felt his erection against my tailbone, but my veins turned to ice as he continued to talk, all excitement giving way to fear: "You deserve to be tamed by a man, by a husband," he said. "You're like a wild beast, defying your father and then tempting me as you have. Your lust is disgusting. Unfit for a proper wife, a proper princess."

I dared not speak, then, I dared not provoke him.

And then, quite suddenly, I was free. He had sliced the ropes with a razor-sharp knife and pushed me away. I whirled to see the knife still in his hand, but a composed and serious look on his face. He cleared his throat and bowed. "Apologies, princess, for scaring you, but I thought it better to show you rather than lecture you about the danger."

"You're really twisted, you know that?" I said, my heart still pounding but my adrenaline ebbing. "I could have you fired, you know. You've been taking ridiculous liberties with me."

"Testing you," he said, his composure never cracking.

"So, what, you report to my father that I'm a too much of a slut to marry? Is that it?"

He shook his head. "No. But I could tell him it is urgent to marry you before you make any scandalous mistakes."

"You came on to me first!" I insisted.

He shrugged. "Did I? I do not think so."

"Ugh. Enough. I've had enough of this."

He bowed to me as I marched back to my room. I reactivated my iWand on the way. "Kumi, when is my father due back?"

"Oh, hey Ami. Self-defense lesson done for the day?"

"Very very done."

"I see. Your father is due to return tonight."

"Good."

"Good? Ami, what's up?"

"Meet me upstairs and I'll tell you."

Once we were in my room I linked our iWands and texted her in English, which was the most secure way we could communicate. Taka's been mindfucking me all week. I swear he wants to get into my pants and he was getting off on the fact that he could mess with me. Wrestling and defense lessons, yeah right.

She rolled her eyes. I thought you were having an affair with him, honestly.

You did? If I were I wouldn't have needed that vibrator!

You have a point.

He was making me horny as hell but it was all some kind of fucked up test. What did you find out about my father making a marriage arrangement for me?

Nothing. Haven't found out a thing. I'm sure he'll tell you when he gets back. You knew it could happen.

I know.

Even if he did give you away, you'd still have a year, maybe even two, before you'd have to actually go through with the marriage, she texted, trying to console me.

She was probably right. But the narrow window of freedom I might have had? I felt it had snapped shut. Taka had only been saying those things to freak me out, but I sensed an urgency behind the whole odd episode.

* * *

I didn't wait to find out. The moment I heard my father had come home, in mid-afternoon, I checked to see if Ryoko was on guard duty for him. She wasn't, probably running an errand for him, so I went to confront him in his office.

"What's this rumor I hear that you've arranged my marriage without even consulting me?" I demanded.

"Sit, Ami," he said, as if by sitting I'd prove I was going to be obedient.

"I won't." I looked around the dark-lacquered, ultra-modern furniture he had surrounded himself with. "This isn't feudal times. Who is it? Is it even someone I've met?"

He sighed. "I'm sure you'll approve of my choice."

"So it's true!" I sat then, only because my knees went weak. He'd really done it.

"We are still in negotiations," he said, as if my future were to be bought and sold like a family heirloom. I supposed it was.

"You didn't even ask me," I insisted.

"This is not about your feelings, Ami."

"What the fuck—"

"Listen to me!" he barked. "There is... great pressure, from the male supremacists."

"Are you kidding me? After Kanda they were utterly discredited politically!"

"The extremists in Manpower were, but there are still many who are sympathetic to their position. Once you are married, that will quiet their voices!"

"Because they'll be assured of an Emperor and not a Bitch Queen on the throne?"

"Ami!" My father acted shocked by my profanity. "How can you say such things! But yes, that's exactly why. And let me tell you, your husband will not be as indulgent with you as I have been!"

"Indulgent? It's indulgent for a woman to want her independence? Her rights?"

"Of course not," my father said, but it was clear I had struck a nerve. "Listen to me, Ami. Ever since your mother, you've been the most important woman on Earth to me."

"And now either you're overcompensating by trying to protect me from things that aren't yours to control or you're selling me out to protect your own political position," I said, rising to my feet.

He shook his head, looking resignedly down at his hands in his lap. "Please, Ami. I've chosen a good man. He'll be loyal to you, a good friend, and protect you."

"You make it sound like he's a pet dog, not a husband!"

"So make him into a pet dog for all I care. That will be between you and him. Though I caution you, please, Ami!" He looked up and I saw the whites of his eyes, he was that afraid. "Do not show this willful, rebellious side with him in public!"

He was serious. He was not only marrying me off, he was apparently marrying me to a soppy pushover? Maybe he thought that would make me happy, because of my headstrong nature? I couldn't believe it. Or worse, maybe he was marrying me to a male supremacist type? Someone who would demand I be subservient. Either way it would be loveless. Either way it would be misery.

All I could think about then was the man I'd seen in the hospital. I could still see his eyes, and the way he had looked at me with absolute need and love.

"You're nearly 24," my father snapped, when it was clear I really wasn't listening to him. "I've waited as long as I could. The wedding should be as soon after the negotiations are concluded as possible. Perhaps a month. I've cleared your schedule with Kumiko. You are to start a new diet and nutrition regimen tomorrow."

"Diet? Is my husband-to-be dieting, too?"

"He will not be wearing a silk dress."

I'd heard enough. "Fine. I'll marry your little puppet. After all, if he's not to my liking, I can cast him aside the way you cast aside mother? Right?"

"Ami! How dare you speak that way!"

I was out of the room faster than I could imagine. I'd said it to hurt him, and to shock him enough that I could run from the room. But I didn't run back to my own room like I usually did.

I was in the elevator to the parking garage before I even knew what I was doing.

And then I was on the street, alone, with no guards, no companions, for the first time in years. The sheer thrill of it made my heart pound. I hurried down to the commercial block and around a corner.

I ducked into a store, my mind racing. Why go back? It suddenly felt as if I had been planning to sneak away all along. How could I do it? Think, think.

I made my way down the aisles, but no one paid me any mind. I had often wondered, when people saw Ami the Princess, was it me they recognized, or the security men, the entourage, the cameras? Right now, maybe I was just a woman who looked kind of like the princess...

All right. I purchased a pair of scissors, sunglasses, eye liner, some other toiletries, a touristy black T-shirt, and a small bag to put it all in. I went to the self-checkout, tapped my iWand against the console, taking out a large amount of cash as well as paying for the items.

So far so good. I passed through the store into the mall it was attached to. My next stop was the public restroom, where I hurriedly cut my hair and applied the make-up. When I was done, I looked years younger, as the black-rimmed eyes of a Gothic Lolita stared back at me. I put my hair in pigtails and licked my blackberry lips. I'd gone through a goth phase in college. Who knew I was learning important skills of disguise?

I threw the iWand into the trash receptacle and went back out into the mall. For a moment my heart stopped as I saw Honda scanning frantically. But his eyes passed right over me. He had no idea who I was.

I made my way onto the street, and then got on a train. All of Tokyo awaited my explorations. Perhaps this would be my one chance to visit the underground clubs where, they said, men could turn women into living works of erotic art with rope. If this was my last adventure, I was determined to make it a good one.

* * *

Tokyo: 2047

"Well, Neko, what do you think about here?"

The kitten purred inside my coat. Perhaps it was the scent of fish that pleased her, or merely the sound of my voice. We took a seat at a noodle bar on the

227

street. At least that seemed somewhat familiar to me. At least everything in the world had not changed.

They say be careful what you wish for, and that was the only thing I could imagine had happened. I had wished for a different world, and here it was, one where everyone spoke faster, and wore more bright colors, and even the cars were more brightly colored than anything I had ever seen before. Maybe Tokyo had always been like that, I thought, but I did not believe so.

There were women everywhere I looked, laughing and carefree. I saw young couples holding hands as they ran across streets evading the traffic. But where was Chiyo?

The doctors had tried to explain. I was mistaken. I had been dreaming. I had dreamed I lived in another time and place, of another woman who could not be her. Could not be her because did I truly not recognize that was Princess Ami? Everyone knew Princess Ami. I must have dreamed that she was my secret love.

And everyone knew of the bombing of Nagasaki, the terrible power that shook the world and changed the course of the war and the entire fate of our nation. It had taken me some time to absorb that. And yet as I did, I wondered again if my past had been some kind of a dream and this the reality. My memories of my father, of Akio, and of the woman who had been my lover seemed paper-thin and insubstantial. Perhaps it truly was as if a hundred years had passed and my memories of them had faded as they would have to an elderly man.

My much more recent memory of Princess Ami seemed much more vivid. Perhaps it was merely that she was the first thing I saw upon waking, but my mind was fixated on her the way a newly hatched chick fixates on its mother.

I ate a bowl of noodles and paid for it using the strange, slick card they had given me upon my discharge from the hospital. Apparently while I had slept, the government had paid for my care as well as a few weeks of rehabilitation afterward. I had returned to the training exercises my father had taught me. Once it became clear there was little reason to keep me prisoner—other than the persistent delusion I was from another time—they brought me as up to date as they could, gave me a little money to get started with, and a directory of agencies to help me find a job and a home. They gave me enough train fare to return to Nagasaki. And then what? I thought. All I could think of was Princess Ami.

I wondered if the monks could be right about reincarnation. Perhaps Ami was my Chiyo, after all? All I knew was that she was in Tokyo and might someday be Empress, they said. A fantasy woman, hardly real.

Except that she had held my hand. She had looked into my eyes. Maybe there were many women who looked like her in this day and age. Maybe my mind was playing tricks, but I had nothing else to go on.

I fed the cat a noodle from the bottom of my bowl. She gobbled it down bit by bit until she was licking my fingers. "How are we going to find her, Neko?"

The cat chose that moment to get restless. She leaped down from my lap and ran a little ways down

229

the street. I ran after her. "Neko! Now is not the time to go running around!"

She dashed down the street toward the entrance to a train station. My breath caught for a moment as I saw yet another woman who could have been Chiyo hurrying into the station. It could not be the princess this time, as she was alone, no guards or entourage with her, but maybe Neko did not make such distinctions. The kitten turned to meow at me and snatched her up.

"That could not be her, Neko," I said. "But I appreciate you looking for her all the same."

Neko hopped down and rubbed against my ankles, but as I reached down to pet her, she dashed away again, this time down the steps of the station. I had no choice but to chase after her.

Chapter Two

The train station was intimidatingly crowded. I knew it would be to my advantage if I blended in with such a massive crowd. If my pursuers were trying to pick me out on surveillance cameras, they'd likely fail. But I was used to being escorted, guarded, moved from place to place to avoid crowds. My heart beat fast like a bird's, already aflutter from my flight, now racing while all the lessons my bodyguards had taught me about crowds sent my mind spinning. Assassination. Terrorism.

I reminded myself that if I was not recognized as Princess Ami, I was no target. I am no one right now. I am safe.

The nagging voice warning me of danger whispered, Is that what the Kanda women thought, though? They were ordinary women, on an ordinary day, before that nano-bomb changed their lives forever.

Where was I going, anyway? I tried to think. Once I had slipped out of my gilded cage my head spun with possibilities. I could get on a train, go out to the countryside, go in any direction. They would have no idea which direction I went...

Except if I purchased a ticket to another region,

the cameras would capture my face. And surely they would be running recognition scans on every female face buying an outbound ticket. With sudden clarity I realized Taka would hunt me ferociously. My escape was his dishonor. I had no doubt that both he and my father would stupidly see it that way. As if my own will had nothing to do with it. What would my father do to him, or what would Taka do to himself, over this? All would be forgiven, of course, if Taka were the one to find me.

Where, then, where? The answer was right in front of my face, the thing I wanted most to try, to taste, the forbidden fruit: a young woman with an elaborate rope harness over her dress stood against one wall, handing out flyers to passerby—or trying to. Most of them were ignoring her, brushing past, or even trying to veer away even though it was too crowded for that. I took the flyer out of her hand without meeting her eyes, without slowing down. I glanced quickly to confirm it advertised an establishment in Yosh-Yosh and I noted which Metro stop was closest. Good. I could snag that ticket from a machine using cash. Within minutes I was waiting on the platform. I stared at the flyer as a way to keep myself from looking around nervously.

They must have found my iWand by now, I thought. Would they assume I was kidnapped or that I was out on my own? Or make no assumptions? How quickly might they determine what direction I went, or could they? I saw no sign of anyone searching. The police patrol on the opposite platform made their way along without any apparent urgency.

I set aside my worry. It was probably not a matter

of if but when I would be caught, and upon resigning myself to that, I ceased to worry. I would most likely have a night of adventure, and tomorrow I would probably go back before things turned into an international incident of some kind. I would figure out how to fight the marriage somehow. Maybe I could talk my husband-to-be himself out of it? Although what were the chances that someone who would cut a deal with my father without even talking to me first would see sense. Zero. I'd have to deal with that later. Tonight was for me.

The train came whooshing into the station and I crowded on with many other people. To avoid making eye contact I stayed against a pole, staring at the flyer again. This time I examined it. The image on it was a photograph of a woman, her body crisscrossed with artful ropes. It might have been the same woman handing out the flyer? Or maybe it was my imagination.

This was a flyer for entry to Rope Club, the most infamous of the new "historical" sex clubs. The fad they had started was only a few years old, but a whole neighborhood of clubs and bars had sprung up around them, each catering to different styles. Yosh-Yosh they called both the neighborhood and the lifestyle, after Yoshiwara, the old "red light" district in Edo, depicted in so many Ukiyo-e paintings and poems.

I had never been into one of these places or anywhere near Yosh-Yosh, but I had read the news, seen the photos and videos. From what I understood, people went there to hook up for fantasy sex, or to pay for it, and there were nightly performances, some of which were "historical" only in the vaguest sense—but who cared if that samurai was wearing 18th century armor and the male courtesan on stage with him was wearing a 14th century kimono? As long as they were going to fuck—or whatever—the audience didn't much mind.

Taka had been right about one thing in his rant when he tried to scare me to be good. I had fantasies. Fantasies of being tied and spread and pleasure-tortured and fucked. I'd watched the porn streams, of course, the girls knotted and made into living works of art, goddesses and sacrifices to desire at the same time. Immobilized by loops and wraps of woven craft, water jets aimed at their clits until they screamed in orgasm and then screamed for mercy when the water did not stop, their cries only silenced when filled by cock. Or tied and suspended in such a way that two or even three men could have their fill of her available orifices.

Of course the biggest fantasy of them all was finding a husband who'd understand that and do it all to me and more. Yeah, right.

I was so caught up in my erotic daydreams it took me a moment to realize we had reached my stop. Fortunately many people were trying to get off so I had plenty of time to work my way to the door and out.

The early evening air was cooling, though the sky was still quite bright, as I approached the narrow doorway on the street level with the words ROPE CLUB in small English letters above the lintel. The door was unlocked. I pushed it open to find a narrow entryway leading directly to a stairway going up. A tall woman in even taller heels was coming down the steps carrying a stool. I stepped back onto the street as she put the stool down with a thump.

"We're not open yet," she said to me, batting her eyelashes. Her voice was deep and I suspected she might be male underneath the exaggerated geisha makeup and kimono. Or perhaps trans. I was certain it wouldn't be polite to ask or to draw attention to it.

"Oh. Um, the flyer doesn't say what time you operate." As if I needed proof, I showed her the scrap of paper in my hand, which had already grown a bit dog-eared and sweat-softened from my carrying it.

"Well. The show's at 10:00," she said as she looked me up and down.

"It also doesn't say how much it is to get in," I pointed out.

Her smile was wide. "Single, unaccompanied women get in free. Men with a partner pay half price. Men alone pay double price."

"Oh, that's interesting."

"Isn't it?" Her expression turned coy. "So, you know, most women who want to meet someone hang around outside on the street. Then once they're in, the man in question is happy to pay the difference in drinks. Plus you get a good look at them out here."

"Who says I'm here to meet someone?" I challenged.

"If you're not, then why are you here? Just to see the show? As I said. That's not until 10:00."

I sighed. The last thing I wanted to do was be standing out on the street all evening. Too risky. "Can't I meet someone inside? Does it have to be out here?"

She perched herself on the stool, which only made her even taller, adding to the fact I was standing a step down on the street—I felt like I was five years old again and asking my mother if I could have a sip of her peach-blossom tea. "If you're only looking for a little... fun... then a partner can be had for a price."

"What's the price?" I demanded.

A window on the floor above us slid open and a man stuck his head out. His hair was overlong and it blew in the breeze like a flag as he shouted, "Rumiko! Stop giving the customer a hard time! If she wants to come in, let her in!"

The geisha leaned out the doorway. "Fine! You give her the orientation, then!"

The window slammed and Rumiko huffed angrily before settling back on the stool with a sweet smile on her face. "Go on upstairs, then. And have a nice evening."

I thanked her with a slight bow and climbed the stairs, wondering what I would find up above.

What I found was the host, the long-haired man, giving me a bow as he welcomed me into a fairly standard-looking bar and lounge area. This part was done retro-1980s, with blue neon strips and some old computer keyboards glued to the wall as a kind of collage sculpture. Behind the bar was another woman, her hair in pigtails, wiping down the black granite surface.

"Sorry about Rumiko, the bouncer downstairs," the host said. "I'm called Zaka."

I recognized the odd name immediately from articles I had read. "Oh! You're the one who started Rope Club. Who started the whole... trend."

He shrugged unassumingly. "People have always played games with sex and people invented rope a very long time ago. I cannot lay claim to have 'started' anything other than this humble establishment, which I am honored has gained such notice. Now, as this is your first time here I should tell you the rules and give you some tips."

"Yes, please!"

"First is that you are not required to use your real name. Most people use an alias. The second is... well... may I assume since you are not carrying any rope that you hope to be tied rather than to do the tying?"

I blushed at the thought that my desire might be so plain to a man like him. "You are correct. Your bouncer mentioned I could hire a... a partner?"

"One thing at a time, my dear. The second tip is when you are new to this sort of thing, we recommend you try out any new partner here in the club."

"In public?"

"Yes, where our staff can keep an eye on you and your safety. Of course if you wish to hire a member of our staff, we will take good care of you. But a young, beautiful woman such as yourself should have no difficulty attracting a match." His eyes sparkled as he appraised me. "Male or female?" he asked, as mildly as a waiter would ask if I preferred my sake hot or cold.

"Male," I said, trying not to look away shyly, but not quite managing it. "Do you ever, um, take on clients?"

His grin showed he was flattered by my question, but also that he was going to say no. "I am tempted, but no, I am too busy with my responsibilities to give my undivided attention to a beauty such as you. And anything less than my undivided attention would be not only dangerous, but a shame as well. Better that I should play matchmaker for you. So, you're looking for a man to tie you up. That we can do."

Hearing him say it aloud made my blood surge, both in a leap in my heart rate and also in my desire down below. "But how much?" I prayed I'd taken enough money out. Who knew how exorbitant the price might be?

I sighed in relief when he named a price not much more than a fancy dinner for two. I handed over the cash without hesitation, thinking that within moments he'd lead me to my Prince Charming.

He cleared his throat. "Most of our regular staff is not here yet," he explained. "I'll be sure to find you the moment someone suitable turns up, however."

My hopes fell. Had I just given my money to a con artist?

He patted my arm. "Why don't you have a drink while you wait? It's only that you're here so early. Don't fret." He told the bartender to fix me anything I wanted.

"Sure thing, Boss," she said. "By the way, Rumi just buzzed. She needs you downstairs."

He hurried away from me and I took a stool at the bar. "Am I really too early?"

She looked around the empty club. "Were you hoping for a quickie and to get out before it gets crowded? Because in my experience, ropes take a while."

I blushed to hear her say it. "Um, no. I was just... impatient to get here, I guess."

"Don't worry. Zaka will fix you up. We've had a bit of a shortage of male tops lately, though. Funny. They keep meeting girls and next thing you know they're married and don't come here anymore."

"How sad—" I started to say, then caught myself. "Wait. You mean they marry the girls they meet here?"

"Yeah, of course. What did you think I meant?"

"Nothing. Never mind." I'm not Cinderella at this ball, I thought. I'm Prince Charming. I was the one who would have to convince my father that the commoner who fit my shoe was magically fit to marry me.

Yeah, right.

* * *

I had one hand on the railing as I hurried down the endless stairs into the station, barely keeping Neko in sight. I had to move faster! But with my leg, my foot... As I reached the long corridor at the bottom of the steps, I broke into what should have been an excruciating jog only to find both feet equally solid under me. What blessing of the gods was this? Although my feet were still unequal, the bad one still turned inward a few inches, and all my muscles were still weak from my long stay in the hospital, there was none of the shooting agony in my leg that my nerves usually gave me. I considered once again whether this all might be a hallucination, a dream. But if it were a dream, would I not have dreamed myself perfect, my feet as symmetrical as a buddha's closed eyes? Also, I had never known what running freely would feel like, so how could I imagine it now? The idea that I was a hundred years in the future seemed more logical than that this was the most realistic and detailed dream I had ever had. The doctors must have healed me while I was under their care.

Then again, what future but one I had dreamed up would have a beautiful woman, brazenly wearing a rope harness outside her close-fitting dress, advertising a sex establishment? She was outside the ticket gates, trying to hand me a flyer. I bowed as I took the flyer which nearly caused me to lose sight of Neko. Nearly. The cat stopped on the far side of the gate and looked back at me.

"Where do you think you're going?" I asked her.

The woman in the rope harness giggled. "Is she yours?"

"This cat has a mind of her own," I said. "I cannot claim to own her in the slightest." I glanced at the flyer in my hand.

"I thought you might be interested," she said, eyeing the rope over my shoulder. "There are a couple of places trying to cash in on the shibari fad but Rope Club is the original, and the best."

Neko ran back to me, leaped up to my arm, and then onto my shoulder and meowed at the woman. "What happens there?"

"It's for anyone into rope," she said.

Into rope. I gathered from the look of the flyer and the woman herself that it was more than just a place to go out drinking.

"Open tonight. Come on by, if you can?" She giggled as the cat hopped from my shoulder to hers and rubbed against her ear, and then hopped back.

I thanked her for the flyer and went on my way, then, thinking that I wasn't sure where I should go next. But why not go see what there was to be seen at Rope Club? The flyer seemed to indicate they would not be open for business for some hours yet, but I decided it would be best to investigate the place in advance.

After tucking Neko into my jacket, I used my government-issued card to enter the train platform and rode to the stop indicated on the flyer. From there I found the address given in a neighborhood that looked rife with interesting establishments.

I could not read the eight symbols above the door, but they appeared to be English and they matched the ones on the flyer in my hand. I approached the woman at the door, anticipation making my throat tight.

She took one look at the coils of rope on my shoulder and hissed, "Go around back! You're late if you want to audition!"

"Au-audition?"

"If you want to ply your trade here, you better prove yourself. You think we let any clown with a hank of rope in here?"

I drew myself up to my full height. "I would be happy to prove my rope skills to you."

She gestured to the alley beside the building. "Around back. Hurry up or you won't be in time."

It was hardly the first time I only had a vague grasp of what was going on in the world around me, but if proving myself with my rope was necessary, that I could certainly do. I made my way around the building and was let into a back room with an open floor. A man with bleached ends to his hair gestured for me to sit beside him at the edge of the mat while two women occupied the center, one tying the other.

As I folded my legs under me, Neko crept out of my shirt and sat beside me. She washed her face with her paw and seemed as unconcerned with the people there as they were with her. My attention, meanwhile, was directed at the walls decorated with photographs, larger than life, of beautiful people artfully bound. I had become accustomed to sexual images on the sides of buildings, in train stations, on screens everywhere, but these was beyond even that. The eroticism of the faces, of the poses, seemed to reach straight into me, igniting my desire. And the thought began to truly sink in that the private uses to which I had put my family's art were now something that many people indulged in. When I had seen the woman in the train station, I had wondered; when I had read the flyer I had dared to hope; now it seemed clear that my idea of an erotic paradise actually existed.

If there had been any question in my mind, the two women practicing their art in front of me would have swept it away. They wore black skin-tight coverings over their breasts and bottoms. The one being tied was standing on one foot while the other bound her other leg in a crooked position. Her eyes were closed, her two hands pressed together in a sacred position. But her buddha-like calm did not last, as it grew difficult to maintain her balance. "Aya! You're about to knock me right over!" she complained.

"Just stay still another minute," the woman with the rope in her hands said, but it was too late. Her partner's knee buckled and a moment later, both myself and the man whose name I still did not know had moved reflexively to catch her before she hit the floor. We lowered her carefully.

"That part of the act needs to change," he said to the two women. "I can't have you toppling right off the stage. Aya, you know better."

The woman with the rope sighed. "I know. We don't have time to figure out something else before tonight, though. I guess we could repeat the same flying-angel act as last week?"

"You'll have to." He looked at me then, kneeling next to him. "Who are you?"

"Call me Jiro." I doubted they would know my family name or history. After all, our lineage probably died out that day in 1945. "At the front I was told I should prove my skills."

"Ah." The man smiled knowingly and got to his feet, leaving it to Aya to untie the woman still wound with rope. "I am Zaka and this is my humble establishment. Are you seeking a man or a woman?"

"A woman, Zaka-san." I said, wondering how he knew I was looking for her, then realized he had meant which type of partner I wished to meet. I supposed I should not tell him that the only woman who truly interested me was Princess Ami.

"Well. As it turns out, we do not have many men here tonight to make the ladies happy. I would be curious to see what you can do." He took a seat again.

I bowed to him. "I would be honored."

"Aya. Are you done there? Would you mind?"

She huffed and stood, while her partner moved off to the side with the rest of their ropes. Neko watched her curiously as the woman coiled them neatly.

I unwound a hank of my rope. "Are you looking for restraint?"

Zaka merely gave me a disinterested shrug. But his feigned nonchalance fell away as I quickly bound Aya's arms behind her back, forcing her to thrust her

243

chest outward. He hopped up, testing the knots with gentle tugs. He opened his mouth to say something, then thought better of it, circling her. When he stood facing her, he said, "This would make a pretty picture without this sports bra in the way."

"You have a one-track mind, Zaka," she said, smirking at him.

"Hmm. Two tracks, I think," he said, and caressed the side swell of one of her breasts. "Jiro, can you put her in a tie she cannot escape?"

"I'm sure I can."

"No, no, I mean while she is trying to escape."

Aya's eyes lit up at that. "Do you think you can?"

I bowed to them both. "I can but try."

I released her from the rope and we faced each other. Her grin was infectious and I found myself smiling in return.

Then she tried to dart away and I grabbed her by one wrist before she could escape the mat. Once I had one loop around her, she was mine. Within minutes I had her on the ground and all of her limbs immobilized.

Zaka stood and bowed. "You humble us with your presence, Jiro-sama."

I bowed in return, surprised by his sudden change of attitude. "You honor me with yours."

"If I may ask you one question, though?" His eyes strayed to where Aya was still struggling to get loose on the mat. I thought he was going to ask me where I trained, but no. "Where did you get this rope?"

"From my father."

"What?" Aya looked up at me. "You're kidding, right?"

But Zaka did not seem surprised "Family heirloom?"

"Yes. I was not deemed worthy of my family's sword, but the rope, yes."

He seemed to understand that. "Come into my office, would you? After you let Aya free."

She gave up the struggle finally, and slumped to the mat while I released her. "That was pretty cool," she said. "Are you busy later? We could work on a performance, you know—"

"Aya," Zaka barked. "Leave him alone."

I followed him to his office, a very small room down the hall, where there was barely space for the desk and two chairs, one behind it and one in front. He offered me the chair in front and he slipped into the one behind. Neko settled herself onto a small side table, next to a stack of books. From a drawer Zaka produced a piece of paper. "This is the disclaimer all our performers must sign."

"Performers? Pardon me, Zaka-san, but I am new to the ways of the big city."

He looked at me curiously. "Okay, I need you to be honest with me. Have you been raised by monks on an island or something?"

"My past is difficult to explain."

He pushed the paper and a pen toward me and then he turned his back. "Go on, sign it. And then I will tell you what family name you put and you will tell me if I am correct."

"All right." I inscribed my first name only, though, curious whether this was a parlor trick or what.

"Mizushi," he said.

The pen clattered on the desk as it fell from my nerveless fingers. "You know who I am!"

He turned to face me again. "No. But I know your family history."

"You do?"

"Ancestors of yours were protectors of the emperor and royal family until the late 19th century," he said. "I don't know why your family fell out of favor."

I thought of my proud but nearly penniless father and felt a sudden wave of longing and sadness. He had been dead for a hundred years now, but I had been too recently awakened from my dream state to grieve for him or anyone else I knew yet. "I don't know why, either."

"This rope was passed down through your family?"

"Yes." I laid it on the desk.

"This is not any ordinary rope," Zaka said. "Do you know that? In the fibers there are strands of the special silk that was made only for the imperial family. Legend has it that the silk had magical powers of protection for those of imperial blood."

"What legend is that?" I had never heard such a story.

"My family's legend," Zaka said, pressing his palm to his chest. "You see why I am interested."

"If you know my family's name, then it is something more than a mere story," I said.

"Of course it is more than a story." He ran his finger along the rope. "I'm real, aren't I? And so are you. And so is this."

I picked up the pen again and signed my family name. "You'll have to tell me what you expect of me, though."

He waved his hand breezily through the air. "We are a place where those who love rope, and who love with rope, gather. I need both performers and instructors. For those who come seeking practice or experience being bound, I need those willing to tie them. Very few know the art as you know it."

"I confess I was taught the way of the rope as a martial art, and I only practiced it as a love art on my own."

He grinned. "That is the story of the 21st century, my friend. Everyone thinks they're the only one to like it that way, only to discover that they are not alone."

Chapter Three

By the time I entered the main section of the club, a crowd had begun to gather around the stage. On it, a woman was tying a man most stylishly, with great flair, but also great concentration. As she circled him and worked her knots, occasionally caressing his skin or whispering in his ear, I felt I was in the presence of a great artist. The dais they occupied was enclosed by what looked like the frame of a house made of iron. I soon grasped the purpose of the set, though, when she looped a rope through the ring at the apex, and lifted her partner into the air. A collective breath of wonder went through the crowd as he soared like a bird that had spread its wings. I blinked, realizing that one of my feet was practically asleep, I had been holding myself so still while watching them.

This is not a dream, I thought, but it is very like one, to have woken into a world where my deepest desires, my deepest fantasies, are such a part of this world. I patted my chest, suddenly aware that Neko's weight and warmth were gone, but I had left her in Zaka's office, asleep in a chair.

Aya caught my attention then, beckoning me to come toward her. I swallowed the lump in my throat then. The woman beside her was another likeness of Chiyo!

"Jiro," Aya said as I arrived. "This young woman would like to experience your talents."

I bowed deeply to them both, saying a prayer to whatever god or goddess had brought us together once again. "I would be honored."

Aya giggled at that: it seemed most were not so formal. But the woman bowed to me in return.

"Keep her clothes on," Aya said into my ear as she handed me more hanks of rope. "She's a first timer. She's not ready for more in such a public setting."

Then she was gone and the woman and I were alone. I wondered if it was my imagination that she was the same woman who had come to me half in a dream while I had been in the hospital. The princess. Surely she would not be here, alone, in a place like this?

I decided it did not matter. Every woman should be treated as if she were a national treasure. Especially one as precious as this.

We moved to an alcove where there were padded seats and footstools and gentle, gem-like lights illuminated the walls with pink and yellow. She smiled a bit nervously.

I'm sure my smile was just as nervous. I indicated she should sit on one of the low tuffets and I knelt next to her. "I have a confession to make," I said. "I am a first-timer also at Rope Club."

Rather than showing disappointment, her eyes lit up. "Really?"

"Yes. I had to prove my skills to the owner, though, so I assure you, I am skilled. My name is Jiro."

Her smile grew in confidence. "That sounds excellent, Jiro-san."

"What shall I call you?" I asked.

She hesitated. "I, um, they told me I don't have to use my real name."

"Of course not." Zaka had encouraged me to choose an assumed name also, but it didn't matter what name I used. No one knew me here. "That's why I'm asking."

She looked indecisive. "Why don't you give me a nickname?"

"So you won't have to invent something?"

"So I won't have to tell you a lie." Her tone was light, but the look in her eye was serious. My noble princess.

"How about Chiyo, then?"

A smile lit her face, surprised and pleased by the suggestion. "My friends used to call me that! That works." She held my gaze wonderingly, as if I'd read her mind. I found myself losing myself in her eyes, my anticipation rising as her nervous breath stuttered a little. "I would be honored if you would show me your talents, Jiro-san."

"And I would be honored to show you." I drew a long breath of my own and tore myself away from her, trying to focus on the task before me. I began laying the rope on the seats, examining what Aya had given me. Varying thicknesses, varying materials. Most of it was silk-smooth yet it was not silk, and the colors ranged from blue to red. I undid some of the coils and then coiled them up again, making sure they would unroll in my hand free of tangles.

When I turned around to look at her again, my

breath caught. She had stripped down to her underthings and was standing there in bare feet—her hands clasped in front of her, though, as if she were unaccustomed to being so exposed. She bit her lip nervously.

I took my own shirt off so that she would not feel she was the only one so bare. I had not realized I had stepped so close to her until I nearly bumped her with my arm as I pulled the shirt over my head. One of her hands fluttered up as if she meant to touch my skin, but then hesitated, unsure if that was allowed.

I caught her hand in mine and held it flat against my chest. Could she feel how hard my heart was beating? She smiled and blushed again, dropping her eyes even as she took pleasure in running her hand over my skin.

Thus began a sensual dance, the steps slow and measured, as I centered my own rope over her breastbone and began to tie her. The bra she wore felt like silk, too, and I slipped the rope around her ribs, over the shoulders, creating a design both beautiful and functional if I were ever to restrain her.

The mere thought sent my blood surging. "Do you like to fight?"

Her grin showed her teeth. "I love to fight. Is that allowed?"

"No one told me it isn't," I said. I looked around at the others in filtering into the club. Aya was greeting a couple near the door who looked like they had stepped out of a Heian era painting of a lady and her loyal retainer. In the niche across from us a pair who looked like they had come on motorcycles had stripped out of their gear and were sorting through a collection of rope that had sparking lights embedded in it like fireflies.

I found myself whispering in her ear. "Struggle."

She pulled against me, then, as if trying to get free. I held the knot I had made against her spine, though, at first merely keeping her from escape. Then I twisted my fist, tightening all the ropes across her back. She gave a cry, the sudden pressure on her shoulders making her go still.

I pulled her back against me then and felt the fight go out of her, as if she had fallen under my spell. I was the one utterly enchanted by her, though. My free hand fit perfectly over the ridge of her hip and one finger slid under the edge of her silk underwear.

I was suddenly aware of Aya watching from a discreet distance away.

"I'll add some ropes here," I said, running my hand across the flat of Chiyo's stomach.

She nodded, pressing against me eagerly.

* * *

When Jiro took his shirt off I think my mouth watered. In the colored lights of the club I couldn't quite tell whether the dark honey tone of his skin was real or my imagination, but nothing could hide the fine, smooth expanse of his chest or the exquisite shape of his muscles. I had never gotten used to how hairy American guys were whereas Jiro, like many Japanese men, was nearly hairless. And this was the man whose job was to please me? I was very, very pleased indeed.

A small part of me was disappointed at first that

he treated me so carefully. I had worked myself up to imagining that a rope top would be all boss, with harsh words and slaps, like they so often were in porn clips. But when he pressed my hesitant hand against his skin I realized this was far better than the movies. This was a man of flesh and blood, a man willing to share something special with me. I felt the throb of my desire all the way down into the pit of my stomach— and lower from there, as well.

The throb only increased when he told me to struggle—ah! There was the commanding figure I had imagined!—and as he took control of me strand by strand, loop by loop, I could feel my panties growing damp.

He pulled my arms back, securing them there. That left my chest thrust outward. Even with my bra still on I felt exposed and brazen. I looked down. The hard points of my nipples were sharply visible through the silk. When he came to stand in front of me, his eyes lingered on them and I could not help but yearn for him to touch them.

His fingers traced the rope from the top of my shoulder downward and I took a deep breath, as if trying to lift my chest toward them. A whimper escaped me as he let his knuckles brush over one erect point. He held still then and I shamelessly panted, letting my nipple brush against his fingers again and again. His eyes were locked with mine rather than looking at my breasts, even as he brought the other hand into place so I could show him how much I needed that touch.

"I can make them even more sensitive," he said, his voice low and tranquil.

"Can you?"

He nodded and began to add a new layer to the ropes criss-crossing my upper torso. Each new strand squeezed my breasts a little more than the previous one, making them stand out from my body. Across the way I could see a woman was being tied in a similar fashion, only more extreme. She was naked and her nipples stood out like dark circles on the strained, tight flesh of her tits.

"Turn around," he said, and I faced into the niche instead of toward the room, as if he wanted to keep this view of my front for himself, at least for now.

Another rope went around my waist, and then, as he stood very close behind me, so close I felt the tickle of his breath on the back of my neck, he pulled a rope between my legs. Then a second one. I sucked in a breath as one of them bumped across my clit. Then he tugged and tightened them and I felt the two ropes spreading my labia apart.

I wished I had been as brave as the woman across the way, fully nude, but instead my clit was trapped in my heavily moistening underwear.

His fingers slid along the rope as if checking how it lay, and I felt his fingertips brush where I was wettest. I bucked my hips, trying to get him to let me rub my clit against him the way he had allowed me to rub my nipples, but he pulled away with a scolding noise.

"But why?" I heard myself say. "What must I do?"

"Obey," he whispered into my ear.

"Yes, yes, please," I moaned. "Whatever you want."

I felt his grip in the center of my back again. "Kneel," he ordered.

I went slowly down, his grip never wavering, as I dropped to one knee, then tucked the other into seiza, my ass coming to rest on my feet in the formal style. The ropes pulled harder on my labia and I whimpered.

He pulled me up a few inches. "Spread your knees if that's where you crave my touch."

I spread as wide as I could and looked up at him, pleading with my eyes.

He sank down behind me, pulling my torso back against him with one hand while the other hand toyed with the ropes that crossed under my navel.

"Remember I said your nipples would get more sensitive?"

"Yes?"

His answer was to brush his fingers across my nipples again, drawing gasps out of me. Both hands now flicked the hard nubs and I bucked, desire pouring through me. I could almost come from such a touch!

Almost. He played and played with my nipples, while I moaned and gasped and thrashed against him, but it was not quite enough. Maybe if I had not been wearing a bra it would have been? Or maybe I required a bit more direct stimulation between my legs.

The pleasurable torment to my breasts ended when he turned his attention at last to my long neglected clit. He slid a finger between the twin ropes and I froze, needing it so very much I dared not move.

"Like this?" he whispered, as he slowly circled the engorged place. I wondered if the same effect that had made my breasts extra sensitive was at work down below, as well.

255

"Yes," I said. "Yes."

There was no hurry in him as he traced every hidden ridge of my vulva between circles of my clit, methodical and delicate as a painter at work.

"Please, Jiro," I begged. "Please."

He held me tight with one arm while his other hand continued to torture me with pleasure. "I have you," he said. "When you are in my ropes, I will take care of you. You are my responsibility."

"I need—"

"I know. If I may, then?"

"Yes, please, please!"

He slipped his fingers under the edge of my panties then, and a single bare finger slid over my desperate clit. Again he did not hurry, but the friction was greater, and as he crooked his finger he could catch the flesh in exactly the right way. I cried out, growing closer and closer.

I feared he would pull away and deny me when the time came, but he did not, upholding his promise to take care of me very thoroughly, continuing to move his slick fingertip against me as I screamed with orgasm. That careful, caring finger wrung every last bit of my need from me and left me panting and limp within the ropes.

My awareness was dim for a few moments after that, my attention all centered on the way his damp hand cupped me and held me fast, comforting and calming. Then the sounds of the couple across the way reached my ears. She was making cries much like my own, but then they were suddenly muffled. I opened my eyes to focus and was amazed to see she was hanging from ropes like a package being lifted into the hold of a ship. What had silenced her was nothing less than the cock of her partner, who had suspended her at just the right height for her mouth to reach him.

I grew very suddenly aware of Jiro's desire, so tightly trammeled I wondered if it were against his principles to show his lust in public. There was something old-school about him; that sort of thing wouldn't have surprised me.

I looked over my shoulder at him. He tore his gaze away from the display across the way and met mine. It all happened in an instant then: I wanted a kiss, he wanted to kiss me, we saw it in each other's eyes, and we kissed, his lips meeting mine in a sudden claiming that I don't think either of us expected. His other hand gripped me by the hair, keeping my mouth against his as his tongue sought entrance, the tip jabbing me even as his fingers below matched the movement. I moaned into his mouth, unsure I would be able to come again so quickly, but his fingers and mouth seemed to demand it, to command it. The scream this time stayed trapped in my throat until his tongue withdrew and allowed me full release.

This time my awareness never left his eyes. He pulled his fingers free of my panties and held them to my face. I licked them eagerly, grateful and obedient at the same time, eager to show him that if he wanted more, I was willing to give.

We both looked around. The Heian couple was on a dais and the retainer had been bound on his back over some kind of low furniture. His cock and balls had also been entwined such that his cock pointed directly at the ceiling. His lady hiked up her robes and straddled him. The folds of cloth hid the actual penetration from our sight but from the way she moved I did not doubt what was going on.

I looked to Jiro again. "Is that... allowed?"

"Apparently, it is," he said carefully, licking his lower lip.

"Would you like...? I mean, that is... with me, could we...?" I could not find the proper way to ask. Perhaps there was no proper way to express what could only be considered too bold.

"I think we should find a more private place," Jiro murmured into my ear. "If you... that is... if you are comfortable with that."

"Yes, please!" All fear that I might be in danger if I were alone with a stranger was gone. Jiro no longer felt at all like a stranger. He felt like the man I'd been waiting my entire life to meet. "I am on NoCept, if you're worried about that."

"Pardon me?"

"A conception blocker," I clarified, in case he didn't know the brand name.

"Aha. Let me free your arms," he said. He helped me to my feet and then undid the ropes binding my arms behind me. I was slightly disappointed that he also let free my lower half, though truthfully with the ropes between my legs as tight as they were, walking would have been uncomfortable. He also loosened and removed some of the ropes around my breasts, but kept the main harness he'd started with untouched.

Zaka was apparently all too happy to rent me a room at a love hotel he owned, one that was conveniently located only a few blocks from Rope Club.

Chapter Four

While Chiyo put her clothes back on, Zaka said farewell to me with a mournful look. "I didn't expect to lose you so soon! But you clearly are meant for each other."

"Do you think so?"

"I know so, my friend. You are clearly utterly smitten with each other." He cleared his throat and adopted a more cynical tone. "Well, I suppose the real test is whether that feeling survives the morning light. Now, the place I'm sending you, the rooms are very special."

"Are they?"

"Well, of course they are equipped with all the usual supplies, but there are some special pieces of equipment for rope enthusiasts. Be careful, though, all right? And if you have any emergency, there is a panic button you can hit that will summon medical help. But try to avoid needing it, will you?"

"Yes, of course." I bowed to him. "Thank you."

"And take your cat, please! She's chewing on my bonsai."

He gave a pay card to Chiyo that would give us entrance to the hotel and to our room.

We stepped out onto the street together. Though

she tried to remain casual, I saw Chiyo's eyes scan around us.

I discerned no immediate danger. "Are you worried?"

She gave me a fleeting smile. "I should tell you. There are some men looking for me. I... I don't belong here."

"I guessed that," I said, without saying what I had thought: this was Princess Ami. I did give her a small bow. "I am at your service."

The slight bow she gave me back only confirmed for me she was who I thought.

At the hotel we let ourselves into the building and then up a flight of stairs.

"Oooh, look at this!" she said excitedly as she hurried down the empty hallway toward something.

I hurried to see what bondage implement or sex aid she had discovered, then stifled a laugh. There was a vending machine. HOT NOODLES proclaimed the lettering.

"I didn't realize I was hungry until now," she said, digging in her pockets for some cash. "Can we? Do you want some, too?"

"Of course, we can. And I would be honored."

"Excellent." She fed money into the slot and pressed a series of buttons. The machine hummed, a cup dropped into a slot, and the sound of liquid pouring reached my ears. So did the scent of soup.

Once two cups had been procured, along with chopsticks, we found our room. The heavy door swung open at the insertion of the card and then shut solidly behind us, sensibly soundproof.

We sat on the edge of the bed to eat, while Neko

emerged from my jacket and explored the edges of the room.

The noodles were not as good as those fresh from a stand, but they were quite edible. She sighed happily while eating them. "I should be honest with you," she said, her face turning serious. "I mean, I feel like, if we're going to have sex, it's only fair for you to know."

"That you're Princess Ami?"

Her eyes widened. "Damn. I hoped I was better disguised than that."

"You look very different from the last time I saw you up close," I assured her.

Now her look turned to one of amazement. "When did we meet?"

"At a hospital. I was the man you woke."

Her hand went over her mouth. "I thought you looked like him! But then I thought, no, it's my imagination. I thought about you so much the last few weeks I—" She broke off, blushing. "But that's not what I was going to tell you. I was going to tell you..." Now she trailed off and looked into her mostly empty cup, her shoulders sagging.

"You don't have to tell me anything," I said. "I am at your service and I meant that sincerely."

Her hand found mine then and squeezed it. I set our cups aside then so I could hold hers in both of mine.

"My father arranged a marriage for me," she said, almost in a whisper. "It's barbaric, like something from another time, but this whole conservative movement, the whole need to uphold tradition in the family... I don't know what to do. I don't want to go through with it. It's so hard to explain."

I blinked away the tears that threatened to form, hearing the sadness and resignation in her voice. "I know what you're feeling," I said.

"You do?"

"My family was also a very traditional family, from an old samurai line. After my elder brother died, my father also arranged a marriage for me. I had fallen for a young woman, though, and convinced myself only she could make me happy." I drew a long, deep breath. My memories of the old Chiyo seemed very dim and far away, as if she had faded during my time asleep. The thing I remembered most about her was her willingness to let me do whatever I wanted to her. At the time it had seemed an act of love but now I saw it for stoicism, for withstanding what it would take to snare the impressionable son of a higher ranked family. I saw now that the ardor had been one-sided, mine.

Nothing made that clearer than the brightness and heat with which the woman in front of me burned. "I had decided to defy my father. But I fell into that sleep before I could tell him."

"Oh, Jiro." Her hand touched my cheek and I felt it was a bit damp.

"While I slept, tragedy befell everyone I had known." Akio. I had mourned the loss of Akio when I had first awoken. He was the only person I truly missed. "I think I would have slept forever, until I died, except..." How could I say this to her? It was too much.

She had no trouble saying what I could not. "Maybe you were just waiting for the right woman to come along."

I had to smile at that.

"So you really do know what I'm going through," she said.

"Yes. Do you think you're going to go through with it?"

"I don't know. I certainly don't want to. My father has this insane idea that the male supremacy movement will die down once I'm married. Or something like that." She sighed heavily. "That's not everything, though. A couple thousand years of tradition. Can I put my personal desires ahead of that? Like it or not, I'm part of the history of this nation. I take that responsibility seriously."

I nodded. The weight of my own family's traditions had been heavy enough. "My family were once protectors of the imperial family."

"Were?"

"My father would never speak of what drove my grandfather to Nagasaki. When he had drunk too much he would occasionally rail at my elder brother to seek a chance to redeem the family name, but I don't think that by dying in the military he managed it."

He had also sometimes ranted that it was the displeasure of the gods that had caused me to be born lame. Was it the pleasure of the gods then, that allowed me to walk without suffering now? Or was that modern medicine? I could not help but wonder if fate had brought me and the princess together somehow. Though at the moment it seemed more that her heart needed protecting than her life. Well, perhaps that was what I was here for.

An inquisitive meow came from above us and we looked up to see Neko perched on a solid metal beam overhead. The beam had hooks and holes that were clearly intended for rope to go through. Chiyo laughed and stood up, trying to coax the kitten down, but she frolicked to the other end and disappeared behind the hanging light fixture.

There were also places to run ropes attached to the bed and up and down the wall. In a cabinet I also found several more skeins, neatly coiled.

The wall was padded. That meant it was not only comfortable to lean—or be tied—against, it was probably comfortable to be fucked against. So long as there weren't too many knots on one's back.

I called Chiyo to me and she came for a kiss, her eyes misty and soft. "Tie me?"

"Of course. I was thinking this wall begs to be made into a work of art." I undid the harness she was wearing, sliding the rope through my fingers while I considered what to do. "This is a family heirloom," I told her, and let her feel it for herself. "It dates back to the time the family served in the palace. My brother would have inherited the sword. Me, this."

"I much prefer this," she said with a sly smile. Her hand slid along my thigh. "This is the only sword I'm interested in." Through the fabric of my trousers, she cupped my cock with her hand and it firmed to her touch.

I decided I definitely preferred the future to the past. "Soon." I slipped the loop of rope around her and she let go of me to hold her arms out so I could wind it about her torso. This time I made a crossing pattern, not to constrict her but to beautify her. Then I added the ropes that squeezed her breasts into prominence. When they were thrust forward so, how could I keep from brushing against her nipples constantly as I worked to tie her to the wall? I could not. I made her into a butterfly caught in a spider's web, ready to be pinned in place. I bound her arms out to the sides, laying kisses along the inside of her arms and the underside of her wrists before immobilizing them with rope.

"Bend your leg," I murmured, and she lifted one. I bound her with that knee bent, her leg to the side, displaying how ripe and wet she was to me. I slid a finger along the exposed cleft and found her dripping with anticipation.

I stepped back to admire the view of her, spread out before me like a mandala, her flawless skin crossed with rope, like perfectly spaced stitches on the hem of a kimono. I stepped forward to do one more thing to make the image perfect, which was to gather her hair atop her head in a topknot, leaving her shoulders bare. Her breasts were swollen and dark now from the constriction of the rope and I brushed them with the backs of my fingers. She moaned, the redolent scent of her desire rising from where her legs were bound apart.

I slipped two fingers between her legs and feeling how wet and swollen she was only aroused me even more. I slicked my already erect cock with her juices, teasing her with my shaft, preparing to do at last what we had come to a private space to do.

This time when I lost consciousness there was not the roar or the light of the previous time, only the pain in my head and then a long dark tunnel that seemed to get longer all the time.

Chapter Five

The smile that spread across Taka's face as he took in the situation was glacial, both slow and cold. He nudged Jiro with his foot to ensure he was unconscious and then licked his lips as he looked up and down my naked form, spread open and helpless before him. "I told you once, didn't I, that being tied up was dangerous?"

I didn't answer him, my cheeks burning with humiliation. "You didn't have to hurt him! He's just a guy."

Taka chuckled and I wondered how long he was going to drag this out before he hauled me back to the imperial penthouse and my father. They'd probably chain me up until my wedding day, and not in a fun way. He looked me up and down again, his laugh growing in strength. Probably imagining how much fun it would be to describe this to my father. He took out his iWand and toyed with it, as if trying to decide whether to photograph me like this.

I huffed. "Going to get some personal porno shots, eh, Taka?"

He stuck the iWand back into his pocket. "Oh no, Princess. I plan to do much better than that."

He stepped close and ran his hand roughly

through the wetness at my crotch. "You deserve this," he said, and thrust a finger into me.

I growled in outrage. "Now you're over the line."

"I? I'm the one over the line? No, princess, you are the one who invited this to happen. It's this kind of wanton disrespect, wanton weakness, that causes bad things to happen to women like you."

Wanton disrespect? "What on earth are you talking about?"

He began to undo his belt. "You need to be taught a lesson. Your father knew he let it go too long. He should have married you to someone with a firm hand long ago, someone who could rein you in. All your love of bondage pornography, you know that's your psyche yearning to be put in your proper place, don't you? The more you need it, the stronger the urge is."

"Oh, so now it's my conscience driving me to like porn, not my moral weakness?"

He slapped me across the face. "Be silent. You have no more to say." He kicked off his shoes, stripped off his trousers, and then balled up his underwear. He stuffed them into my mouth and then taped across my cheeks to hold it in place. "Remember, bitch, you are the one who tempted me into this. Otherwise I would have just killed you."

Wait, killed me? He was going to kill me?

"But you are the one who tempted me with your sports bras and... and..." He apparently was so overcome with lust he could not speak and he suckled on the insanely sensitive tip of one of my breasts instead while his hand worked between my legs, getting a second finger into me. The truly insane thing was how good that felt, because my body didn't know he was a crazed traitor with murder on his mind.

"Maybe I should thank you for making my job easier." He lifted his head and licked his lips. "Now instead of killing you and then myself, I can instead merely frame your lover here. Don't you know it's dangerous to go alone with the men you meet at clubs? And to let them tie you up?" He shook his head in mock sadness. "This sex-crazed maniac who raped you and then killed you. A national tragedy that will surely close down the entire sex club trade and show the rightness of the male supremacy movement."

Taka was a male supremacist! He rubbed his cock against my thigh and I tried to scream through the gag. But I knew it was no use. Surely they were used to people screaming in these rooms all the time. Even if there were security cameras on us, nothing he was doing right now looked out of the ordinary if the porno clips I had been watching were any indication. Not even when he took out a knife. It gleamed as he wove sinuous cuts in the air, smiling like he enjoyed the feel of it in his hand almost as much as his cock in the other.

For a moment I prayed that he was only trying to scare me again, that in another moment he would cut me free, say he hoped I'd learned my lesson, and then drag me away to my father.

But no. "I will fuck you while you're dying," he said. "How many men can say they raped a woman while she bled out? Or that they came in a dead bitch's body?" He got a condom from the dispenser by the bed and put it on, I suppose so he wouldn't leave DNA evidence. He also put on rubber gloves, then made sure to put Jiro's fingerprints all over the handle of the knife.

He slid his dick between my legs and the condom felt cold from the lubricant on it. He dug around with his fingers, trying to find the right angle to penetrate me, but I squirmed as best I could, thwarting him somewhat. Perhaps that's what drove him to decide to stab me first.

"Good night, Princess," he said as he drew back his arm to thrust the knife straight into my heart.

But as he lunged, the knife twisted out of his hand and clattered to the floor, as if he'd struck a Plexiglas wall. He stared in disbelief, picked it up, and tried again. Same result, and this time he shook his whole hand and wrist as if they'd taken the shock of running into brick. He picked it up a third time, and this time ran his hands over the rope harness on my chest.

"This must be Kevlar or something," he muttered to himself. He slipped the knife under one loop and tried to saw it through, but it did not cut. He made a grunt of frustration and carefully touched the tip of the knife to my bare skin, making sure the rope did not block it, gripping the handle in one fist and pressing the palm of the other hand against the butt. I wanted to spit in his eye but the gag prevented it.

Before Taka could drive the knife into my chest, though, he suddenly had a face full of clawing kitten. He stumbled back, the knife falling to the carpet with a thud, Neko landing a few feet away with a vehement hiss. Taka wiped at his eyes, while I held my breath: Jiro was climbing to his feet and brandishing a length of rope.

Taka's vision cleared before Jiro could move in,

269

though. Taka snatched up the knife. I could see they were both on the balls of their feet, ready to spring into action. I pushed at the cloth in my mouth with my tongue, trying to dislodge it. The tape was not well applied and I could feel it pulling away from my skin.

Taka lunged so quickly the knife was a blur, but Jiro danced away.

I was accustomed to seeing the focused look of a fighter on Taka's face, but now Jiro wore the same. They were measuring each other, I realized. Taka lunged again. This time Jiro twisted away and they circled slowly. I shook my head and pushed and finally got the wadded underwear out of my mouth. The tape hung loose from one of my cheeks.

Taka lunged a third time and Jiro twisted, but this time instead of twirling away, he stayed in close, looping the rope around Taka's neck.

Taka dropped the knife to claw at the rope tightening around his windpipe.

"Should I kill him, princess?" Jiro asked me.

"No," I said immediately. "He should stand trial for this."

"As you wish." Jiro held fast to the rope as Taka struggled, trying to kick out his legs but failing to free himself. He eventually went limp from lack of oxygen and Jiro quickly tied his hands and feet before sitting him up.

"What are you doing now?"

"Reviving him," Jiro said, and bent Taka forward, then struck him between the shoulder blades. Taka jerked awake. "Now we can interrogate him about what other plans there may be to assassinate you, princess."

He had a point. Normally I would have left that to our family's private security force. But Taka was the head of that force. Could any of his men be trusted?

"You had better let me loose, then," I pointed out.

Jiro bowed. "I am sorry for the interruption, my princess."

"As am I."

But as he stepped toward me to undo the ropes, Taka swung his bound legs around, catching Jiro in the ankle. Jiro went down and the next thing I knew, Taka had gotten his legs around Jiro's neck. Jiro's face was starting to look like Taka's had before he had passed out from lack of oxygen.

The little cat hissed at Taka then, and I wondered if she were going to try to attack him.

"Neko!"

She batted at Taka's shoulder with her claws extended but then ran to the end of the bed and pounced directly onto the panic button.

The lights immediately brightened and I heard a sound that must have been the door unlocking automatically. "Help!" I screamed. "Help!"

I could see Jiro's eyes were closing.

"Help!"

The door burst open and Zaka and Aya came in. Aya kicked Taka in the face and he went limp while Zaka began cutting me free. My leg came down and I shook it. Then my arms, then the bindings around my breasts... no. The knife flew out of his hand. He chuckled. "Whoops. I must have gotten too close to Jiro's rope. I mean you no harm, princess."

"You know who I am? And you know about... Jiro's rope?"

271

"I had my suspicions about you, princess. And I know more about that rope than Jiro does. Come, there will be many explanations to make tonight." He handed me a kimono and then assisted Aya in helping Jiro to his feet. "Is the building secure?" he seemed to ask the general air.

"It is now," came a voice from a speaker hidden somewhere near the door.

"Then let us have tea. Come, Neko." Zaka held out his arm and the little cat jumped onto his elbow and clambered up to his shoulder, where she rode, her eyes scanning back and forth for any more trouble. But that was the end of the trouble for that night.

Chapter Six

If I thought my father was going to be difficult to convince of the conspiracy to kill me, I was wrong. I contacted him after Zaka smuggled us out of the city to a village where he assured us we would be well taken care of. The village was quite quaint, but the house Zaka brought us to was equipped with a full net feed and video conferencing.

My father's face on the one-meter wide screen showed only relief when he saw me, and he reached out to touch the screen as if he could cup my cheek. I smiled. "Are you safe?" he asked. "Ami-chan, I've been so worried. At first Taka claimed you had run away, and I believed him! Now he's in the hands of the police and I find out he is part of the plot to kill you?"

"Wait, you knew there was a plot to kill me?"

"Well, yes—"

"And you didn't think maybe I should know that?"

"We canceled your appearances to protect you. I told you that."

"I thought you canceled them because you were being a controlling dick," I said, far more coldly than I thought I could. "I've tolerated your treatment of me for too long already. Honestly. You knew there was an active assassination plot and you did not bother to inform me?"

"Well, it might have been only a rumor." He would not meet my gaze now. "I didn't want to worry you."

"Why, because women shouldn't ever have to worry our little empty heads about anything? I'm going to have plenty to worry about when I'm empress, you know."

"Ami-chan." He tried to talk to me like you would a child. "You've had a scare, you're not rational."

"No, *you* are not rational, speaking to a grown woman that way." The scare had been a full day before, anyway. "You want to know what saved me? I have a new protector now."

"What? What are you talking about?"

"Don't be stupid about this, Father. I don't trust any of Taka's men after this. My new head of security is this man here." I gestured for Jiro to step forward where the camera could see him. I introduced him formally to my father and he bowed deeply toward the camera without looking up at my father's face.

My father frowned. "That name is somewhat familiar."

"He is from a samurai lineage that formerly served as protectors to ours. He is the one who incapacitated Taka when Taka was attacking me."

My father appeared to digest this news. "And he is pledged to protect you?"

"Yes," I said at the same time as Jiro, who bowed again.

"You clean house," I said, "and tell me when it's safe to come back so I can take the Chrysanthemum throne from you." I had used up all my coldness, though. Now my anger flared hot and bright. "You allowed this to fester right under your nose! You and your blind, backward, idiot ways!" The look on his face said I drove a knife into his heart when I screamed: "You don't deserve to be emperor." And I twisted it: "You don't deserve to be my father!"

He bowed his head, shame-faced. "You're right. I do not. To think I almost lost you! Ami, you must understand, because you are my only child, I've lived in fear—"

"In cowardice."

His nod was almost a short bow, not speaking.

"Everyone has fear. Everyone, Papa. You can't let that control you and pretend it's love."

Again the short nod. This time I could see a single tear shining on his cheek. This is a man I had never seen cry. Not even after he drove my mother away. The supposed reason had been her inability to bear another child. Yet he had never remarried.

He mastered his emotions and stood with his back straight. "Very well. How shall we handle the opponents to female succession?"

"We must use this as an opportunity to swing public opinion against the male supremacists once and for all. Send Kumiko to me. She's taking over family PR as of right now."

"She is highly qualified," he said, as if he had any choice in the matter, but I let him save face. Then he looked at me directly for the first time since the video call had begun. "You are the same age I was when I

275

took the throne," he said, his voice gruff with suppressed emotion.

The same year I was born. "You're not even 50 yet, you know. You could still re-marry."

A look of surprise flitted across his face. "I did not think you would tolerate another woman in your mother's place, Ami-chan."

Another flare of anger went through me, but I tempered it with the knowledge that this was a major confession for my father to make. For him to say anything about his emotions was unheard of. "No one will ever replace my mother. But you shouldn't live without love, Papa."

I could not miss the scarlet color that flushed his face. And I suddenly knew. Ryoko, his assistant. Talk about being blind to what went on in one's own house.

"Marry Ryoko," I said. "Marry her and have a son. Then I can abdicate in another 20 years or so."

I saw then a glimpse of another emotion on my father's face: joy. "Somehow you have grown wise and I have grown foolish," he said. "I love you, my daughter. I love you more than I can say. I realize I have been poor in demonstrating it with my actions. I will do better with that from now on." He bowed to me then and a lump caught in my throat at the sight. My proud father bowing so low. It felt like a new beginning.

* * *

Zaka's clan took good care of us. They had been here forever—in this village of silk weavers who made quite a fuss over Jiro's heirloom rope. They also knew better than to try to separate us.

Jiro laid the rope aside as we sat at a low table for a late meal.

"What happened to your family's sword?" I asked.

"Lost in the bombing of Nagasaki," he said, his eyes somber.

"Oh." It was a subject every schoolchild learned, the seriousness of the event carrying down from generation to generation even though it was no longer within living memory for anyone. Or so I thought.

"I believe I was thrown forward in time so that you could have a protector. Something in the rope drew me to you in your time of need."

I folded my hand over his. "But you left everyone you knew behind, then."

"Yes." He bowed his head. "Maybe I was chosen to come forward, though, because I was the one thinking of running away. I am honored and blessed to be the one to restore my family's name."

I squeezed his hand. "You could have been killed. Taka was stupid to let you lie there without tying you up."

He raised my hand to his lips and kissed it. "He thought I was nothing more than a random man you picked up in a bar. And he was completely distracted by the naked beauty in front of him."

I pulled his hand to me and kissed it in turn. "Speaking of my time of need. We were interrupted." I sucked on his index finger then, tonguing it gently and sliding my lips down the length lewdly.

"So we were."

"Are you going to have a problem taking care of me in bed now that I'm going to be empress?" I asked.

In answer he flattened me against the tatami and suckled my neck until I squirmed, trying to free myself. It tickled! And aroused. And I could not get free, no matter what tricks I tried—not even the escape Taka had taught me!—for Jiro had braced his own legs wide to keep my hips in place.

When Jiro lifted his mouth from my neck, his lips were swollen and glossy, and I wanted him to kiss my mouth. "Tie me?" I asked.

"No, empress. Not this time. If you want me to serve you, you'll lie perfectly still now."

"Will you kiss me if I do?"

"Put your hands above your head. Grasp the leg of the table. Do not let go and I will kiss you," he said.

I did as he asked and was rewarded with a deep kiss that left me gasping. He worked his way downward then, unbuttoning my shirt to expose my breasts and leaving a trail of kisses from one nipple to the other. Then working his way lower, until he was pulling my pants off. I lifted my hips to help him but did not let go of the leg of the table.

His kisses then began at my ankle and worked maddeningly light, maddeningly gradual, up my leg, grazing my knee and dotting my inner thigh. When his lips nudged my labia aside, hunting for my clit, I cried out with the intensity of the pleasure those gentle touches brought me. And cried out again as his tongue increased it tenfold.

He raised his head and I made a whine of dismay that the pleasure had stopped, then saw that he was making sure I had not let go of the table leg. I had not. His eyes met mine with a nod of approval and he dipped his head again to continue his task of bringing me to orgasm. This time he did not pause, but carried right on until I was thrusting against his mouth, crying out and drumming my heels with abandon. Perhaps it was all the interruptions, all the excitement, all the many times I had been aroused but not released over the past two days, but it was by far the most intense orgasm I'd had in my life. I saw sparks fly before my eyes and it felt as if I were plunged down into the depths of the ocean, from the rushing sound in my ears to the feeling that I was being enveloped in something larger than human life.

And still he did not stop, his tongue lapping at my center bringing me back to awareness of my skin, my blood, and my pleasure rising again like a diver, up and up until I had another peak, this one bright and hot like the sudden sun on my face.

I was still in its throes when he slipped a finger into me and sent ripples across my entire body. "You are truly blocked from conceiving?" he checked.

"Yes," I said, glad that the answer could be given in one syllable, since I didn't think I could manage more than that. "Yes, yes!"

"I suppose the same medical miracle that healed my lame leg could do no less." He got to his feet, looking down on where I lay, debauched, still clutching the wood between my fingers. He smiled when he saw that, as he disrobed completely.

I marveled again at the beauty of his body, sculpted by movement rather than chemicals or weight-lifting, and the elegant taper of his cock, a natural and organic shape.

He knelt between my legs and leaned down to plant a kiss upon my mons. "It is an honor to serve you."

"Your sword, please. Onegaishimasu."

He bent one of my legs toward my chest, clutching it against his own, as he aligned himself and I felt the blunt tip of him searching for the right angle. Then, swift and sure as a blade, it cleaved me. He held still, his eyes closing for a moment, and I wondered if he was feeling the same sweet rightness as I was. When his eyes fluttered open to meet mine, I wondered no longer.

That feeling blossomed as he withdrew slowly and then thrust again, never taking his gaze from mine. I was not a virgin, but I had never been taken like this, never been loved like this, with such connection. Sex with the boys I had known in college had been about making sure we both got off. That was "equality." This was something else entirely: a joining. Each movement, each thrust, was for our mutual pleasure, a step we took together in a dance. My hips rocked in time with his as we fell into a rhythm as old as the sea.

I felt myself being swept up again on a tide of pleasure, threatening to plunge me down into the depths again, but I didn't want to lose the connection between us by falling into my own pleasure. I held my breath, holding back, yearning toward him with my eyes.

"Let go," he said, and I didn't know what he meant.

"Let go of the table, and hold onto me," he went on. "I have you. I have you my princess, my empress, my goddess. I have you."

I let go the table and clung to him then like he was a raft on a raging wave, as pleasure did sweep me away, drowning me in the ultimate ecstasy, every fiber of me singing as if I had become one with the universe.

And then the tide receded and left me lying there, gasping and blinking. His mouth descended to mine and I breathed in the sweet, vibrant air from his lungs as our tongues and lips slid against each other. He was still pumping in and out of me, but his hips moved with short jerks now, as he neared his own flood of ecstasy.

"You now, Jiro," I said. "Hold onto me."

He did the same as I had, locking me in a rigid embrace. He gave a shout when orgasm struck him and carried him like a rip current. And then he came to rest atop me, his head against my chest as he let out a long sigh.

You may not believe that the gods destine lovers for one another, but I do not have to doubt it. We feel it to the very depths of our bones that we were meant for each other, and so long as we feel that way, it is no one's job to question otherwise.

About the Authors

Laura Antoniou, Midori, and Cecilia Tan are three of the best-known writers and educators in the erotic world of leather and BDSM. All three of them regularly teach workshops at BDSM conventions and conferences, write articles, and create fiction bringing together the passionate fantasies of dominance and submission with memorable characters and stories.

Laura Antoniou

Laura is the author of *The Killer Wore Leather* (which won the Pauline Reage Novel Award and the Rainbow Award, and was a finalist for the Lambda Literary Award) and the creator of the ground-breaking, bestselling (over 400,000 books sold) "Marketplace" series of books about an underground BDSM society. Originally published under the name Sara Adamson, the first three Marketplace books became instant classics, "must reads" for anyone discovering bondage for the first time, and various volumes have been published in Germany, Japan, Korea, and Israel. She has also edited several anthologies of erotic fiction, including *Leatherwomen* and *Some Women*. Her short stories have appeared in *Best Lesbian Erotica, SM Classics, Once Upon a Time,* and many other anthologies. She can be found on Patreon at http://patreon.com/kvetch

Midori

Dubbed "the super nova of kink" by Dan Savage, Midori is a globe-trotting sexuality educator and writer. Her classes are humanistic, funny and warm, revving up sex lives, and encouraging self discovery and personal growth and include her trademarked Rope Dojo and Forte Femme women's intensive weekend workshops. She is originally from Japan, but now is based in San Francisco, and is the author of several books. In her nonfiction portfolio are the how-to volumes *The Seductive Art of Japanese Bondage, Wild Side Sex*, and the *Toybag Guide to Foot & Shoe Worship*, and on the fiction side she created a sexy, cyberpunk future with the short story collection *Master Han's Daughter*, which was a finalist for the Lambda Literary Award. When not writing or teaching, she is deeply involved with HIV/AIDS fundraising and develops interactive museum art installations. You can support her art via her Patreon account at https://www.patreon.com/PlanetMidori

Cecilia Tan

One of the leading erotica writers and editors of the past 25 years, Cecilia Tan is the author of many novels, short story collections, and online serials, editor of over a hundred anthologies, and the founder and editorial director of Circlet Press. She is a 2014 recipient of the RT Book Reviews Pioneer Award and the Career Achievement Award for erotic fiction, and her novel *Slow Surrender* won the Maggie Award for Excellence and the RT Reviewers Choice Award for Erotic Romance in 2013. Her other books include the Secrets of a Rock Star Series from Hachette/Grand Central Publishing, the Magic University Series (Riverdale Avenue Books), *The Prince's Boy, Mind Games, White Flame*s (Running Press), *Black Feathers* (HarperCollins), among others, and her short stories have appeared in *Best Women's Erotica, Best American Erotica, The Mammoth Book of Best New Erotica, Ms. Magazine, Asimov's*, and *Nerve*. She was inducted into the Saints and Sinners Writers Hall of Fame in 2010 and won the 2010 Rose & Bay Award for fiction. Her Patreon can be found at http://patreon.com/ceciliatan

If You Liked This Title, You Might Also Like:

The Circlet Treasury of Erotic Wonderland
Edited by J. Blackmore

The Circlet Treasury of Erotic Steampunk
Edited by J. Blackmore & Cecilia Tan

*The Circlet Treasury of Lesbian Erotic Science
Fiction and Fantasy*
Edited By Cecilia Tan

*The Siren and the Sword:
Book One of the Magic University Series*
By Cecilia Tan

*The Tower and the Tears:
Book Two of the Magic University Series*
By Cecilia Tan

*The Incubus and the Angel:
Book Three of the Magic University Series*

Spellbinding: Tales from Magic University
Edited by Cecilia Tan

*The Poet and The Prophecy
Book Four of the Magic University Series*
By Cecilia Tan

No Safewords2
Edited by Laura Antoniou

Made in the USA
Middletown, DE
20 September 2022